SANE ENOUGH TO KNOW SHE'S CRAZY

Written by Ruth Thomas Hansen

Edited by Natalie Fowler

Cover Photo by Ellen Hansen Rhoades

ISBN 9781730937651

Acknowledgements

"Give thanks to the Lord, for He is good; His love endures forever."

Among the many blessings God has given me, some of the greatest are the people He has placed in my life. As I think about the amount of help and support I've received in writing this book, I am in awe of His perfect love. I am incredibly thankful for the many people who had a part in making this happen.

I'd like to give special thanks to the following:

Janet Reid and Nathan Bransford You so generously share your knowledge and expertise with a whole world of writers who are trying to find their way. Your public and personal guidance have been invaluable to me as I wrote, and sought to publish this story.

Ben LeRoy You helped me to find purpose, in my story and in my life. You heard me, even when I didn't know what I needed to say.

Natalie Fowler I couldn't have hoped for a more perfect editor. You patiently stuck with me, making sure my words made sense. I cannot thank you enough for believing in this story and helping me find the best way to tell it.

Ellen Hansen Rhoades Since the beginning, I dreamt of using one of your photos on the cover of my first book. You didn't let me down! The pictures turned out better than I imagined. Your commitment and talent amaze me. I am proud to have your work be the face of my story.

Christy Calkins More than once, you walked with me through this story, page by page, chapter by chapter, offering the feedback I so desperately craved. Thank you for helping me sort through the cheesiness.

My Early Readers My precious friends and family, you gave me much needed hope throughout this journey. Thank you for that beautiful gift!

Dad and Nita Thank you for being a constant source of support. In everything I do, I can always feel you rooting for me. No matter the distance between us, you are forever close in my heart.

Mom You are my biggest fan! You've been cheering me on since I wrote the first page of the first draft. You saw me through years of rejection, never letting me give up. This is our book, a product of my passion for writing, and your passion for supporting your children.

Ed Dear, I'm sorry I didn't write about a Job Johnny killer like you wanted me to. Thank you for indulging me in this venture anyway. I loved driving through Iowa with you, looking for Carrie's house. You are an awesome dream partner, and an even better life partner. Let's make lots of happy endings together.

And My Children I hate that your lives had to experience any of the difficult realities that inspired this story. Please know it was you who inspired me to fight back. Writing was my way of trying to spin the hard times into hope. I wanted to finally be strong for you. Of course, each of you has proven you have strengths of your own.

Sam Despite your struggles, you manage to hold on to that punderful sense of humor. You have a way of making me laugh, which isn't always easy. Your eye for detail makes me take a closer look at the world and your exceptional memory helps to fill in the gaps that my own brain can't find. Thank you for coming to me, no matter what, and for sharing your beautiful daughter, Velouria.

Ellen You try to hide your emotions, but I kind of love how you can't. You have a sweet, beautiful soul and I am lucky to have you to join with me in all the feelings. Now that you are a mother yourself, those feelings have multiplied. I am happy to have Aran, Bella, DJ, and Graham on our team.

Jordan Publishing this book terrifies me, but you knew all the right things to say. Patient and kind, you have helped me through countless freak outs. As the unofficial manager of our family, you keep us all together. You are a model of grace and class. Your strong sense of family has brought Nick and Genevieve into our lives, and I couldn't be more thankful.

Thomas When you were little, you told me to write a story with a lot of exclamation points so everyone would be able to hear me. Your support continued over the years. You gave me hugs when I felt like this dream would never come true. Then, you'd tell me to try again. Thank you for a lifetime of encouragement. I pray that your own wise advice will follow you through life. Be heard. Dream. Hug. Never give up.

Dedicated to my great big, sassy, and caring family. You keep me grounded, and you keep me going. I love every single one of you more than words could say. Thank you all for supporting me and my dream.

SANE ENOUGH TO KNOW SHE'S CRAZY

By Ruth Thomas Hansen

CHAPTER 1 – THEY'LL NEVER EVEN FEEL A BUMP

The baseball cap looked better on her husband, but that wasn't his fault. Adam's head was normal. Carrie wiggled the crown of his hat over her eyebrows and pulled her ponytail through the opening. She released a long reddish curl over each of her ears. Good enough.

"Adam, I'm going out," she said to him. "I have to… um… see a friend." The excuse sounded lame, even to her. She shoved her hand into a pocket of her faded "mom" jeans, trying to look casual.

Gripping the sports page, Adam looked up over the rim of his reading glasses. He twisted his lips a little and crinkled his forehead, a sure sign he had questions. Before he could ask, she kissed him goodbye. Then she rubbed her cheek against the small patch of grey in his beard. The subtle change in color had started to show a few months ago—the first admission of age his face had allowed. To her it was a reminder their "ever after" had come true.

"You look cute," he said. She smiled her biggest smile, hoping to make herself worthy of the compliment. "You okay?" he asked.

The dimples in her chubby cheeks disappeared. "I'm fine," she said. "Fine."

Adam's gaze returned to his newspaper. She paused behind him, then hugged his broad shoulders. "Good bye."

"Beth!" Carrie called up the stairs. "I'm going out." Her daughter didn't answer. She was probably on the phone with her boyfriend. Again.

Daniel stood to give his mother a hug. "See ya' later, Slugger," he said, straightening the hat on her head. She responded by raising her hand to the brim and saluting him, a reverse of the ritual they'd started with his first little league game. It was a bittersweet nod to the fact her freckle faced little boy, with shaggy red hair, was now a man with a crew cut and a copper goatee. Standing there beside him, she felt small, but not because he was a good three inches taller than her now. Her role in his life was shrinking.

"I put your keys on the hook," he said. "You left them in the door again."

"Thanks, sweetie." She set her purse down on the back of the couch. "Want some ice cream?"

He laughed a little. "Mom, I'm eighteen. You don't have to wait on me. Go. Have fun with your friend."

She went to the freezer anyway, pulled out a carton of his favorite cookie dough ice cream, and heaped two big scoops into a dish.

"He's not your baby anymore," a man's voice said. She tried to dismiss the hallucination, but the voice persisted. "Daniel is a grown man. He doesn't need his mommy."

Leaving the ice cream on the counter, she grabbed her purse and walked out the front door. Nobody tried to stop her. Of course they didn't. Nobody knew.

#

Carrie drove past the empty little league field. "Daniel Jenkins takes the mound," she whispered.

Her son's old baseball glove appeared on the seat beside her. It looked so small. She blinked, and it was gone.

She reminded herself that Daniel would be leaving for college in September. Soon he would be gone too.

With a deep breath, her senses found the familiar scent of fabric softener. She tucked her nose into her t-shirt and inhaled.

"Gone." She hated that word.

The radio scanned through stations without stopping. Songs played for a few seconds, then left. It didn't occur to her to push the button to make them stop until she heard Beth's four-year-old voice above the noise.

"Sing with me, Mommy," it said. "We can be Dorothy."

But her baby girl wasn't with her. Beth wasn't a baby anymore.

Carrie clicked the radio off and sang her daughter's favorite song alone.

But she couldn't feel the music. She looked down at the floor, longing to see the ruby red shoes little Beth had loved to wear, then stopped herself.

"Don't seek illusion," she told herself. "Seek peace." The ache was too real to let her go. Her fingers tapped the song's rhythm on the wheel.

"Sing with me, Beth," she whispered. Her daughter's voice could soothe her inner chaos better than any cookie ever had. She was Carrie's closest link to peace. "Oh, honey. Let me hear you now. Help me be normal."

Instead, an answer came from the stranger inside her head. "Normal doesn't exist," the voice said. "Kook."

Carrie pulled her car over, stopping on the side of the road. She found a napkin and a pencil in the glove compartment and wrote one sentence before the point broke. She snapped the wood in two and watched the pieces bleed. "No!" she screamed and flung the broken pencil across her car's dashboard.

With that, the gruesome image disappeared. "There's no blood," she assured herself. She held her hands in front of her face.

"I'm in control," she scolded.

Avoiding the steering wheel, she dropped her hands onto her lap and frantically rubbed them on her jeans. The friction created by the motion freed her from the moment. She reached under her seat, hunting for a pen, but all she found was half of a cookie. It tasted like oatmeal, or maybe stale peanut butter. She reached down again to recover the napkin that had fallen. Carrie silently read the words she had scrawled across the top of it, unable to process how they'd sound out loud.

"A good story doesn't require a happy ending."

She would have added, "But it has to have meant something," if her pencil hadn't betrayed her. Those were the words she needed to see. The napkin crumbled in her hand.

"Screw you," she told the wad of paper. "You don't get to choose my ending."

The Honda's motor started again. Her hands gripped the steering wheel like only they knew what they were doing. Her sneaker stomped the gas pedal. It felt like someone else was driving.

"He can't make you do this," she told herself. "He's the one who isn't real." She rolled down her window. The car slowed as she drank in the fresh air. A cut on her forehead stung with perspiration inside of Adam's hat. She took the hat off and placed it on the seat to dry. Running her fingers through her damp bangs, she tousled her hair and stretched it over her eyebrows.

A red car pulled alongside of hers. The teenage boys inside were laughing and making faces. One yelled out the open window, "Get off the road, Grandma!"

Ignoring the tired reflection of the forty-year old crazy lady in her rearview mirror, she glanced at her speedometer and accelerated from twenty miles per hour to thirty. The limit was forty-five, but the red car kept pace with hers. She slowed again, hoping they'd pass. As they did, two shining white tushies smiled back at her, bare asses in the rear window.

She heard a boy yell, "Oh, crap! It's Daniel's mom!"

"Coach is going to kill us!" another boy shouted. Their tires screeched as they cut in front of her to speed away.

Daniel's Mom. Beth's Mom. Adam's wife, even Coach's wife. That's who she was, who she was supposed to be. She twisted her ponytail around her fingers. The other mothers were all so perfect. Some of them even ate salads.

She steered her car into the empty church lot and parked in her usual spot. The large stone building was dark. She walked up to the door and tried to open it. The handle wouldn't turn.

"Coach's wife is locked out of church," she mumbled. She waited, as if the situation could change, then pounded on the door with both fists. "Please…" she cried.

"He's not home," the voice said.

"But God, I need You," Carrie whispered, but God was quiet. She hung her head and found her way to her car.

Again avoiding eye contact with the mirror, she dug through her purse, cursing the collection of useless antidepressants her gynecologist had prescribed. She found a Snickers bar at the bottom that had somehow eluded her earlier in the week. The emptiness and fear were temporarily replaced by chocolate, caramel, and appropriately, she thought, nuts.

"Pathetic," the stranger said. But she already knew. For the moment, though, the candy soothed her nerves and sweetened her spirit. With the last bite, the comfort was gone. She thought about going home. The old farmhouse had been a comfortable place to raise their children.

"No," the voice said.

"The children…" she started to say.

"Don't need you," he interrupted. "You're in their way."

Carrie sat alone in her church's parking lot. The building stood there, waiting for Sunday. She wanted to pray, but the words wouldn't come. She quietly licked remnants of caramel from her teeth.

Locked out.

#

I was somebody's baby once, too. Carrie buried the thought as she drove toward the train station. She'd never known her mother. She couldn't miss her. She had no right. Refusing to acknowledge her own tears, she stared ahead.

Soon the train tracks came into view. Her car slowed. "Control," she reminded herself, but the word felt foreign now. She had sworn she'd never give in to the man's voice, but the fine line between hearing it and listening to him was a delicate place to battle.

She'd denied the stranger for twenty years. Now he struck with a truth she couldn't fight.

"You're in their way," he said again.

She dried her eyes with her t-shirt. He was right. Her family had never needed her. She needed them. She had no right.

"I'm in their way," she told her car as she pulled into a parking lot near the train station.

Her best defense against the man had always been her children. Now, Daniel and Beth had become his weapon. The fight consumed her. Staring ahead at the tracks, she felt like she was about to be digested.

With the touch of a button, hazard lights flashed in the dark. She wished the blinking orange glow could scream on her behalf. "No," she told the button. "Make it say, 'no.'"

"Whore," the voice said.

She pushed the button harder and the lights stopped.

Habit guided her step on the emergency brake. The safety belt clicked open, offering mixed freedom. The train should be leaving the station soon. It wouldn't take long for it to reach this spot.

Her wounded mind didn't know how to fight anymore. Her body was like an old tattered rope, holding together the broken pieces of a soul that had torn itself apart.

She stepped out of her car.

"They deserve better than you," the voice said. "Get out of their way."

The thick summer air held a lingering skunk odor.

"Tomato juice," she said over the voice. "Tomato juice would take care of that smell." Somewhere in her memory, images of a pink dog whimpered in the distance. "Tomato juice worked on Sassy's dog."

"You left that life a long time ago," the voice said. "You can't go back."

"Sassy is still my best friend," Carrie said.

She watched the tracks move toward her, mocking her stillness. Biting down on her tongue, she willed the vision away. With a first step, motion became hers again. The path of the tracks stayed flat and straight, leading beyond her view. If nothing stopped it, the train would leave Iowa and go all the way to Pennsylvania. At least, that's what she imagined.

Her sneakers crunching across the rocks stole silence from the moment. She reached a patch of grass beside the tracks and sat. Her body felt heavy against the earth. Through the artificial light of the streetlamps, her eyes instinctively searched for clover. In all of her life, she'd never been able to find any with four leaflets. Normal clover only had three.

She pulled her legs up to her chest and hugged her knees against the "East End Bull Dogs" logo printed on her t-shirt. She closed her eyes, desperate to absorb every ounce of quiet in the night air. A threat of relief challenged her as the plan played out in her mind. She wasn't sure if it was his relief or hers.

Imagination took over. She could see herself on the tracks, boldly facing the train. Staring into the light, her darkness was illuminated by the great locomotive racing toward her. Soon, her body would be struck with a moment of exquisite pain. Her mind would be released.

Carrie shook her head, as if she were allowed to resist the delusions it had created. A train filled with babies and daddies roared through her mind. *What would happen to them?*

"You can't hurt them. It's not their fault," she said out loud.

"They'll never even feel a bump," the stranger answered.

The twisted reasoning settled her some, and her mind drifted. She could see the home she shared with Adam; her grown up home; her children's home. The soft blue walls of her bedroom felt real around her. She stilled herself, aching to hear the creak of the floorboards beneath the old rocking chair as she rocked her babies.

Shh. Rest, baby Daniel. Sleep, my love. You're safe now.

But the walls of her home weren't there to protect her tonight.

Beth, sweet little Beth, please don't cry. Mommy's here. He can't hurt you. He can't hurt you.

Mommy rocked alone in the grass now. The scent of the skunk nudged at Carrie's senses. The ground that held her felt damp, and safe. She didn't deserve safe.

"Mommy has to go now," the voice said. She ripped at the ground, unable to hold on. "He can't hurt you," she said to the babies that weren't there. "I won't let him."

Carrie stretched her legs out flat and took a deep breath. "I won't let him," she repeated. She ripped up a handful of clover. Each stem only held three leaves. She covered her empty lap in a blanket of freshly torn grass. "Kook," she heard. Blades of green drifted away with a warm breeze. She brushed the rest into the dirt beside her and with a small twig, carved the words she wouldn't let herself say: "Couldn't handle being a mother."

"Grown children don't need their mother's lap," said the voice.

"But…" she started to say.

"You can't hide in the past." The hallucination roared at her like a hungry lion. "You weak coward. Stop being so selfish. You can't hide."

From the train station, bells began to clang. She was far enough away to hear the rhythm take motion.

"They don't need you! They don't need you!" the stranger sang with the chorus.

Carrie's head pounded in unspoken agreement. The rumble of the approaching train didn't stifle him. "You're in their way."

She climbed to her knees. A mournful whistle called out to her, growing louder as it chugged closer. Breaths of steam poured from the monster's snout.

"It's time," the stranger said.

Rising to her feet, she could feel the power of the train vibrating through her sneakers as one hundred tons of steel reality drew closer.

"NOW," he commanded, "NOW!"

Her legs waited for a decision to move. Life with the man, the voice, had to end.

Above the noise of the train she heard the word.

"Gone!"

Images of her childhood flashed through her mind. A mermaid doll. The tree house. Sassy.

"Gone!" she heard.

"Gone," she said.

Carrie felt her toes curl inside of her sneakers. If only the church doors hadn't been locked. But she needed more than man-made sanctuary. God. She needed God.

"God, I am Yours," she said, and held her breath. Summoning every bit of faith within her, she let go of her fear. A burst of strength rushed through her.

For an instant, she saw the bright light. She felt the movement in the air and could hear the sounds around her. The noise was real. She was real. Her arms reached out. Her knees bent and her feet pushed. With all of her might, she jumped away from the tracks. She fell onto the ground and rested her head on the cool grass as the train whistled past her. She smelled the dirt and cried.

"God, I am Yours, not his," she said. "Please never leave me." She felt His presence as she claimed the words that kept her just beyond reach of the invisible stranger.

She rose and yelled into the thunder of the passing train. "You can't have me! You can't have me!"

The voice that had been haunting her stayed silent, for now. Bells sang out as the train's clacking continued down the tracks. The stranger said nothing. She was alone at last.

Adam would be so proud, if only she could tell him. But then he'd know his wife was crazy. She knew in her heart she needed to save herself. She was meant to be a kick-ass heroine in this story, not a princess depending on a kiss.

She thought, again, about telling Sassy. They'd been friends forever, despite the fact they hadn't seen each other in twenty years. They talked all of the time, but a cry for help had never left Carrie's mouth. She'd come close many times, but those calls always ended the same way—the phone hanging up, words left unsaid. She thought about sitting across the table from Sassy, face to face like real friends should. Like always, the thought filled her with dread.

We used to tell each other everything. But something in the pit of her soul told her that wasn't true. She brushed some dirt from her jeans. *Why can't I be normal?*

She left the tracks and got back into her car, locking the doors. Her hands trembled as she reached for her purse. She fumbled through empty prescription bottles and candy wrappers until she found her phone. "Should I?" she asked it. "Can I?"

She sat up straight and called home, bracing herself with each ring.

"Yeah?" Adam answered.

"Adam, it's Carrie." She pulled the Snickers wrapper from the cup holder and searched for crumbs of chocolate.

"I know that, dear."

"Adam…"

"Yep. I'm here. What's up?"

She reached for the crumpled napkin. *A good story doesn't require a happy ending.*

"But it has to have meant something," she said.

"What?" Adam asked. "I can't hear you, Carrie. You're mumbling."

"I'm on my way home," she heard herself say. She knew something in her voice was crying out to him, *Come to me. Hold me. Fix me.* Damn. Part of her wished he'd hear that too.

"I'm on my way home," she said a little louder.

"Could you bring me some pretzels?" Adam asked.

CHAPTER 2 – IF THE NAME FITS

The phone didn't ring. After a solid month of three a.m. calls, the bastard had stopped cold. Sassy had refused to let the nightly ring concern her. Such a cowardly prank didn't deserve her time. Yet, on the third night of silence, she still had trouble sleeping.

Rolling over, she opened her eyes and took a deep breath. She slid herself to David's side of the bed and snuggled in his empty spot. The silk sheets felt annoyingly cool against her warm skin.

"Damn it," she scolded the darkness. "Not again."

It was three thirty. No call, and still, no husband. Tonight was the fourth night out of seven that he hadn't come to bed. The accountant in him clearly failed to assess the potential ramifications of that majority. Her analysis, however, came from a different book.

She knew work never kept him from their bed as well as she knew he hadn't told her the truth about the night he had gotten arrested. She'd never known him to hit anybody. She wasn't falling for the lame road rage story he'd tried to sell. His Volkswagen modeled courtesy like it was on a date with the Queen.

Sassy yanked the plug from the wall and pitched the phone into the trash can. She ripped the linens off the bed and stuffed them into the hamper. Wiggling out of the lacy red teddy she hadn't planned to sleep in, she swore she'd never have sex with him again. *At least not until he tells me what's going on.* She reached for her old Phillies sweatshirt and a pair of track pants.

She got dressed and ran a brush through her short brown hair. With a sigh, she did a quick inspection. *Damn. Another strand of grey. Pluck you.* Trying not to look forty, she dabbed on the moisturizer that vowed to make her appear ten years younger. Fifteen would be better, really. She'd settle for five. She brushed a touch of pink on her cheeks and a hint of green over her hazel eyes, finishing with a generous coat of vanilla lip gloss.

The dog padded into the bedroom with a running shoe in her mouth and dropped it at Sassy's feet. "I'm sorry, Barbie. I didn't mean to wake you," Sassy said, stroking the lab's golden fur. "It's still dark outside. We should wait for David." The dog rubbed up against her long legs and whimpered. Sassy looked at the empty bed. An early morning run around the lake sounded good right now. "Okay, girl. Where's my other sneaker?"

Barbie wagged her tail and ran downstairs. Sassy followed her down, but stopped in front of David's home office. She opened the door a crack and peeked in. There he slept, reclined in his favorite chair. That stupid chair had become the mistress she'd never expected. The soft black leather got to hold him on restless nights. He hid with his papers while Sassy flopped alone in bed.

She shut the door. "Let's go, Barbie."

When they stepped outside, the sweet scent of lilacs touched her senses. Fickle Pennsylvania weather hadn't let her down. She took a deep breath, inhaling the freshness of a new summer morning. The lake was still for now, but not without life. A light mist hung over the water. Loons sang into the silence. Calls of the osprey cried out in the distance.

They kept a steady pace as they ran. She struggled to balance her thoughts. Two weeks had passed since David's night in jail, the night he didn't call her. Their friend, Joseph, said he would take care of everything. He had the nerve to tell her not to worry. Ha! After all these years, he should know her better than that.

She looked out at the lake. Little ripples spread across the water. *David's lying,* she thought as they continued to run.

Professional skills demanded she not take his silence as a direct insult. But damn it, David was not a troubled client, and she was not his therapist. A husband should trust his wife enough not to worry the crap out of her. *Her* husband should not stroll in from jail in the middle of the night like it's no big deal and not tell her anything.

Sassy dabbed her forehead with her sleeve, wiping away the perspiration. Her inner-therapist reminded her that her worry was her own. In his own way, he was trying to save her from it. Still, there was a matter of trust.

David must have heard her tell dozens of girls they needed to keep away from guys that can't be trusted. He could probably quote the speech word for word. "Always be real. Respect yourself. Be a person you'd want to spend your life with." Blah, blah, blah.

But David had never given her a reason not to trust him. Even all those years ago, when he first walked into the diner and told her he barely had enough money for a cup of coffee, she'd believed in him. Since then, he'd proven her faith was justified more times than she could name.

Sassy ran a little faster. She could see the house now. The home they shared was so much more than the place they lived and worked. Their life here was proof that they believed in each other. They had history and a future. She could be patient and allow him to hold onto his secret for a while. Whatever happened that night, he was still the man she loved. He'd talk to her when he was ready, like always.

The heaviness of the dark began to ease as the sun crept higher in the sky. With Barbie at her side, Sassy sprinted toward home.

#

Taking an afghan from the hall closet, Sassy tiptoed into David's office. She kissed his bald head, leaving a hint of vanilla lip gloss on his scalp. Then she climbed onto his soft lap, hanging her feet over the side of his chair. Pulling the afghan over both of them, she rested her head on his shoulder. His face nuzzled in the chestnut waves of her hair. He wrapped his arms around her and squeezed.

"I'm here," she said.

He gently tasted her sweet mouth. "Mmm. I love you," he answered.

An hour later, they were awakened by the sound of Barbie, barking at the paper boy.

"Quiet, Barbie," Sassy mumbled. But the dog had already had a taste of morning.

Sassy felt her husband try to ease his way out of the chair. She let herself move with him, under him, on him. She touched him with both hands, desperate to feel him feeling. Her body begged his to communicate, offering assurance and comfort. He devoured her passion with confidence, exploring her like a world he knew how to travel. His flesh spoke to hers. She welcomed him in, eager to experience what it had to say. Without words she knew, everything would be okay.

#

Sassy started a pot of coffee and brought in the newspaper. Without so much as a glance at the headline, she placed the paper at the head of the table for David. The ink blackened her fingertips.

"No wonder you won't fetch it for him," she said to Barbie. She patted the dog's head and turned to the sink.

Through warm, sudsy water the diamond on Sassy's finger shone in the morning's light. The gem held a few minor flaws, but the beauty enhanced the lifetime it celebrated. An anniversary gift from David on their tenth year, the ring fit like a doting husband.

Sipping coffee from her giant mug, she studied the day's tasks on the memo board. She made a note for her new assistant to reschedule her outpatient clients and her meeting with social services. She'd handle the rest when she got back.

Then Sassy left a note telling David she was going to the train station and signed it with a kiss.

THIRTY- FOUR YEARS EARLIER...

CHAPTER 3 – BIG BROTHER

(Sassy, Age 6)

"Oli, wake up!" said Sassy. "Something's wrong."

Oliver opened his eyes and squinted at his little sister, then he turned his head to look at the clock. It was after midnight. "What? What's wrong?"

"I don't know," Sassy said.

"That's stupid," he grumbled. "What are you doing in my room? I gotta rest." He tried to roll over and away from her.

But Sassy wasn't about to let him go back to sleep until he did something about whatever it was. She grabbed his blanket away from him, reached for his hand and pulled. "I heard something…a creepy noise. Come downstairs with me for one second."

"Was it a monster?" he teased.

"Jerkface," she said, letting go of his hand. "I'll go by myself."

Oliver grunted as he forced himself out of bed and followed her to the top of the stairs. "Hold up," he said. "Let me go first."

They crept halfway down the steps and sat to listen. It sounded like a ghost.

"You hear it too, don't you?" Sassy asked.

Oliver put his fingers to his lips. "Shh."

Together they peeked through the opening in the staircase and saw their mother. She was sitting in the dark near the window. Her head hung low. Her body was curled up like she was trying to hide. The noises were soft and deep, sadder than anything Sassy had ever heard. Her shoulders bounced with a sharp whimper. The children jumped, startled by the break in rhythm. The sobbing continued.

Oliver turned and eased his way back up the steps. Sassy hesitated, then tiptoed up behind him. He opened his parents' bedroom door. The bed was empty.

"Where's Dad?" Sassy asked. "We have to tell him."

Oliver went to the window in Sassy's room and looked down at the driveway. "Car's gone."

"He probably went to get her some flowers. That's what men do when their wives cry."

"That's dumb. It's the middle of the night. I bet they had a fight."

"Maybe he went to the fair again," Sassy said.

"What are you talking about? What fair?"

Sassy put her hands on her hips. "I heard them last time. Mom was mad 'cause Dad keeps on working late. She told him the fairs had to stop."

Oliver made a smarty face like he was about to take charge. He was only eight, but he knew a lot about fairs. One time he even won her a giant teddy bear.

"Go back to bed. I gotta think."

"But I wanna think with you," Sassy said.

"Get in bed. I'm gonna be right here."

Sassy got into bed. Oliver settled himself at her window to wait for their father to get home.

"Oli?" Sassy whispered.

"Yeah?"

"I hate the fair. Every time I win a fish it dies." She sucked in her cheeks and made a fish face at him.

Oliver laughed. "Girls are so dumb."

#

Sassy woke up the next morning to the smell of banana bread. Oliver was sleeping on the floor, covered in a blanket from his room. Their father's car still wasn't in the driveway. She looked across the street.

"Carrie's father hasn't even started his car yet," she said. "He usually leaves first."

Oliver didn't wake up, so she went downstairs.

"Good morning, Elizabeth," her mother said. "Did you sleep well?"

"Where's Dad?"

"Oh, he left already. He has a meeting today. Are you hungry?"

Her mother had always told her it was a sin to tell lies, but Oliver would have heard the car in the driveway. He was on watch. Boys were good at being on watch, even if they fell asleep, 'cause they could still hear with their eyes shut.

Sassy stood with her hands on her hips. "Oliver slept on my floor last night," she said.

"I know. I covered him."

"He was watching for Dad to come home." Sassy looked at her mother, waiting for a reaction. "Dad wasn't here."

"Carrie will be here soon," her mother said. "You better get ready for school. You have library today. Don't forget your book."

"You promised you'd take us to get our ears pierced after school today."

Sassy's mother opened the oven and stuck a fork in the center of her banana bread. "And I will," she said as she reached for her oven mitts.

She removed the pan from the oven and set it on a cooling rack. Then she set three places at the table and poured three glasses of milk.

"Go tell your brother to come down for breakfast."

Sassy went up to her room, but Oliver wasn't there. She walked across the hall to his room. The blanket was back on his bed, and the bed had already been made. She saw the open window and smiled. Sticking her head out, she looked for her brother's homemade rope ladder. "Aha!" She grabbed the rope and climbed out. Shimmying her way down the side of the house, she ran across the yard to Oliver's tree house.

"Oli!" she called in a loud whisper. "Whatcha doin' up there?"

"Get outta here," he called back. But she was already halfway up. He stopped her at the entrance. "Sassy, get out. I have stuff to do."

"Hey!" she said pointing past him. "You can't have that! Dad said no more weapons."

"Too bad. Dad's not here." Oliver grabbed his slingshot. "Tell Mom I'm walking to school with Adam today."

"Only if you tell me where you're really going."

He moved past her and started down the ladder. "The fair," he said.

He jumped from the rope and started to run. He paused for a moment and yelled back to her, "Give her those flowers."

Sassy looked at the tree house floor and saw the pile of wildflowers that Oliver had picked. She scooped them up and made a small bouquet. Finding a loose sprig of something pink and pretty, she stuck it behind her ear and climbed down the ladder.

Carrie was sitting at the kitchen table when Sassy came inside. "Your Mom went upstairs to look for you guys," she said.

Sassy put the flowers in her mother's empty coffee cup and put it in the middle of the table.

"Oli's gonna be in trouble again," she said. She took the pink thing from behind her ear and put it in Carrie's hair. "We may have to wait to get our ears pierced."

#

By dinnertime, their Dad was home. Their mother, for the first time in her life, served corn dogs. Store bought corn dogs out of a box- and no vegetables. Oliver ate four, then spent the night alone in his tree house. Sassy never went to a fair again.

CHAPTER 4 – DADDY'S GIRL

(Carrie, Age 10)

Carrie and Sassy didn't play dolls together anymore. They hadn't since they were eight. Sassy thought they were too old for little girl stuff. Now that they were ten, she always wanted to do things like listen to music or play Atari. Or spy on the boys. Sassy loved spying on her older brother and his friends.

Carrie watched from her bedroom window as Sassy and Oliver walked out of the big brick house across the street and got into their father's car. Mr. Lingle honked the horn, waited, then honked again. Soon, Sassy's mom hurried out with her pocketbook and her Bible. The kids looked up and waved at Carrie from the rear window as the car backed out of the driveway.

"Okay," Carrie said as she waved back. "They're gone."

Sassy had to go to church every Sunday. This week they were going to her grandmother's house for dinner after the service. Carrie's father was home today, so she didn't have to go with the Lingles this time. She closed her frilly pink curtains and stood to open the bench she had been sitting on.

"You can come out now," she told her dolls. "We have to get ready for the wedding."

She lifted the bride first, carefully inspecting the long white dress, the mini veil Mrs. Lingle had helped her make, and the shoes she'd borrowed from an old Cinderella doll. She liked the way the pink polished toenails showed through the glass slippers. Satisfied, she tucked the bride into the pocket of her own flowery sundress. Then she dressed the guests in their best ball gowns, with matching plastic shoes, and sat them in rows on her bed. She stood the groom against her pillow next to the GI Joe that Oliver had given her for her birthday when she was six. On Joe's first night in her room, she had tried to put a smaller doll's tuxedo on him, but the shiny pants ripped. Four years had passed. Joe was still in fatigues and the little shiny pants were still held together with a duct tape belt.

She went down the hallway into the bathroom and shut the door. Clicking the lock, she paused to listen. Her father's footsteps stomped across the floor downstairs. His busy work voice rambled. He was on the phone again. Good. She took the doll from her pocket and propped her up against the soap dispenser. Then she dug her mermaid doll out from her hiding place under the sink. Turning on a slow stream of water, she gently placed the mermaid in the "ocean."

From the shore, the little bride called out, "Momma, are you here?"

Momma swam to the edge of the sink. Carrie moved each doll as she spoke, changing her voice for each one. "You are the most beautiful bride in the whole wide world," Momma the mermaid said.

"I wish you could come to my wedding."

"I have something special for you," said Momma. Carrie made the mermaid fly to her dress pocket. She pulled out a small blue box and opened it. "I want you to have this," she continued, in her flying mermaid kind of voice. "It was a gift from the king."

Carrie popped off the bride's head and put the diamond ring around her neck. "Wear this and know I will never leave you," Momma said as Carrie put the bride back together. She reached for the mermaid again and made her fly some more. "I will be with you always and forever," she said. Then she wrapped the mermaid doll in a towel and returned her to the hiding spot underneath the sink.

She was on her way to the wedding when her father stopped her in the hallway.

"Good morning, lil' miss," he said.

She spun around, startled.

"I'm not too early, am I?" he asked. "It's almost ten o'clock."

"No, Daddy. The bride had to put on some makeup and stuff. We're all ready."

Her father took Carrie's arm in his. "Let's play," he said.

She held her bride doll like a bouquet and hummed as they were escorted to the canopied church. Standing at the side of her bed, she handed the bride to her father. Holding the doll, he froze.

"Kiss her on the forehead and put her next to the groom," Carrie whispered.

Her dad didn't move. She reached up and tapped his shoulder. "Daddy, what's wrong? Why aren't you playing?"

"Carrie!" he finally said. His voice was scary. "What are you doing with this?"

Carrie stood on her tippie toes. It was time to act like a grown up again. She pushed a curl away from her eye, but it bounced right back. "I was putting away laundry. I found it in your drawer."

He ripped the doll's head off and dropped it onto the carpet. Removing the ring, he yelled, "This is not a toy!"

"I- I'm sorry, Daddy!" she cried. "I didn't break it. I promise!"

Her dad wiped at her tears. His face looked sorry. Sorry and sad. She wanted to touch it, but she was afraid. He picked the head up off of the floor and fixed his daughter's doll. He kissed it on the forehead and put it next to the boy dolls on the pillow.

"Daddy, we don't have to play anymore. I'm sorry." She took the blue box from her pocket again and handed it to him. "Please don't be mad."

He held up the ring. "This is your momma's," he said. "I gave it to her when I asked her to marry me."

"But you said she's gone."

Now, she wiped his tears. "She is gone. Almost ten years." He sat in the rocking chair in the corner of her room. "You were only two weeks old when she died." Carrie climbed onto his lap. "I found her ring when I came home from the hospital," he said. "It was in this box. On this chair."

That night, when Carrie went to bed, the mermaid doll was under her pillow. She pulled it out and hugged it. On Monday, her father would be going out of town for work again. She'd have to be a big girl and stay with the Lingles for a few days. She wondered if Oliver's friend, Adam would be there.

CHAPTER 5—MIDDLE SCHOOL

(Carrie and Sassy, Age 12)

It was eighty-five degrees outside on their first day of sixth grade, their first day in the middle school. Carrie was wearing four shirts. The first tank top was too small to reach her belly button, but it held her new boobs down flat. The second tank ensured the first was doing its job. The pink t-shirt hid the tanks, and the baggy sweatshirt safely covered it all.

She rang the Lingles' doorbell and walked in.

"She's not ready," Oliver said. "Been hoggin' the bathroom all morning."

"Is she scared?" Carrie asked.

"It's only school." He playfully punched her arm. "There's nothing to worry about."

"Who's worried?" Sassy asked from the top of the steps. "Care, it'll be fine," she said, coming down the stairs. She was wearing a red V-neck top, emphasis on the "v," and snug designer jeans. Carrie noticed Sassy had a little more boob than she'd had yesterday.

"You look pretty," Carrie said.

"Ha!" Oliver said. "Mom's not gonna let you wear that."

Sassy put her hands on her hips. "Mom bought it for me. So there." She walked into the kitchen and grabbed the lunch bags off of the counter.

Mrs. Lingle reached into Sassy's shirt and pulled the tissues out of her training bra. "No," she said as she adjusted the shirt to its proper fit. "I bought that." She rambled about being a "proper young lady" as she followed Sassy to the door.

Carrie stood with her hand on the knob. Sassy handed Oliver his lunch and gave a bag to Carrie.

"My dad gave me money to buy lunch," she said.

"Nonsense. That cafeteria serves slop," Mrs. Lingle said. "And you're going to have a heat stroke in that sweatshirt." Then she whispered too loudly, "You need a bra, dear. You'll feel much better."

"Mom, stop!" Sassy yelled.

Oliver took his jacket off of the hook behind her. He put it on and zipped it to his chin.

"Let's go," he said.

#

It was the middle of English class when Sassy began to hear the sniffs.

"What's wrong, Care?" she whispered, turning around to her friend.

"Nothing," Carrie said, wiping her eyes.

"Damn," Sassy said. "I don't have any tissues." She patted her boobs, hoping Carrie would laugh.

Carrie smiled, but lost hold of her emotions. The tears started and wouldn't stop. The sniffs got louder. The harder she seemed to fight it, the worse it got. Kids were staring. The teacher turned away from the board.

Before Mrs. Thomas could speak, Sassy stood at her desk. "I need to take Carrie to the nurse's office. She's not feeling well."

The teacher pointed at the hall pass hanging near the door. "Come right back," she said.

Sassy took Carrie into the hallway and hugged her as hard as she could. "It's no big deal. I've seen lots of eighth graders with boobs," she said. "You look older, like them." Then she guided her into the girls' room and lifted the sweatshirt over her head. "Awh, Care," she said when she saw the tank tops. "Go in the stall and take those off."

As Carrie did, Sassy unhooked her bra, worked it out her shirt sleeve, and threw it over the stall door. "Here. Let me know when you're ready. I'll hook it for you."

"Thanks, Sassy. It's pretty."

"It's not very comfortable. The lace is scratchy."

"Sassy. Remember that thing your mom told us about? The gross woman stuff. I think it's happening. Like, right now."

"Really? No way! Does it hurt?" The commercials always made it look so glamorous, but she had heard that some girls couldn't even take gym class when they got it.

"Do you…need something? The machine out here only has the innie kind. Damn. I should have put some of those panty pillows my mother bought in my purse."

"No. Eww. This is too weird," Carrie said. "Ick. I have to go home."

"Okay. Don't worry. Wrap a bunch of toilet tissue and put it in your undies for now. We'll go to the nurse and tell her you puked. She'll call my mom to come get you. Oliver says the puke excuse works every time."

They got to Miss Moroney's office minutes before the bell rang for the next class.

"She threw up," Sassy told the nurse and waited to see if her brother had been right.

"Awh. Poor thing," Miss Moroney said. "Go ahead and lie down."

Sassy nodded her approval, holding back a smile.

But then Miss Moroney added, "I'll call your mom to come and get you. What's your name, sweetie?"

A wounded look crossed Carrie's face. Sassy spoke for her. "My mom will come get her," she told the nurse. "Her dad's at work. It's in the file." She waited for Miss Moroney to look up Carrie's information, then she verified the phone number.

Carrie shrunk onto the nurse's hard bed and pulled at her shirt. "Thanks, Sass."

After Algebra, Sassy walked by the nurse's office to see if Carrie was gone yet. She was lingering in the hallway when she saw Oliver sneak out a side door. She ran to the door and slipped out with him.

"What the hell are you doing here?" he asked.

"Mom's coming. Carrie's sick. What are you doing?" Sassy asked, following him toward the parking lot.

"Lookin' for someone. Mom's coming now?"

Before Sassy could answer, they saw their mother in the parking lot. She was talking to the high school football coach, Adam's grandfather.

"Duck!" Oliver grabbed Sassy's arm and pulled her down behind some shrubs. "Adam was right. He is here," Oliver said. "I have to tell him I got a "B" on my English test. He's gonna pick a few eighth graders to practice with his team, but ya' hafta have good grades."

"Football with high school kids? Cool. Think he'll pick you?"

"I'm as good as Adam." Oliver said. "I bet he's asking Mom if I can play. Let's get closer. I wanna hear what they're talking about."

Crouching down behind cars, they worked their way through the parking lot until they were close enough to hear the adults' conversation.

"He'll be home by six," Coach Jenkins was saying. "I promise."

"That'll be fine," their mother said. "Now if you'll excuse me, I need to pick up Carrie."

"Eddie's little girl? I heard you help him out with her. Poor kid. I don't know how Donna could do that to them like that."

"She was very ill."

"I don't get it. My boy would have done anything to get to see his kid grow up. If it weren't for the accident, Adam would have two parents. With Donna, it was no accident. She done it to herself. She done it to that kid."

"I'm not going to pretend to understand," their mother said. "Nor will I judge."

"Still, it's not right. Bailing on her kid like that. How's a kid supposed to grow up normal knowing her mother wasn't sane enough to love her?"

"I beg your pardon, Coach. You're out of line."

"Think as you will, Margaret, but I'm warning you…"

"You stop yourself right there," she said waving her hand like a preacher calling for an "Amen!" "Carrie's mother did love her. I saw it with my own eyes. The night that Donna died I held her baby in my arms and I promised the Lord I'd love her just like her momma had. Because, sir, she did. And I'll not allow you, or anyone else, to make that little girl think that her momma didn't love her."

Mrs. Lingle walked away without hearing the coach mumble, "Kid's gonna grow up to be a bitch and a psycho. Just like her damned mothers."

Oliver spit his gum out onto the pavement. Sassy wiped a tear from her eye so he wouldn't see it. They waited for Adam's grandfather to go inside the building, then they ditched school and walked to the baseball park.

CHAPTER 6 – CREEK

(Age 14)

The girls were practically in high school and Sassy was bored with Thanksgiving break. Every other eighth grade girl on the planet was at the mall, and her lame mother wouldn't let her and Carrie go. Instead, the two of them were decorating the front of Carrie's house with Christmas lights. It had been fun for the first five minutes, but Sassy was already sick of it.

Sassy saw Adam pedal his dirt bike up the road and stop in her driveway. He wasn't wearing his Phillies jacket. Weird. Just a plain old coat. She watched as he pushed the bike through the gate and disappeared into the backyard.

"Adam's kinda cute, don't you think?" she asked Carrie. "I mean, for a jock."

"I don't know," Carrie said, burying her focus on the string of multicolored lights that she was trying to hang around the window. The plug ended up six inches from the outlet. She yanked at it and the whole string fell down. She scooped them up and shoved the mess back into the box.

Sassy picked up a wreath and hung it on the door. It was crooked.

Across the street, a giant manger scene graced the Lingles' front lawn. In every window stood a tall white candle, with fresh batteries in the candlestick. As soon as it got dark, the shrubs lining the porch would twinkle with a thousand lights. Oliver opened the front door and the wreath he'd hung for his mother barely moved. He looked over and saw the girls. He hesitated, then hopped off the porch and headed to the backyard.

"Hey! Maybe Mom will let us go to the mall if the guys go too," Sassy said.

Carrie fussed with her crooked wreath. "Oliver hates shopping," she said.

"They can hang out in the arcade. He has, like the top score, in Pac Man."

"I guess we can ask."

"C'mon," Sassy said. "I'll do the talking."

The girls abandoned the Christmas decorations and crossed the street. As they stood at the gate, they could hear Oliver and Adam talking. They stopped to listen.

"I told my mother I was going to your house," Oliver said. "The girls saw me, but they don't know anything. Let's get down there before they come lookin' for us."

"We should take them," Adam said. "They can watch."

"No way, man. Sassy would want to try it."

"Damn right I wanna try," Sassy whispered to Carrie. "Whatever it is." They peeked through the gate and saw Adam pushing his bike across the frozen ground and into the woods behind the Lingles' yard. Oliver walked with him, carrying some kind of board.

"They're going to the trail down by the creek!" Sassy said.

She and Carrie followed at a distance, careful not to be seen. It had been awhile since they had last spied on her brother. The girls crept from one bare tree to another. Sassy had forgotten what a rush being stealthy could be. The feeling grew as bits of excited guy talk cut through the cold air.

"…ramp…jump" she heard. Ooh, this was going to be good.

"Your mom is going to freak," Carrie whispered.

"Shh." Sassy scolded. "They'll hear us."

"…dare…" they heard. "…water…"

"Holy crap! They're gonna jump the creek," Sassy said.

"What do we do?" Carrie asked.

"Watch 'em," Sassy answered.

Without another word, the girls followed Oliver and Adam until they stopped at the edge of the creek. Two older boys were there waiting. Sassy didn't recognize them.

"He showed," one of them said.

Oliver punched the guy's arm. "You bet your ass he did. And he's gonna make it over."

Adam stood his bike against a tree. With rocks and fallen branches, the four of them built a ramp. Packing it with snow leftover from last week's storm, they added the board.

"Dude, you got this," Oliver said, patting Adam's back.

Adam rode his bike up the hill. Carrie gasped like an old lady when the bike started to roll. Sassy put her hand over her mouth before she could shout. Gaining speed, Adam pedaled toward the ramp. His feet spun faster and faster. Oliver cheered. The creek stretched twenty feet across. Adam hit the ramp and pulled back, launching himself into the air.

"He's doin' it! He's really tryin' to jump the creek!" a guy yelled.

Adam's face hit the handlebars as his front tire barely touched down on the other side. The back tire splashed into the creek. Adam flipped off the bike, plunged into the icy water and flowed with the current. His head bobbed. He tried to pull himself up on a rock but his pant- leg was caught in the bike's chain. He fought to wiggle out. Wet denim clung to him as the bike pulled him under.

Carrie and Sassy screamed. The older boys ran off. No-good cowards. Oliver pulled his Scout knife from his pocket, then ripped off his clothes and dove into the water. With a few swift strokes, he reached his friend and released the jeans from the chain, sending the bike drifting away. He swam under Adam's limp body and raised him on his back. Oliver swam to shore with Adam's arms around his neck. Despite their closeness in size, he lifted him from the water like a father lifting his child and settled him on the ground.

"Carrie, go get help," Oliver said. He rolled Adam onto his side and pushed on his stomach.

Carrie took off her coat and covered Oliver's bare back. She tossed her fuzzy accessories down on the ground next to them before following orders to run for help.

"C'mon, man. Let it out, damn it," Oliver said.

When Adam didn't respond, Oliver laid him flat and tilted his head back. He pinched his nose and blew into his mouth a few times. Sassy helped move him onto his side again. Oliver pushed harder on his stomach and Adam coughed. Some water came out of his mouth.

"That's it," Oliver said. "Let it out. Breathe."

Adam coughed again. Then he spewed a lungful of creek water all over her brother.

"Oli, you did it," Sassy said. "You saved…"

Oliver had already started toward the water to clean himself off.

Adam shivered in his wet clothes. Sassy helped him out of his coat and laid herself across his chest for warmth. His heart pounded against hers. He closed his eyes again and her young mind thought he died. She slapped his face. He wasn't allowed to die.

"Bully," Adam said. His strained laugh embarrassed her. She wasn't supposed to be the one freaking out, that was Carrie's job. But this wasn't their world. Their world wasn't cold and scary. It had hot chocolate and mini marshmallows. Adam never stayed down when Oliver tackled him. Boys were supposed to be sweaty, not frozen.

Sassy had to be the fun one. She had to make the fear go away. She sat up, took off her coat, and covered Adam. Oliver was dressed again, with Carrie's coat around his shoulders like a cape.

"You look pretty in Carrie's pink coat, Oli," she said. "Doesn't he, Adam? Maybe when she gets back she'll let you borrow the matching boots."

"Hubba… hubba," Adam said, forcing a smile.

Oliver took Carrie's scarf and wrapped it around his head. He put her coat on backwards. With sleeves halfway to his elbows and his long arms stretched out like a movie zombie, he stomped toward them.

"Eek! A monster!" Sassy yelled. Then, refusing to be a good little damsel in distress, she scooped up a handful of old snow and whipped a snowball at him.

Adam sat up, enjoying the game.

"Give me that," Sassy said to Oliver, pointing at his head. She took the scarf and wrapped it around Adam's neck. Then she tried to make her voice sound sexy. "Adam, you know this really isn't swimming weather."

Her pink zombie brother grunted and pretended to eat her brains. She found Carrie's hat on the ground and put it on for protection. Adam's coughs mixed with laughter as he forced himself up from the ground. Soon Carrie returned with Adam's grandfather.

"I hear you lost your bike," Coach said.

Adam stood up straight, "Yes sir."

"Everybody okay?"

Oliver moved closer to Carrie, creating a six- foot tall barrier between her and Adam's grandfather. "We're fine," he said, giving Carrie back her coat.

Coach Jenkins looked from the ramp, to the hill and back down to the creek. He shook his head. "Son, you better get yourself to the gym early tonight. This little stunt earned you twenty laps around the court."

"Football season ended three weeks ago," Sassy said with her hands on her hips.

"It's always season," Coach replied. He turned to Oliver. "That's what I came to talk to you about."

"No thank you," Oliver said. "I don't play football."

"That's crazy. You were one of the best offensive players Wayne Valley Middle School ever had."

Sassy held her breath, afraid Oliver would tell the coach why he really didn't want to play for him. She took Carrie's hand in hers, a small protection from this old man who had called her a psycho.

"Everyone's a little crazy," Oliver said. "The trick is staying sane enough to appreciate it."

#

Adam's grandfather scraped the last bite of turkey pot pie from his bowl and filled his mouth. Before he finished chewing, Sassy's mother offered him more. He nodded and held up his bowl. She dipped the ladle into her good tureen and filled his dish with her famous homemade noodles. Then she refilled Adam's bowl and cut him off a hunk of warm bread.

"This soup is awesome," Adam said, dunking his bread into the hearty broth.

Mrs. Lingle handed him an extra napkin. She paused, then gave him another. "You children have had quite a day," she said. Making her way around the table, she refilled everyone's bowls. "This will warm your bones."

Carrie was sitting between Sassy and Oliver. She watched Adam from across the table. His square chin moved up and down as he chewed. His jaw was bruised from hitting the handlebars of his bike. She wondered if his teeth were okay, especially the little crooked one on top. That one was her favorite.

"Crazy," Adam's grandfather said, breaking her daydream. "What were you boys thinking, pulling a stunt like that?"

"Oliver's a real hero," Sassy said.

The old man turned and spoke to Adam. "Boy, you'll never get to drive the Mustang if you don't grow up."

"He had to do it," Oliver said. "Those punks from Westside dared him."

The coach's white, bushy eyebrows sunk. "Dares are for fools." His gruff voice was almost a whisper. "You should have learned that from your father."

Everyone at the table went silent. Adam fidgeted with his collar as if he suddenly realized the Hershey Park t-shirt Oliver had loaned him was a size too small. Oliver took the crusts that Carrie had picked off of her bread and used them to sop up the last of his soup. Mrs. Lingle didn't scold him for it like she usually did. Even Sassy was quiet.

Carrie nervously gulped her soda. She wanted to hug Adam. She understood how it felt to lose a parent. He'd lost both of his. Sure, he had his grandparents, but it wasn't the same.

She opened her mouth to tell him she was glad he was okay, but instead, a loud burp erupted. She put her hand over her mouth, but it was too late. Everyone had heard.

"I'm sorry. Excuse me. I'm sorry," she mumbled through her hand.

Sassy laughed so hard she snorted. Oliver reached over and smacked his sister on the back of her head. Carrie shrunk down in her seat, certain she was the grossest thing Adam Jenkins had ever seen. Or heard.

Oliver pushed his chair back and excused himself from the table. "C'mon, Care," he said, taking her by the arm. "I'll help you finish hanging your Christmas lights."

As she stood to leave, Carrie caught a look at Adam. Through teary eyes, she saw him smile at her. The crooked tooth looked perfect.

#

Two years later, Carrie and Sassy sat together in the stands as Adam scored the games' third touchdown. Carrie clapped excitedly.

Sassy looked up from the guy she was talking to. "Is it over?" she asked.

"There's still one more quarter," Carrie said.

The guy nudged Sassy's arm.

"I can't go yet," she told him. "My friend wants to see the rest of the game." Then she cupped her hand around her mouth and whispered loudly, "She has a crush on one of the players." She pointed toward the field at Adam. "That big dude scoring all the points."

Carrie almost choked on her gum. "We're only friends," she said. Even that felt like an exaggeration, but she heard herself saying, "It's his last high school game. You guys don't have to stay. I'll be fine."

The guy put his arm around Sassy. "See? She doesn't mind," he said.

Sassy coughed and nodded toward Carrie. "I'm not leaving her here by herself." She had that hopeful look in her eye, the one she always got when she wanted to be released of Carrie's constant neediness.

Carrie faked a laugh. "Don't be silly. Go," she said. "I'm fine. Really."

"Well, if you promise to meet up with me later at the pizza shop."

"Sure." Carrie hugged her and said, "Be careful."

"Always am," Sassy said. Then she whispered into her ear, "Have Adam give you a ride to Andaloro's. He loves their Stromboli."

#

After the game, Carrie waited for Adam outside of the locker room.

"Great game," she said when he walked out. "Congratulations."

"Did Sassy abandon you again?" he asked.

Carrie breathed in the scent of fresh deodorant. He always smelled so good right after he showered.

"Nah. She met a guy." Looking down at her shoes, she noticed her laces were untied. "She said she'd meet us at the pizza shop later. Would you mind giving me a ride to Andaloro's?"

Adam grinned. Maybe he was thinking about Stromboli. "You stayed for my game? All by yourself?"

The back door of the locker room burst open before she could answer.

"Adam!" a player yelled. "The coach! He collapsed."

Carrie followed as Adam ran back inside. His grandfather was passed out on the floor.

"Pop!" he yelled. "Pop, can you hear me?" He shook his arm. There was no response. Adam felt for a pulse. "Baker, call for help!"

The guy hurdled the bench and rushed away. Adam bent down, putting his ear near his grandfather's mouth. He knelt over him. "No!" he demanded, beating up and down on his chest. "Pop!" Adam covered his grandfather's mouth with his own, breathing life into the awful stillness. Again and again, the chest fell flat. Adam refused to give up. Over and over he repeated the motions.

Beating, beating, breathing. Beating, beating, breathing. Carrie stood helpless, bound to the rhythm as she watched Adam desperately try to save the man who had raised him.

Coach would have been proud of how well his grandson performed the CPR he had taught him in Health class. But he never woke up.

CHAPTER 7 – MAN OF THE HOUSE

The moving truck left at supper time. Carrie noticed Adam waited until it was out of sight to stick the "For Sale" sign into the ground. He and Oliver had taken Adam's grandmother to the airport that morning. Now, her stuff was gone too. She hadn't left in a funeral procession of a hundred cars like her husband had last month, nor did a sea of maroon and gold pennants wave through the bleachers in her honor. She wasn't the least bit dead, but she was gone just the same.

Carrie had never thought of Adam as an orphan. He used to say that his parents were especially grand. Towering over that awful real estate sign, Carrie could see traces of a little boy within the man Adam was trying so hard to be. She wanted to hug him, but she wasn't sure if she should, or if she even could. She didn't know how to act.

"It's getting chilly out," she said. She chose the prettiest pumpkin cookie from the tin she had brought and handed it to him. Cream cheese icing was stuck to the bottom from another cookie. She hoped he'd eat it fast enough not to notice. "Oliver and Sassy are starting a campfire out back in your fire pit. Could be fun."

"It is kind of empty inside the house," Adam said. He ate the cookie in two bites.

"You can stay at the Lingles' for a while," Carrie said, putting the tin on the top step. "Sassy already asked her mom. She said it would be okay."

"I have some stuff to take care of here." He picked a football up off of the front lawn and tossed it through the hole of an old tire swing.

Carrie ran to get the ball, tripped, and fell into a pile of leaves. She lay there for a minute, feeling like a dork for tripping. But before she could get up, Adam jumped in the pile with her. She laughed and threw a bunch of leaves on top of him. He buried her up to her neck. The leaf war continued, scattering the pile all over the lawn until they fell to the ground and lay looking at the stars.

"Pop had been promising to take Gram to Florida for years," Adam said.

"It's good she finally got to go," Carrie said.

"I guess. She loves the sunshine. Shame she had to go alone though."

Carrie was quiet.

"He should have retired five years ago when the doctor told him to slow down." Adam sighed. "I tried to talk to him. Lots of people did. He was great with advice—as long as he didn't have to follow it."

A hint of smoke from the campfire out back crept into the crisp autumn air.

"Tell me more about him," Carrie said. "Something that makes you smile."

Adam's words flowed naturally. His hand fell against hers as he spoke. She kept very still against him, never wanting to lose the connection. He told her everything she already knew about the Mustang his grandfather had driven around so proudly. Then he told her the story of how his father had bought it without consulting Pop.

"Sheer spite," Adam said imitating his grandfather's gruff voice. "I benched that boy for cutting class and smokin' cigarettes in the men's room. He turns around and spends an entire summer's worth of grass mowing money on a beat up old Ford. Sheer spite is what it was."

Carrie laughed. "You sound just like him," she said.

"Of course," Adam said in his own voice. "My parents met and got married soon after. The accident was three years later—her car. Pop inherited me and the Mustang. The car sat in his garage for years, untouched. We didn't start working on it until I turned ten."

Carrie desperately wanted to say something comforting, wise, or, at least, charming. She thought about the time Adam's grandfather had told her that her mom wasn't in Heaven. Mrs. Lingle said he had no right to say such a thing, but she didn't say it wasn't true. Carrie couldn't bring herself to talk about Heaven. She wiggled her hand, unable to feel his anymore.

"Adam," she said. "Do you mind if I share something with you?" She held her breath, waiting for him to answer. She had never talked with a boy like this. Sassy was all the way in the backyard. Carrie was in over her head. Adam needed someone better, someone who knew what to say.

Adam turned onto his side and faced her. His gaze held her from falling into herself. "Breathe," he said. "You don't have to be shy with me."

"It's just… I say this prayer. It's really short. I thought… maybe… it might help you, too."

He smiled the best smile she had ever seen. Then he folded both of his hands over hers. She bowed her head, like she did when she was alone.

"God, I am Yours," she said. "Please never leave me."

#

The campfire had burnt down to a few glowing embers. Oliver poured a bucket of water over the pit. It hissed at him. A thick white cloud drifted into the air. The rugged scent of smoking walnut clung to them like a frightened child.

"I guess I better get you girls home," Oliver said.

Adam waved as they drove away. Carrie imagined him walking back into the big, empty house: The hollow sound of his own footsteps slapping across the kitchen floor, the creek of the stairs as he went up to bed, the silent ache of abandonment that wouldn't let him sleep. And all that was across the street was some lame insurance office. The lights were never on over there.

CHAPTER 8 – FIRST KISS

"Is the coast clear?" asked Sassy.

Carrie looked up the basement stairs. The door was still shut, and she couldn't hear anything. She was pretty sure Sassy's parents had left for the New Year's Eve party up the street, and Oliver hadn't been home since Christmas. "I guess so."

Sassy flicked the light switch off and on twice. Carrie heard a tap on the window. It made her jump. The guy Sassy had been flirting with at the mall peered through the window.

"They're here," Sassy said to Carrie. "Are you ready?"

"Why did you tell them we're in college?" Carrie asked.

"We will be next year. Close enough."

"What if his friend doesn't like me?"

"Relax. I'll be right over there." Sassy winked and nodded toward the big ugly chair in the corner. She opened the window and the boys crawled in.

"Happy New Year," she said to them.

They took off their coats and set a bottle of rum on Mr. Lingle's bar. Carrie nudged Sassy and whispered, "You promised no drinking."

"Shh. Don't worry," Sassy whispered back. She hung their coats. "Alex, you remember Carrie," she said.

"Ah, yes. The girl who had to leave the mall early to buy cheese," he said.

"Uh, yeah. She's an awesome cook," Sassy said. "Wait 'til you try the Stromboli she made for us."

"Pete here loves Stromboli." Alex nudged the smart-looking guy that had crawled into the house with him. "Isn't that right, Pete?"

Pete glared at his friend. "Actually, I don't eat meat."

Sassy touched his shoulder. "It's just pepperoni. You can pick it out."

"Do you like football?" Carrie asked, pulling at her shirt.

"I golf," Pete answered.

Sassy took out four glasses and filled them with ice. She poured a diet soda and handed it to Carrie, then mixed rum and cola in the other three glasses. They took their drinks and sat around the old coffee table.

Carrie recited the details she had rehearsed, "Sassy is a Psychology major. I'm in Elementary Education." Both guys seemed more focused on Sassy's butt as she got up and walked over to get coasters.

"Sorry," she said as she bent to slip one under each of their drinks. "The rings are really hard to get out."

They watched her like she was sculpting ice with a chain saw. Carrie sat back and hugged a throw pillow as they listened to Sassy talk about her fictional professor in her fictional Psych class. She laughed to herself when Alex pretended to know the professor personally. Pete went along with the story, sharing a few anecdotes of his own.

Carrie tried to participate in the weird conversation but slipped up and mentioned something about forgetting a hall pass. She stopped herself mid-sentence. "Wait," she said with a panicked look toward Sassy. "That was high school. Last year. We were in high school last year."

"Carrie made these cookies," Sassy said, trying to recover. "Chocolate chip is her specialty." She took a bite and fed a piece to Alex. He licked chocolate from her finger.

It was almost eleven o'clock when Sassy turned down the lights and led Alex over to the corner of the room. Carrie gripped the arm of the couch. She stared ahead at the television, wishing she couldn't hear the sounds of her best friend making out in that ugly chair.

Pete moved closer to Carrie on the couch. "Want to watch the ball drop?" she asked.

He put his hand on her knee. She inched away from him, but his fingers slid up her thigh. It tickled. Gross. She squirmed out of reach and grabbed the plate from the end table.

"Would you like a cookie?" she asked.

He leaned closer. His breath smelled like rum. She shoved a cookie into his mouth. Suddenly, the lights came on. Startled, Pete jumped up, knocking the plate out of Carrie's hand, dumping cookies all over her lap.

Sassy and Alex hurried to straighten themselves as Oliver stormed down the stairs. "What the hell is going on down here?" he demanded.

The boys scrambled to get away. Oliver tackled Alex to the floor. Pete tried to pull him off but got flung into the ugly chair.

"Keep your damn hands off my sister."

"Oli, we were just…" Sassy tried.

"I know exactly what you punks were doing," he said to the boys over her protests. "You don't even know her."

"Knock it off, Oli. I can handle myself," Sassy said.

"You don't know men."

"So punch every guy that kisses me? I kiss back, you know. Want to give me a black eye? Maybe I'll kiss this guy, too?" She grabbed Carrie's stunned date by the collar and kissed him hard on the mouth. "How 'bout it, big brother?" she asked with her hands on her hips. "Want to beat us all up?"

Carrie brushed crumbs from her lap as Alex and Pete bolted up the stairs. The night's humiliation continued with an argument.

"Now look what you've done," Sassy said. "Poor Carrie liked that guy and you chased him off."

Adam loves pepperoni, Carrie thought, trying to blend into the background. She wondered who he was with tonight.

"That guy's a toad," she heard Oliver say. She imagined Pete, shrunk down and standing on a lily pad, swinging a golf club and chewing on broccoli.

"You stay out of her love life!" Sassy said. "You know Carrie's …shy. She has a hard enough time."

They both looked at Carrie, who was doing her best not to cry. Oliver picked up a cookie that had fallen on the floor. She must've missed that one. He examined it like evidence from a crime scene. "You baked cookies for those guys?" he asked.

Carrie could only nod.

He dropped it on the plate with the others. "She's too good for Toad Boy," Oliver said to Sassy. Then he flipped the ugly chair on its side, breaking its back.

Carrie would never admit it to Sassy, but she kind of liked the brotherly love of his protection. She grabbed her coat and slipped away as Oliver and Sassy debated the propriety of each other's actions.

At least her first kiss hadn't been wasted on a toad.

#

Across the street, Carrie was greeted by a locked door. Her father had already gone to bed. As she dug through her pockets for a house key, tears sent an icy burn down her red cheeks. She buried her face in her mittens at the sound of footsteps crunching in the snow.

"You can't hide from me," Adam teased. "I'd know those fuzzy pink mittens anywhere."

Carrie lowered her hands. "Adam. Thank God it's you. I thought Sassy's friends might be back."

"Good cover," he said. "They'd have never found you. Lucky for me, I could still see your boots."

She faked a laugh. "I guess I'm not as stealthy as I thought I was." She turned her head away as he got closer, trying to hide the fact that she had been crying.

"I thought we were meeting across the street. Oliver told me to come over before midnight."

"I don't know. He didn't even tell us he was coming home." Carrie jiggled the doorknob. "I forgot my stupid key again. Crazy, right? Locked doors are supposed to keep the bad guys out. Instead, it's keeping me out."

She checked her pockets again and sighed. "I can't get in… I definitely can't go back…"

Adam stopped her. "What happened, Care? You okay?" he asked.

Carrie slumped down onto the stoop and hugged her knees. "It's almost midnight. Go ahead over there. I'll be fine."

"I'm not going anywhere." Adam wrapped her scarf around her and petted her like a kitten. "There, there." The lame, but well- meaning sentiment made them both laugh.

"Meow." Carrie rubbed her head on his chest and purred.

"Ha ha. At least I didn't slap your butt like they do on the field."

"Does that really work for guys?"

"I've never seen one cry. Do girls really fall for that mushy stuff?"

"Well, I probably would," Carrie said. "I'll let you know if someone ever tries it on me."

"I'm trying," Adam said. He took off his coat and wrapped it around her shoulders. "Wanna talk about it?"

"It's silly, really," Carrie said, trying to resist Adam's coat. "Sassy's date brought a friend. He was more interested in her than me."

Adam put his coat over her again, snapping it up to her chin. "Um. There's other fish in the sea?"

"Oh, it's not that. I just feel so stupid." She snuggled in the warmth of his gesture. "He couldn't care less about me. He stared at Sassy all night. He didn't even try to stop her when she kissed him."

"Wait. What? Sassy kissed your date?"

"Ugh. He wasn't my date, really. I don't get why she even thought I'd like the guy. He was a dud. A toad. She only kissed him to spite Oliver after he tackled the other guy. It meant nothing. I guess I just wanted to be the one to be stared at for once."

"Hmm. I see. Sort of."

"I want to feel special. Guys don't look at me the way they look at her."

Adam held her face in his hands and looked deep into her eyes. "Wow. They have no idea what they're missing."

Carrie embarrassed herself with an awkward giggle. "You smell like Old Spice," she said.

Sitting side by side on the stoop with Adam, Carrie didn't feel like a high school girl with a crush on a college football star. She was here with her friend. He didn't make her hands shake or her voice quiver. With Adam, she felt real. He knew her. He saw her. She wanted him to touch her again.

As if she had willed it, he put his arm around her. She fit against him like she belonged there. They were huddled together, enjoying each other's warmth when the fireworks went off at midnight. The bright lights crackled in the brisk winter air, shining on a relationship that was ready to change.

She turned to look up at him. "Happy New Year," she said. He kissed her on the nose and she giggled again. Their faces stayed together, now just a whisper apart.

He kissed her mouth so gently her eyes watered with the sheer joy of it. Then he kissed her again and she followed his lead, their lips moving in sync like a sweet dance.

CHAPTER 9 – JERRY ROCK

Sassy slid a butter knife between Oliver's locked bedroom door and the door frame. With a little maneuvering, the latch moved and the door popped open. She entered the room and pulled open his desk drawer, looking for his stash of batteries. She didn't find any, so she tried his nightstand. The drawer was stuck. She pulled harder, but it wouldn't budge. She was sitting on the floor trying to jimmy it open with the butter knife when Oliver came in.

"Hey. Do you have any batteries?" she asked. "My Walkman died and…"

He ripped the knife from her hand like it was a deadly weapon. "What the hell are you doing?!" he yelled. His breath had that gross yeasty smell he always brought home after college parties.

"Geesh, Oli. I was just looking for batteries. I'll clean up."

Sassy stood and took a quick look around. Not a thing was ever out of place in Oliver's room. "Lighten up," she said, adjusting the collar on his polo shirt. "Lots of guys have dirty magazines."

"Stop," he said, pulling himself away. He stumbled backward, knocking the Bible on his nightstand to the floor. "Damnit. You're gonna wake Mom." As Oliver bent to pick up the book, Sassy spotted a small hickey below his ear.

"You didn't tell me you're seeing someone," she whispered. "Afraid I'd beat her up?" She put up her fists and pretended to fight an invisible girlfriend.

"Stop," Oliver said. His face was getting red and his nostrils were flaring.

"C'mon." She poked his stomach. "You never bring any of your girlfriends home. How am I supposed to judge who's good enough for you?"

He didn't poke back, or even crack a smile, so she tickled his ribs. "What's the matter, Oli? Are you embarrassed of your baby sister?"

Oliver took hold of her wrists and pulled her hands off of him. His fierce grip overpowered her defenses but kept her from falling.

"Stop," he said again.

His glare struck her spirit.

"Ouch. Oli, what are you doing?"

His hands locked tighter around her wrists, sending the pain up her arms. Trying to wiggle away, she looked into his eyes, expecting to see anger. Instead, she saw fear, something she didn't know how to fight. For a moment, Sassy let him hold on to her. As her fingers went numb, she imagined she was absorbing his pain. She hadn't seen him this angry since he was in high school. Even then, he'd never laid a hand on her. A jolt shot through her pinky, startling her back to reality.

"You're hurting me," she finally said.

"Stop," he said, and she realized he was talking to himself.

His hands released her, but she could still feel his grasp. Her little finger was crooked, and already starting to swell. She stepped back from him. His heavy breaths hung between them. Annoyed by her own tears, she rubbed her moist face with her sleeve.

Oliver's fist came out of nowhere, swung past her, and into the wall. The moment froze. Her arms felt like they were still being squeezed. Her brother's fist remained clenched. Sassy stared at the hole as white dust settled around it.

#

Carrie heard a car out front. It was two o'clock in the morning. She got out of bed and looked out her window. Adam's car was parked across the street.

I knew he'd come back.

When he'd brought her home at midnight, she hadn't told him she never slept there if her father wasn't home. She was eighteen years old. She didn't need a babysitter. Mrs. Lingle didn't even wait up for them anymore anyway. So, Carrie had gone by herself, into her own house, to her own room. Like an adult.

Now, she ran a quick brush through her hair and hurried downstairs. She turned the lock and swung the front door open just as the Lingles' door opened across the street. Oliver looked back at her, then hung his head. He had the blue duffel bag he used to take on camping trips. It appeared to be full. He shoved it into the back of Adam's car, then hopped in the front seat next to Adam. She figured he must've had a fight with his father again. Except, his father's car wasn't in the driveway.

Carrie looked up at Sassy's window. Her room was still dark, but the curtains moved a little. She waited for the guys to leave before running across the street in her pajamas. Sassy met her on the front porch.

"Are you okay?" Carrie asked. "What happened?"

"Nothing," Sassy said. "He's pissed at me for going into his room. He always hoards the batteries."

"He took a bag with him. He's more than pissed, isn't he?"

Carrie caught a quick glimpse of her finger as Sassy hid her wrists inside the sleeves of her robe.

"Care, can we sleep at your house tonight?"

,

#

Adam wondered what Oliver had done this time, but he didn't asked any questions when the duffel bag hit his back seat. He would have preferred one of Mrs. Lingle's Tupperware containers, but he couldn't complain. He'd seen his share of those over the years.

"You left Carrie home alone," Oliver said, rolling down the car window. "Your little girl's afraid of the dark." His words slurred, somewhere between sarcasm and concern.

"She said she was fine," Adam answered. "She was going right to bed." But he glanced in his rearview mirror and saw Carrie and Sassy crossing the street back to Carrie's house.

Adam stopped at the intersection. It was late, and there was no traffic. He waited an extra minute at the stop sign, watching for the girls to reappear in his mirror. All he saw was the dark emptiness of the road. He hesitated, then drove toward home.

"Who'd you hit?" he asked, noticing Oliver's busted hand. A hand like that never came without a story, and Oliver always had a good one.

Oliver looked at it like he was seeing the injury for the first time. He curled his hand into a fist and swore at himself. Then he pulled the sleeve of his sweatshirt over it and hid it under his armpit.

"So, did your father kick you out?" Adam asked, thinking he was changing the subject. "I guess he finally made good on his threat."

"Ha! My father. He's not even home."

Adam thought about going back to check on the girls but decided to settle Oliver first.

"What a hypocrite," Oliver continued. "He bitches at me for drinking too much. Then he shows up at my bar and finds himself a whore!"

"Holy shit," Adam said, slowing his car to turn onto his street. "Your poor mom. I'd have hit him, too."

Oliver paused, then continued. "He walked into the bar like he owned the joint. Sat his ass down right next to Esther. He's a pig. Had his hands all over her."

"Who's Esther?" Adam asked.

Oliver rolled up his window as Adam parked in front of his house. "Nobody. Some girl I knew a long time ago."

They got out of the car and Adam realized Oliver's face was unmarked. He shook his head in disbelief. "He didn't even have the nerve to hit back?"

Oliver shrugged, then reached for his duffel bag. "Got any beer in there?" he asked, walking toward the house.

"I think you left a few cans in the fridge the last time you were here." Adam opened the door and Oliver followed him inside.

"Left a few?" Oliver slapped Adam on the back. Then he mockingly rubbed his chin, as if to ponder such a strange scenario. "That doesn't sound like me," he said.

"Well, you were a little preoccupied with your date when I left."

Oliver dropped his bag at the bottom of the stairs and headed to the refrigerator. He tossed a beer to Adam and got one for himself. "Ah, yes…I never did get her name," he said. "Like father, like son… like father, I guess," he said. "Why fight it, right? A swine's gotta slop in the mud."

Adam plopped himself down on the couch. "But the girl at the bar…Esther. You knew her name."

Oliver drank his beer. "She works there," he said. "I see her once in a while." He belched and went back to the refrigerator and grabbed another beer.

"Your father was hitting on a waitress?"

"More like hiring." Oliver chugged his beer. "She's not a waitress. She's a hooker. They left together."

Adam leaned forward in his seat, unsure if he had heard correctly. "Shit, man. The same girl… you… *see*?"

"Nah. It's not like that. I just see her around. She probably doesn't remember me." He emptied the can and crushed it with his busted hand. "We met at church. I was fifteen. She was sixteen, maybe seventeen. Whatever. It was just that one time. My first. Definitely not hers."

"No way. With a prostitute? At church?"

"She wasn't a hooker back then." He chuckled under his breath. "She used to sing in the choir."

"You're full of shit."

"Seriously, man. We snuck out of a Sunday service together. She told me she knew a place where we could be alone. We went down to the church basement and she pulled me into a storage closet." He shook his head and smiled. "She wasn't wearing any panties under that choir robe."

#

Sassy hadn't been to Chippi's Park with Oliver since last autumn. Being here without him now distorted the view. She dismissed the ache around her wrists. She moved her pinky. It still hurt, but she was able to touch her palm. As long as it worked, she didn't care if it looked a little crooked. After last night, everything looked different.

The early morning glow along the horizon singed the sky. The height of the mountain had never made her feel so vulnerable. The stream that flowed through the ravine below moved swiftly with yesterday's rain. She sat on a large rock, looking out over Wayne Valley. From the top of the mountain, her hometown looked like an oil painting, but even in the distance, it was marred by the ugliness of reality.

Oliver had started bringing her to this park when she was fourteen. They nicknamed their rock "Jerry Rock" after their favorite philosopher, Jerry Seinfeld, because it was where Oliver liked to go to think. Coming to Chippi's Park with her big brother used to make her feel grown up. She was eighteen now, and still didn't feel old enough to be here alone.

Sassy sipped her water. She wasn't sure what she had come to find at Chippi's. Maybe something could help recapture the peace this place had allowed her to share with her brother in the past. She slipped off her shoes and dangled her bare feet over the edge.

She didn't understand the spiritual connection Oliver felt to Jerry Rock, but she liked that he shared it with her. He was different here, calmer. He talked about things like nature and miracles. Up here, his anger never spoke.

She tossed a pebble over the edge like a penny into a wishing well. *Don't let it be true.* But last night had still happened.

His bedroom wall would be fixed. That damage was small. The swelling in her finger had already started to go down. The bruises around her wrists only needed time to heal. The pinkish grey marks on her flesh would fade, little by little, until her skin appeared normal. Oliver, however…

Sassy turned when she heard a dog bark. He was only a few feet away from her. His brown and white fur was dirty and matted. He watched her as she twisted the lid off of her water bottle and stepped toward him. She let him sniff her hand. "It's okay," she said, patting his head. She tipped water over his mouth. He lapped at it, drinking until the bottle was empty.

She walked him through the park to look for his people. He followed right along and never left her side. Nobody was around to claim him. He sat with her on the rock for a while. She wondered how long it had been since he had eaten. They took another lap around the park. An elderly couple was sitting on a bench tossing crumbs to the birds. They said they hadn't seen anyone else either. The dog gulped their last piece of bread when they weren't looking.

"Oh no! I'm so sorry," Sassy said to the couple. "He must be starving." They smiled sympathetically and shook their heads when she again asked them if they had seen anyone who could be searching for him.

After one last look around the park, the dog followed Sassy back to her car. "I guess we better go home," she said to her new friend. "We can come back tomorrow. I'll make some signs." He sat next to her in the passenger seat, wagging his tail. His sweet face made her smile. "You are a work of art," she told him. "Mind if I call you Jerry?"

CHAPTER 10 – STRAY

Sassy took Jerry for a run early Sunday morning. Adam's street was only two miles away. She noticed a new realtor's sign on the front lawn as she approached his house. She couldn't remember if it was the third or fourth agency he had used over the past year. Jerry followed her to the door and barked as she knocked. Adam came out, pulling the door closed behind him.

"Hey, Sass. You're out early. Who's this guy?" he asked.

"This is my friend, Jerry. I found him at the park yesterday. Can we come in? I need to talk to Oli."

Adam petted Jerry's head. "Yeah, um. He's not here. Can you come back later? Or tomorrow, maybe. In the afternoon. Come back tomorrow afternoon."

"Damn, Adam. You're a horrible liar." She tried to push past him, but his large figure blocked the door.

"C'mon, Adam. I know he's here."

Adam didn't deny it this time. Instead, he bent to pet the dog again. Sassy waited as Jerry enjoyed the attention. Adam lingered. Jerry licked his face. She was in no mood to appreciate the sweetness of it right now.

"I guess I'll come back tomorrow- *in the afternoon.* Wouldn't want to wake anyone." She turned to leave. "C'mon Jerry. Good boy."

"Sass, wait…"

She stopped but didn't turn around.

"Sassy," he started again. "He's still sleeping it off."

"Since Friday night?" she asked.

"Well, his Friday night didn't end until late Saturday."

She spun around to face him. "What? Where'd he… what?"

"Don't worry. He was here the whole time. He was so… I don't know… restless…"

"Restless," she repeated. She hugged Adam and whispered, "Thank you for keeping my brother safe."

"It's the least I can do," he said.

He stood at his front door as she walked away. Jerry followed her to the edge of the property, then stopped beside a patch of bushes and growled.

"C'mon, boy," she called. She stepped toward him, looking into the bush to see what the dog was after.

"Sassy, stop," Adam said in an even tone. She didn't listen.

She saw a patch of black fur. Then a white stripe. Jerry growled again. The skunk hissed and the dog jumped into the bush.

A sticky yellow film sprayed out. She turned away but was already covered. Jerry yelped and ran off. Sassy coughed and spit.

"Un-freakin'- believable," she finally said.

#

Sassy waited with Jerry in Adam's backyard while he went for supplies. The dog followed her around as she gathered twigs for a fire, making a pile near the firepit. She turned and saw Jerry with a stick in his mouth. He dropped it next to the pile. "Hey! Good job, Jerry!" she said with a laugh. His name rolled off her tongue. For a split second, she forgot about all the drama. She had yet to introduce her dog to Oliver. "Jerry! Wait until I tell him your name!" The joy quickly faded as she remembered.

Adam came home from the store with a dozen large cans of tomato juice, a kiddie pool, rope, and lots of soaps and shampoos. He even got a new collar for Jerry. They stood him in the pool and doused him in the tomato juice. Adam held the dog still as she scrubbed. He whined when they tied him to the tree.

After they showered, they made a fire to burn their clothes.

"You still reek, Adam," Sassy said.

He laughed. "Yeah. I shouldn't have gone near that skunk like that."

She ignored his sarcasm. "Thanks for helping me." Sassy tied a knot in the end of the long t-shirt Adam had loaned her. She felt weird wearing his clothes. "I don't know what I would've done without…"

"Sassy." Adam gently turned her arms. The bruises looked darker in the sunlight. She pulled away, but it was too late. "What happened?" he asked.

"Nothing." She reached for another can of tomato juice. "Where'd I put that can opener?"

Adam took the tomato juice from her and set it on the ground. "Let him air out. He'll be fine." He put some lawn chairs near the fire and added another log. They sat in awkward silence. Finally, he took her hands in his and studied the marks on her arms. "Sassy," he said. "Talk to me."

"Oh. That." She looked down at her arm. "Yeah. No big deal. Oliver didn't mean to…"

"Oliver did this to you?" Adam jumped to his feet, ready to attack her brother, his best friend.

She stood up in front of him. "No," she said. "No, it was an accident." It sounded ridiculous as she heard herself say it.

"An accident? Bull…"

She put her hands on his chest, desperate to stop him. "It was an accident," she said sternly. She told herself she was defending Oliver, not what he did. She'd work out what that meant later.

Adam walked over to the woodpile and heaved the biggest log up onto his shoulder. "Okay," he said. "I guess you're right." Holding it with one arm, he brought it back and dropped it near the fire. "Accidents happen."

The baggy sweatpants Sassy had put on dipped below her belly button and she hiked them back up.

"If I had known we'd be having this party, I'd have brought marshmallows," she said.

Adam stared into the flames. "Maybe Oliver should stay here for a while," he said.

"I don't know. Maybe he will." Sassy stood and walked over to Jerry. "Do you have a tennis ball or something? This guy needs to play."

Adam picked up a stick and launched it across the yard. Jerry bolted after it. He came running back with the stick in his mouth. Adam threw it again.

Every time Jerry brought him the stick, Adam ruffled his floppy ears until his tail wagged. "No matter how far I throw it," he said. "He brings it back." He stretched his arm back and sent the stick flying. Jerry ran for it. "Look at him go!" Adam laughed like a little boy.

She wished they could all be kids again. Trouble used to be exciting. Of course, Oliver always had her back then. Now, she felt so lost.

"Adam, something happened Friday night," she said.

His smile disappeared, but he said nothing.

"Why was he so pissed? Did he tell you anything?" she asked.

Adam didn't answer. Sassy huffed and took the stick from Jerry. She tossed it for him a few times. She played until he was worn out. He plopped onto the grass and chewed his stick. Sassy sat down next to him. Her emotions nagged at her. She felt silly and weak. She hated Oliver for making her feel this way. Even more, she hated not knowing how to help him.

"Damn it," she said to Adam. "Give me something. No excuses. Just make me understand."

Adam picked up some twigs and piled them onto the dying fire. "Okay. He had a few beers and punched a guy. Busted his hand pretty good," he said. The flames kicked up and he added a small log. "He didn't want you to know he was fighting."

She knew very well how he busted his hand, and it wasn't in a bar fight. "He hit a guy in a bar? Is that what he told you?"

She didn't wait for an answer. "Adam, I need to know what's going on," she said. "He wasn't himself. I mean, I know he'd been drinking. He's been doing that a lot lately. But there was something bothering him, something he was fighting to restrain."

Adam laid his giant hand gently on her shoulder. She flinched at the touch, but she stopped him when he tried to pull away.

He looked up at the house as if he needed permission to talk to her. Or maybe he wanted a place to hide. Then he spoke like he was afraid Oliver would hear him.

"Oliver saw your father at the bar," he said. "With a woman. She was uh… a professional. You know, a prostitute."

"What? That's why he was so mad? That's crazy," Sassy said. "It couldn't have been Dad."

Adam drew in the dirt with his shoes. "I'm sorry."

"Maybe it was a lady from work," she tried. "A client- or an intern or something."

"Sass…"

"He was sure? It really was our father? Picking up a whore? I don't think so. Oli was drinking. He must've made a mistake."

Adam threw Jerry's stick into the fire. "Sassy, please. Stop. There was no mistake. Your father left the bar with a hooker."

His gentle tone didn't make it any easier to hear. There was nothing left to debate. "I don't understand. Why didn't he tell me?" She raised her hands in the air and yelled, "I don't need to be protected!"

Adam hung his head and rubbed the back of his neck. He took a deep breath. "When we got back to my place that night, we had a few beers," Adam said. "You know how he gets when he's drinking. You can't shut him up."

Sassy thought about the hole in the wall and the way he'd hurt her. The only thing he had said then was, "Stop."

"There's more," she said. But she was thinking. *Stop. Stop. Stop.*

She looked to Adam. His jaw was clenched. His chest moved up and down as he breathed. She couldn't make herself tell him she was afraid of her own brother. Instead, she tipped her head and rested on his arm. But his muscles stiffened.

"Yeah," he answered. "There is. Oliver knew her." He mouthed the word "knew" like a cuss at the dinner table.

Sassy stood, unable to bear any more. "I need another shower."

#

When she got out of the shower, Oliver was still sleeping on Adam's bed. The sheet and blanket were bunched around his feet. His clothes were in a ball on the floor. Sassy picked them up and shook out the wrinkles, then folded them into a neat pile. She straightened the bedding and eased the covers over him.

She looked around. An empty Pop Tart wrapper was with some tools on Adam's dresser. She wondered what he had been fixing. The thought was refreshingly uncomplicated. A man, living alone in a two-bedroom house, eating Pop Tarts and fixing things. Adam was easy to understand.

His bedroom wasn't anything like her brother's. He had text books and comic books. Hats were everywhere. She counted eleven as she gathered and stacked them on her head. Dressed in his clothes, the ball caps, and the Tom Cruise sunglasses she'd found on his nightstand, she went downstairs.

Adam was standing at the kitchen counter. He laughed when he saw her.

"I see you found something that suits you," he said.

She strutted across the room like a runway model as he described the hottest new trend in women's fashion.

"The 'Adam Jenkins Collection' is versatile enough for any occasion, but who wouldn't want to get skunked wearing this ensemble?"

She stopped to strike a pose and the hats tumbled to the floor. As they both bent to pick them up, the sunglasses dropped and their heads bumped together. She fell down, giggling.

"I'm sorry, Adam," she said between snorts. "I'm not always this graceful."

"You have a really hard head," he said, helping her up from the floor.

She saw two ham and cheese sandwiches on paper towel "plates" waiting on the counter.

"Awh. You cooked for me."

"Don't get any mustard on my good t-shirt."

She wiped a little yellow glob from the corner of his smile. "Yeah, I can be a slob sometimes."

He blinked. She shouldn't have noticed his deep brown eyes, so caring and gentle. She wrapped her arms around him and hugged. "Thank you," was all she meant to say. She felt his hands on her back. His tender strength comforted her, as her body rested against his. She squeezed him harder, afraid of what she might do if she let go.

Their faces touched and she couldn't stop. Her lips slid into his. Her mouth was moving, daring his resistance to shatter. Her heart silently begged him to push her away, but his lips opened. His fingers slipped into her shirt; his shirt. Her skin tingled as his hands moved around her waist. She reached down and opened the button on his jeans.

The floorboards above them creaked, startling them both back to morality.

"Oh my God. I'm so sorry," she said. They apologized to each other like they were apologizing to Carrie.

Sassy and Jerry were gone before Oliver even made it out of the bathroom.

CHAPTER 11 – UNBURIED

Carrie stood on Adam's front porch with a plateful of lemon cookies. She pulled back the plastic wrap, making sure the rain hadn't gotten to them. Relieved the cookies were dry, she stuffed the wet wrap into her pocket. *That was stupid. Now I'm going to look like a goof, standing in the pouring rain with uncovered cookies.*

The lights were on inside, and she could hear his stereo playing. *I should have called first. Give him space. Don't be clingy.* But the idea of being alone tonight was worse than letting Adam know she needed him. She knocked, but he didn't answer. Opening the door, she called out to him, "Adam… It's just me."

It's too late to turn back now. Kicking off her muddy shoes, she stepped inside. The music from his room was louder than the rain now. She put the cookies on the counter and took off her coat.

She heard movement upstairs. "Your door wasn't locked," she yelled up to him. "I hope you don't mind I came." Adam still didn't answer.

She waited a minute, then started up the stairs. "I would have gone to Sassy's," she said, "but she isn't home." Her words slowed with her steps as she got closer and closer to her boyfriend's bedroom, but she couldn't quite stop herself from talking or walking. "I didn't see her much all week, really. She's probably making so many friends at college."

Adam's door was shut.

Just go home. She didn't follow the advice. Instead, she knocked, hating herself instantly. The music stopped. She thought she heard him say, "Come in."

"Honey, something happened," she said, opening the door. Oliver stood in the middle of the room, still naked and wet from the shower. "Oh!" she shrieked, slamming it shut.

"Carrie! Shit. I didn't know you were here," Oliver yelled through the door.

"I…I thought you were Adam…not naked Adam… regular Adam… with clothes… lots of clothes… and a hat."

"Adam left an hour ago."

#

Carrie's socks squished across the soggy grass. "Shoes!" she scolded herself out loud. But she couldn't go back in that house. "Now what do I do?" she mumbled. "Adam's gonna see my muddy sneakers and know I saw his best friend's thing."

Carrie was already soaked, and the rain kept falling. She got into her car and realized she'd also left her coat. "Of course," she grumbled. "The keys are in the pocket with the stupid plastic wrap."

The front door of Adam's house opened, and she ducked. "Carrie!" she heard Oliver yell.

"Maybe I can hotwire it," she told herself, as if she even knew what that meant. Instead, she got out of her car and ran.

"Carrie, wait!" Oliver called.

She splashed through the puddles, helplessly aware of how ridiculous she was acting. She reminded herself she was a grown up. Yet, she still felt like the seventh-grade girl who'd vomited on the worm she was dissecting in science class.

She slowed down, and her foot stepped squarely in a pile of dog poop, causing her to slip. She fell, face first, into the mud. Any hope of Oliver not seeing her disastrous getaway was dashed when she realized he'd caught up to her. He lifted her to her feet and wiped mud from her face with the sleeve of his shirt. She was relieved to see he was wearing clothes.

#

Carrie wrapped her hands around the hot mug of tea. She held it up to her mouth, hiding behind the cup as she spoke. "Thank you, Oliver. I… I'm sorry for, uh, well…"

Oliver bit into a lemon cookie. "Wow. Did you make these?"

She lowered her tea. "Yeah," she said. Looking at the plate, she wished the cookies were nice and round like cookies are supposed to be. "A new recipe."

"Mmm. Write this one down," he said. "You should make them again some time."

As she watched him eat another cookie, she noticed his knuckles were bruised. His eyes caught hers looking at his hand. She lifted her mug. It was still too hot to drink, but she sipped it anyway.

"How was your first week of school?" Oliver asked. "Nobody's giving you a hard time or anything, are they?"

Carrie swallowed another sip. "Oh. Fine. College is great. It's really great. It's fine." She had only made it to one class all week.

Oliver got up and went to the fridge for some milk. "Great, huh? That's what you used to say about high school." He filled a glass to the top. "Yep. Four years in a row. First week of school, you'd tell me everything was great. Then I'd find you crying in the treehouse."

Carrie hung her head. She'd only hidden in his treehouse once. She'd been at the park twice, and in her closet the other time. She still had no idea how he'd found her there. She looked up at him and said, "Sometimes it's hard to fit in, ya know? Then you finally get used to things and it all changes."

"You're a big girl now," Oliver said. He lifted her chin with his finger. "A grown woman."

She blinked away a tear. "But I feel like such a freak."

"I know it's hard for you." He gently wiped her eyes. "But you have to be strong. Don't let the feelings own you. You get to choose who you are. You don't have to be like…" his words trailed off to nowhere. He shook his head and bit into another cookie.

She was certain she knew who he'd meant. This wasn't the first time a conversation had suddenly been censored. Her mother's name had been treated like a four-letter word throughout her childhood.

Carrie sat up straight and crossed her legs, like a lady. "Why?" she asked. "Why won't anyone talk about my mother?"

"Sure they do."

"No. I mean really *talk*. I want to know more than what she looked like. I want to know who she was, what she was like…why she was so sick." Carrie didn't know where her rambling was coming from. She hadn't expected to be talking about any of this tonight.

He paused and took a big sip of his milk. "I didn't know her either, Care. I was too little."

"But something," she said. "You know something."

The sound of thunder rumbled into the conversation. "That storm is really kickin' up out there," Oliver said.

She looked into his deep grey eyes. "Please," she said.

He blinked hard, then he gulped down the last of his milk. He stood and put his glass in the sink. Slowly, he paced across the kitchen, gathering his words. "They say she was crazy."

"Crazy," Carrie repeated. *Crazy*.

"She lost control." He cleared his throat. "Killed herself."

The thoughts had been floating around in her mind for years. Questions. That's all they used to be. "How?" she whispered.

Oliver stopped at the sink and turned on the water. He scrubbed the glass with a sponge.

"How?" she asked louder. "How!" In her heart, she'd always known it was the truth. But nobody had ever said it to her, so she never had to believe it. *Why hadn't anyone ever told her the truth?*

The glass cracked in his hand. He slammed it into the trashcan. "You ask 'how?' like it matters," he yelled. "What good is that now?" He washed his hands. His voice settled. "What you need to figure out it is, 'how not.'"

Carrie closed her eyes and saw an image of her mother, rocking a newborn baby. The questions that had been crashing around in her head for years battled for priority. But one of them won out and she asked it out loud. "What if I'm like her?" she asked. "I'm not strong."

Oliver turned and walked across the room. "Listen to that rain, Carrie," he said as he opened the window. "It's playing a kind of music." The sound of the raindrops was steady and peaceful.

Carrie joined Oliver at the window. Looking out from here, the storm didn't seem so bad. He took her hand in his and her pain no longer felt alone. He spoke over the darkness they shared.

"Rain is beyond our control," he said. "It comes, so we get wet. But we don't have to drown."

The curtains danced with a misty breeze. The dampness warned against forbidden comfort. Their hands fell apart.

Oliver reached out and raised the window higher. A chill passed through her, making her shudder. She stepped back. "Some storms can be absolutely terrifying," she said.

He looked at her and smiled. "But they can also be beautiful."

#

The next morning, Carrie went to school wearing flip flops.

"You're in the wrong building," a guy told her. He smelled like coffee. She smiled and nodded as he explained where to go, but her mind drifted.

Coffee Guy pointed. "Across the quad…" he was saying.

Her brain turned the word quad into quadratic formula. *Not now, Algebra. I'm trying to learn Geography.* She smiled but was glad she hadn't said the silly joke out loud. It didn't matter though. Coffee Guy had already left.

She wandered back outside. She looked at her schedule again, then at her watch. Class had started ten minutes ago. She'd never even heard a bell. Stupid college. *Couldn't they at least ring a damn bell when it was time for class? High school rang bells all day. All day! Here, people wandered around quads drinking coffee and pointing.*

She plopped down on a bench with her books and no coffee. No use trying to find the class now. It was too late. Damn college. Everyone else was probably sitting in that classroom laughing at all the things she'd never know.

She thought about Oliver. *Maybe she knew too much.*

#

Carrie parked her car in the garage and shut the door. She wasn't supposed to be home from classes until after three. She hurried into the house, hoping nobody would notice she was five hours early. Her father wasn't home.

She went directly to the medicine cabinet and opened it wide. Before she could find the bottle she was looking for, the doorbell rang. Her headache would have to wait.

She peeked out and saw Sassy's mother standing on the porch with Tupperware.

"Hi," Carrie said. "Sassy's not here."

Mrs. Lingle smiled with her whole face. "I know," she said. She was wearing the beaded necklace Sassy had made in girl scouts years ago. It looked like the pearls mothers wore in old black and white sitcoms. "I saw your car pull in. I thought you might like some breakfast." She tilted her head. "We have so many leftovers now that Oliver isn't home." In her warm brown eyes flashed a hint of sorrow.

Carrie took the Tupperware and peeled off the lid. Cinnamon buns with cream cheese frosting. Oliver's favorite. "Come on in," she said. "I'll make tea."

"Don't be silly. You go and fix your hair. I'll make it."

Carrie swept her bangs out of her eyes. She'd been meaning to cut them.

Mrs. Lingle fussed around the kitchen. Carrie liked that she was wearing an apron, like she always did at her own house.

"Did my mother wear an apron?" she asked.

"No, Dear. She didn't cook."

"My dad never told me that." Carrie said. She studied the floral pattern on the apron. The dress it covered was blue; not an ugly dress, but very plain. "Was it because of me?" she asked.

"Nonsense," Sassy's Mom said. "She was ill."

"What else?" Carrie twisted her ponytail, then made herself continue. "Dad didn't tell me things. But I know now. It was because of me. She was sick because of me."

Mrs. Lingle adjusted her apron around her thick waist. The kettle whistled and she filled the pot. "Where's your brush, dear? I'll help you. Follow me."

Thankful she didn't have to be an adult right now, Carrie followed obediently into the bathroom and stood in front of the mirror. Sassy's mother pulled the tie from her hair. She brushed with long, firm strokes. "See how beautiful you are," she said. "Set it free."

Carrie closed her eyes and imagined she was a little girl again. Her mother had never lived long enough to brush her hair. "Was I too hard for her to love?" she asked. "Daddy said I was two weeks old. That's not enough. She didn't give me a chance."

"Sweet girl, love goes beyond life. It's timeless. Your mother loved you before you were here, and her love didn't leave when she died. It's yours forever." She handed Carrie the brush and smiled. "I'll be right back."

The tea was still warm when she returned with her sewing box. She opened it and removed the tray of buttons and threads. She took out her embroidery and set it on the table. At the bottom of the box was a small plastic bag full of white fabric. Mrs. Lingle handed the bag to Carrie.

"Your mother was making this for you when...she was sick."

Carrie pulled the fabric out and studied it. She traced the pink stitching with her finger. The letters were crooked and bumpy on the snow-white cloth.

"C-a," she read.

"She asked me to help her sew something special. She wanted to do your name herself."

Carrie rubbed the silky fabric against her cheek.

"My Dad thinks I don't know," she said. "She did it on purpose."

#

Dear Mom,
    You don't know me. I'm the girl who grew up without you. I'm the girl who just found out why you died. Well...sort of. All I really found out was that you killed yourself. That doesn't explain why. But at least I understand the whispers now.
They tell me you were sick. I guess some words are too hard to add. Daddy wants me to have sweet images of being rocked by my mother as she sang lullabies, not crying alone in a crib while you up and died.
    I hate it. I hate that you left us. I hate that you were hurting so much that you thought killing yourself was the only answer. And I hate that I can't tell you how sorry I am that having me did that to you.
    I wish I could thank you for loving me enough to bring me into this world. Yet, I feel unfinished and abandoned. I want to tell you I forgive you. And I want to hear you forgive me too. I want you with me in this rocking chair when I can't sleep, when I'm scared, when my pieces are falling apart. I want you to know me. Love me. Take it all back and let me love you.

Sometimes, I get scared and I'm not sure why. I can't keep up with my thoughts. It's like I'm running around inside my head, trying to catch my mind. But at the same time another mind is chasing me. So, I'm left watching strangers pretending to be me. I hate them too. The strangers. Or maybe I hate myself for not being strong enough to live out from under them.

Part of me always feels confused or lost. Is this how you felt when I was inside you? Are you who I am? Am I you? I can't be the one who took you away. There's too much of you left in me. And I can't be your second chance. I have to be someone new.

It's weird to say that I miss you since I didn't really get to have you. I do though. I miss you a lot. Things are happening and I need my mother. I need to tell you that I love you, too.

Amen. So be it.

Love,

Ca

Carrie ripped the letter from her notebook and buried it underneath her dolls.

CHAPTER 12 – CONFESSION

Sassy sat on the bench in Carrie's bedroom and looked out the window. She could see her front door open across the street. She watched as her parents came out. Her father had his Bible tucked under his arm. Her mother looked silly, standing there waving as he drove off.

Sassy wondered if he was wearing the cologne she'd bought him last Christmas. She wished she had never gotten it for him.

"She has to know where he's really going. How can Mom let him leave like that? 'Bye, Dear. Go rent yourself a nice whore. I'll stay here and make a Bundt cake.' She probably packed him a lunch," Sassy said.

"Sass, that's not fair. He's the one who's cheating. Sooner or later, he'll have to answer for that. Your mother is hurting. She has to handle it her own way," Carrie said.

"He's never going to respect her if she can't respect herself."

"Lies have a way of sucking the respect out of a person."

Sassy closed the curtains. She couldn't hold it in any longer.

"Care, I did something awful. It wasn't Adam's fault."

#

Alone in the dark, Carrie rocked in her mother's chair. Hours passed as her mind twisted. The past. The present. Whispered secrets and fractured trust.

Nagging guilt taunted her. She couldn't beg for forgiveness the way Sassy had. Carrie hadn't even been allowed to be sorry. She wasn't supposed to know that her mother killed herself. It was because of her. Because of her.

Sassy had promised over and over that what happened with Adam was an accident, misguided comfort, a one-time mistake. The argument probably eased her conscience. Carrie's conscience had no help. She couldn't tell her mother she was sorry, and she couldn't promise it would never happen again.

Carrie brought herself to the window but didn't look out. She opened the bench and unpacked her dolls. She counted them as she set each one in a row on her pink carpet. Thirty-seven well-dressed bodies lined her bedroom floor. She removed the males from the group and buried them back inside the bench. Thirty-four dolls remained. She laid herself alongside of them. The dolls didn't move. They didn't love her, and they didn't just confess to kissing the only boyfriend she had ever had. She picked one up and threw it against the wall.

"Forgive me," she said. "Please, forgive me."

The words echoed in her mind. She had never imagined hearing

them from her best friend. She picked up another doll. Perfect hair. Perfect

face. Perfect body.

"Adam pushed her away," she said. Then she swung the doll by

her hair and whipped it into the corner. One by one, the dolls flew across

her room. "It was such a weird day." Thud. "I'm so sorry!" Smack. "It will

never happen again." Boom. The plastic storm continued.

Finally, she was left with her stupid little bride. Carrie squeezed

its head as hard as she could. Then she took off its clothes and threw it.

"He pushed her away," she mumbled. Curled into a ball, she cried herself

to sleep.

#

Carrie woke up on her bedroom floor, snuggled in her softest

blanket. Her dolls were resting safely back in the bench and the letter to

her mother was gone.

CHAPTER 13 – UNBREAK MY HEART

Sassy sat cross-legged on her bed with a pile of books and notepads. There was a soft knock on her door.

"I'm not hungry, Mom," she called.

The door opened. "Mind if I come in?" Carrie asked.

Sassy looked up from her notes. Carrie hadn't been in her room in almost three months. They'd spent time together, but it hadn't felt like Carrie was really there. Sassy hated herself for hurting her. She'd tried to talk to her about it countless times, but Carrie always got flustered and changed the subject.

Sassy moved her books aside now, clearing a spot for Carrie to sit. "Hi," Sassy said.

Carrie stood by the door. "Looks like you have a lot of work there."

"American Literature. Hoo Rah."

Carrie laughed nervously. "You don't fool me, Sass. You're into it. You're analyzing the authors again, aren't you?"

You're back, Sassy thought. There was so much she wanted to ask, so much to say. But she couldn't. "Some of 'em were seriously disturbed," she said instead.

"You know your class is mostly fiction, right?"

"Still, it's not normal for some of this stuff to come out of a person's brain."

"Imagination is healthy."

"Sometimes," Sassy said. "Want to study together?"

"Actually, I have to go. I have a job interview at the insurance agency by Adam's house. They need a secretary."

"Oh. Okay. Cool. Want to borrow my new scarf?" She reached for the green scarf tied around her bedpost. "Oliver got it for me for Christmas. It'll look great with your hair."

Carrie took the scarf and wrapped it around her neck. The splash of color brightened her whole look. "Thanks, Sass. I... I miss you..."

"I love you, Carrie," Sassy said.

"I love you, too," Carrie said. Then she hurried out the door.

#

Sassy took a large pan of lasagna from the oven. Her mother set three places at the dinner table.

"It's Friday," Sassy said. "Is Dad actually going to eat with us tonight?"

"He has Bible study," her mother said. "But he may have time for a quick bite."

"Mom…"

Her mother raised a hand, signaling she didn't want to talk about it. Sassy put the third plate back into the cupboard. "He's not going to be here for dinner," she said gently. "Maybe Oliver will stop by for leftovers later. It looks delicious."

"He better not forget to bring back my Tupperware. He can take some lasagna with him."

"He won't, Mom. He knows better." Sassy kissed her mother on the cheek. "By the way, I changed my mind. I don't want to move into the dorms next semester. Mind if I stay home a little longer?"

CHAPTER 14 – SASSY MEETS DAVID

Sassy had only started working at the diner a few months ago, but she was familiar enough with her customers to notice when a new guy walked in. Thick black hair. Clean-shaven. Ooh, a suit. He looked like he had just stepped out of a JCPenney catalogue. Surely, she would have remembered him if she had seen him before.

She stopped to freshen her vanilla lip gloss before bringing him a menu.

"Only coffee today, please," he said. His empty stomach growled in disagreement.

"Just coffee?" She raised an eyebrow at his conflicted mouth and tummy.

"I'm meeting with Logan and Reed to discuss an internship."

"Ah, they're making you fast first," she teased.

"Honestly, my wallet is a little thin these days…but it's only temporary. This job will help me through the rest of school. They don't know it yet, but that's just the beginning. I have a future with this company. In a few years, I should have my own office. If you can wait until then, I'll gladly order the day's special. Maybe even dessert."

"A man with a plan. How refreshing."

"How about you? Do you have a plan?"

"Psychology. I'd like to help people really find their souls. Know what I mean? I'm not much of a nine to fiver, though. I may have to hang my own shingle."

A man across the room hailed for more coffee. Oh yeah, there were still other customers.

"Someday," she said. "Guess, for now, the souls will have to wait."

Sassy worked the restaurant, hoping he was watching. There were lots of demanding customers. She knew most of them by name. She'd listen to their joys or woes, and made certain all were fed. She walked past his table way more than she needed to.

"That's quite an impressive building," she said. "The big boys over there don't come over here much. Sometimes we deliver though."

He smiled at her. "I'll probably be here a lot."

Sassy topped off his coffee. "I hope so."

She bopped about like she was the best waitress in the world. She liked how he pretended to stare out the window of the diner. She could tell he was watching her in the reflection of the glass. He turned and caught her looking back. Their eyes locked for one hot second before he looked away.

She tried to keep on with the rest of her work. She could feel his eyes trying not to watch her. The job she normally loved was becoming a nuisance. His presence was getting to her. The preppy young college man dressed to impress in his fancy duds made a nice package. The depth behind those eyes left her wanting more. He was drinking his coffee way too slowly.

She looked for an excuse to stop at his table. She thought of the chocolate cream pies she had brought out that morning and his poor grumbling tummy. She cut him a generous slice of pie and layered it with extra whipped cream. After a quick glance in the mirror, she delivered it to his table.

"Nobody should have to wait years for dessert," she said.

"Thank you kindly, Miss…"

"Sassy," she said, intentionally adding a hint of dare to her tone. "I'm Sassy."

"You certainly are. It's a pleasure to meet you. I'm David."

He reached for a fork and their hands brushed against each other, sparking a current of seductive energy. Trying hard not to try too hard, she walked away.

"Damn!" he said a little too loudly.

It wasn't quite the reaction she had wanted. She turned to see what had prompted his mood swing. Kindness had backfired. The bit of sweetness she had hoped would spark a promising romance was now a chocolate plop on his starched white shirt.

Sassy laughed out loud at the surprise direction her plan had taken, but she rallied quickly. With only twenty minutes until his interview, she wasn't about to let a meltdown spoil his dream.

"Breathe," she commanded as she took his hand and marched him to the back room. She took off his tie and unbuttoned his shirt. His biceps flexed a little as she pulled it off. In a stellar performance, she acted like she didn't notice his firm chest and the thick muscles that had been hiding underneath his businessman persona. *Mmm. Sweet honey. This boy is fit.*

Forcing herself to turn away, she tended to the shirt. Like it or not, her mother had taught her a few things. Despite the woman's intent to raise a proper young lady, Sassy chose to use lessons from home to hit on guys once in a while. Bold as she knew it was, this time she needed the help. So, she rubbed the spot with ammonia and water and rinsed it with a damp cloth before patting it nearly dry. A quick trip to the hand dryer in the ladies' room, and the chocolate cream plop was a delicious memory.

She didn't have the heart to tell him he had somehow gotten a bit of pie in his hair as well. She combed it out by hand, gliding her fingers through his silky locks. Pretending a little less not to notice the body being covered, she helped him back into his clean shirt. Button by button, she eased her way up his chest. She held her breath and fixed his tie. Once again, he looked the part. For a last shot of confidence, in a move that would have horrified her mother, she kissed him smack on the mouth.

"You'll be great," she assured him.

As he grabbed his coat to leave, he licked her vanilla reassurance from his lips. "I'll see you later," he said.

#

Sassy managed to keep Oliver and David from meeting for a good three months. Then one day Oliver pulled into the driveway as they were about to get into David's car. He didn't bother offering to move so they could get out.

"Going somewhere?" he asked her.

"Yep," Sassy said. "There's a new band playing at The Hub. Supposed to be pretty good."

Oliver glared at David. "Just you and this guy?" he asked.

David reached a hand out to shake, but Oliver didn't take it. "Hi. I'm David."

"What do you do, boy?" he asked.

Sassy held her tongue, knowing better than to point out the fact that David was a few months older than her big brother.

"I've just begun an internship with Logan and Reed. Investment banking."

"Don't you work?"

"Of course. I also do some landscaping, odd jobs, whatever it takes."

"So, nothing stable."

"Keeps the bills paid while I finish school."

"How 'bout girls? Lots?"

"Nothing serious."

"So, you're a player."

"No, sir. Guess I was just waiting for the right one." David winked at Sassy.

"Smart Ass," Oliver said.

Sassy shot Oliver a stern look, signaling him to stop.

"Shake and be nice," she said.

He paused a moment as if there might be a chance she'd let the issue go. With a slight cough, she informed him that she wouldn't. Oliver huffed and extended his hand. David grabbed it in a burst of relieved enthusiasm. Their hands locked. Each, in its own way, declared a grip on the relationship it represented. She giggled as both men looked to her for an end to the awkward exchange.

"Good boys," she said with a grin.

Oliver kissed his sister on the cheek and whispered, "Be careful, kid," into her ear. Then he slipped a ten- dollar bill into her pocket. "In case of an emergency."

She didn't bother to argue. "Mom made meat pies," she said. "Please eat."

"Guess I better move my car out of your way first," he said. He eyed David's sensible blue Volkswagen. "Even his car's a smart ass," he called over his shoulder as he walked away.

Sassy got into the Volkswagen with David and sighed. "I think he likes you, David."

"Sassy, he growled."

"He always makes that noise. It's his nerves."

"Yeah, I guess I was pretty hard on him. Poor guy. Maybe I should have sung him a lullaby."

"I know he seems a little rough, but he's a teddy bear."

"Maybe you're right. He's just looking out for his baby sister. It's actually kind of sweet."

"I think Carrie is the only one who gets away with calling him that."

"Okay. I wouldn't want to upset the big sweet teddy bear. I'll do my best not to piss him off. Even if he did call my car a 'smart ass'."

"Aw. You'd do that for me? You're an angel. Oh, and don't worry. To a guy like Oliver, 'smart ass' is a term of endearment."

CHAPTER 15 – UNDOUBTED

Sassy flipped through the calendar, mentally assessing her situation. *David and I have been together for ten months… we've only been really serious for four… I'm not that late…ugh, my stomach… I can't be pregnant… I'm not ready… I have to finish school… Damn, I wish Carrie wasn't away at that stupid insurance conference.*

She crossed another day off on March's page, as if she could make today disappear. *She'll be home soon… I can talk to her tomorrow, she'll be home tomorrow…*

She looked at the number Carrie had given her. It was dinner time. She probably wasn't even in her room. Sassy picked up the phone anyway. She called the hotel and waited to be transferred to Carrie's room.

*Please be there…*she thought as the phone rang. Both girls knew that Sassy's mother had taken her to the gynecologist in eleventh grade. *This wasn't supposed to happen. It couldn't happen.*

Carrie answered on the third ring. "Hello?" she said into the phone.

"I think I'm pregnant," Sassy blurted out.

"Sassy? Wait. What did you say?"

"I'm pregnant. It's been a few weeks since… and I've been sick to my stomach… and … and… I don't know. I wish you were here." Sassy forced a bite of the corn muffin she had been trying to eat into her mouth, then gave the rest to Jerry. The dog ate the bits off of the floor and licked her hand.

"But, what about the…?"

"I forgot a couple times. And those pills are so tiny. Once I dropped one and I couldn't find it." She watched Jerry sniffing for more crumbs and wondered if he could have eaten the lost birth control pill that day.

"Maybe you should talk to your mom."

"You know I can't tell her. And Oliver! Crap, Care. He's gonna lose it." She put her hand over the pain in her stomach. "But David. I have no idea what he'll say. Or do."

"David's not a bad guy," Carrie said. "He'll do the right thing."

Sassy stroked Jerry's soft fur. "It's just…he has this plan. He works all the time. I don't know. We're not ready."

"Maybe you're not even pregnant. It could be the flu. Do you have a fever?"

Sassy felt her forehead with the back of her hand. "I don't think so. It's more of a pain than queasiness. All around my stomach. It's weird. What do you think pregnant feels like?"

"I can't imagine."

"Do you think he'll freak out?"

"You need to take one of those tests. There's a drug store across from the hotel I'm at. I'll get one before I come home tomorrow night. We'll figure it out from there."

"Thanks, Care. Promise you won't tell anyone?"

"Of course. I promise. Go drink some tea. It'll help settle your stomach."

#

The hotel's dining hall had been booked and set up for a hundred people. When Carrie walked into the room, there was only one seat left available. Her boss was standing behind a podium at the front of the room, speaking without the note cards she was supposed to have brought. She slunk into the empty chair, hoping he wouldn't notice that she wasn't only incompetent—she was also late.

Sitting with a table full of insurance agents, she picked at her salad and laughed at jokes she didn't get. Clapping with the crowd as the man she worked for spouted numbers and rattled on about potential and growth, she bumped her glass of water, spilling it all over herself and the guy next to her. A waiter rushed over to help, and to accentuate the drama.

When her boss finished speaking, he came over to her table and put a hand on her shoulder.

"Secretaries are down at the bar, hon," he said into her ear. "You're in my seat."

The important people laughed at Carrie as she stood, patted the chair with her napkin, and left. Her pathetic image looked back at her through the mirrored doors of the elevator as she waited for them to open and let her in. She had forgotten her sweater and her nipples were standing at attention in her wet dress. Her hairdo had fallen out, and she had greens from her boss's salad in her teeth.

When she stepped onto the elevator and pushed the button for her floor. A woman and a little girl got in after her. The child must have been about five or six years old. She was holding her mother's hand. Her hair was braided, all fancy, with blue ribbons that matched her dress.

Carrie reached into her purse and found a pack of Starburst. Glad they were still dry, she held the candy out to share.

"Stranger! Stranger!" the girl yelled at the top of her lungs.

The woman gave Carrie a nasty look. Panicked, she pushed a button and got off at the next stop. Crying in the stairwell, she climbed six flights to her floor and tried to settle herself with the candy bar she had bought at the drug store earlier.

An hour later, there was a knock on her hotel room door. Carrie could see her boss through the peephole. She held her breath and waited. He knocked again. "Carrie, I found your sweater," he called. There was a pause, then he lowered his voice. "C'mon, sweetheart. I brought some wine. I was hoping we could talk or something."

Carrie ran to the bathroom and locked herself in. She stayed hidden for half an hour, then crept out. She packed her suitcase, then made her way back down the stairs to leave.

#

Sassy took Carrie's advice and went downstairs to get a cup of tea. With each step, the pain got worse. Oliver and Adam were sitting at the table eating leftover chili when she entered the kitchen, doubled over in pain.

"Help," she could barely say.

The guys jumped up and helped her to a chair.

"Sassy! What's wrong? What happened?" Oliver asked.

"I don't know. My stomach. It wasn't this bad earlier."

Adam soaked a dishtowel in hot water and laid it across her abdomen. "Try this," he said.

"It hurts when I breathe." Tears covered her face.

"Oliver, help me get her to the car."

"Mom's at the church," she told Adam. "Please call."

"I'll go get her," he said. "As soon as we get you to the hospital."

At the hospital, Oliver stayed with Sassy. He was standing by her side when the nurse asked her, "Is there any chance you could be pregnant?"

"Well …I…uh…" Sassy avoided eye contact with Oliver, but she could feel him waiting for an answer.

"Sir, why don't you have a seat in the waiting room?" the nurse said. "We'll take good care of her."

Bless you, Sassy thought.

Oliver hesitated, then squeezed her hand and left the room. Sassy motioned for the nurse to come closer.

"Please make sure the baby's okay," she whispered into her ear.

#

When Carrie got home, she didn't see David on her front porch until she reached the first step. She hid the bag from the drug store inside her shirt.

"Oh. Hi, David. Isn't Sassy at her house?" she asked.

"No. Nobody is. I told her I was coming over after work. I thought maybe I'd find her here," David said.

"Wow. You worked late tonight. I just got home from an insurance conference."

"Did you talk to Sassy at all today?"

The bag crinkled inside Carrie's shirt as she squirmed. "No. I was out of town. I couldn't have talked to her. Maybe they went for ice cream? Sassy loves mint chocolate chip."

Darn. Why'd I say that? she thought. *Sassy likes cookie dough.* "Maybe they're getting pizza," she said out loud.

David looked at her funny.

He knows I'm lying, she thought.

Carrie changed the subject, bringing up the experience she wasn't really ready to talk about yet.

"I'm back early. My creepy boss came up to my hotel room. I didn't know what to do, so I left. I had to leave. I guess I'm probably fired. Or maybe I quit. Either way, I'm not going back."

"Creepy? What did he do?"

"Nothing. It's fine," she said. "He brought a bottle of wine. I don't even drink. It can make people crazy."

"Maybe he was trying to be nice," David said.

"I guess. Maybe I should have at least opened the door."

Oliver's car came flying up the road and screeched to a halt in front of the house. He got out and ran at David. Carrie jumped back, frightened. The pregnancy test fell out of her shirt and hit Oliver's shoe, losing the bag on the sidewalk. The three of them stared at it for a second, then Oliver and David looked to Carrie.

Carrie bent down to pick it up and put it back into the bag. Oliver reached over her and grabbed David by the front of his shirt.

"I've been looking for you, punk! My sister's at the hospital. Let's go."

Carrie stuffed the pregnancy test into a bush and ran after Oliver and David as they hurried to the car. She hopped into the backseat right before he peeled out. Oliver drove like a maniac, yelling at David.

"You're in deep shit, you little smart ass," Oliver said to David.

"What happened?" David asked. "What's wrong with Sassy? Is she okay?"

Carrie leaned forward in her seat, desperate to know the same answers.

"She'd better be. And if you knocked her up…"

"What are you talking about?"

Carrie wanted to say something. Anything. But her mouth wouldn't speak.

"Don't you dare, you bastard," Oliver was saying. "You're not bailing on her."

"I'd never," David said. "What? Is she sick?"

"Don't play dumb. You know what you did to her." Oliver ran a stop sign. "Hope you saved your receipt for that pregnancy test," he yelled at Carrie. "They're doing their own at the hospital."

"Why is she at the hospital?" David pleaded. "Tell me, damn it! What's wrong with her?"

David wasn't defending himself. Even with Oliver yelling at him, all he cared about was Sassy. He sounded worried.

He really thinks she's sick.

"Sassy's not pregnant," David finally said. "She can't be. No way. It's not possible. It's just…not. She must be sick."

Something about the way he spoke struck a nerve with Carrie. There wasn't a trace of doubt in his voice, yet Sassy had seemed so sure.

#

They found Adam outside of the hospital's emergency room entrance.

"Oliver, I've been looking for you," he said. "It's her appendix. She's in surgery now. Your parents are in the waiting room."

"You're lucky," Oliver mumbled to David as he went inside.

"Don't worry," Adam said to Carrie. "Sassy's going to be fine."

"Thank you for taking care of her." Carrie meant it and hated herself for being jealous.

He rubbed the back of his neck, then stretched. "You're home early," he said, touching her hair. "Honey, I'm so glad you're here."

"Me too," Carrie said. As she hugged Adam, she looked over his shoulder at David. "Me too," she said again.

Carrie wanted to be thankful that the man she loved had been there for her best friend. Sassy was sick. Of course Adam had taken care of her. But David's words to Oliver kept replaying in her mind.

It's not possible. Not. Possible.

He had spoken with confidence, not fear. David knew without doubt that he hadn't gotten Sassy pregnant.

Emotion distorted Carrie's thoughts as buried pain resurfaced. There was still a pregnancy test at home in her bushes. David's proclaimed innocence corrupted the fragile trust she had rebuilt with Sassy.

Adam pushed her away, Carrie reminded herself.

#

Sassy was supposed to be discharged within the hour, but Carrie couldn't find the right room. Things looked the same as they had yesterday—big windows…lots of doors…and bright lights reflected on polished floors.

She looked at her arm, trying to read the room number she had written in marker, but it had faded. She passed a nurses' station…wheel chairs…a room with little baby cribs.

Cribs? Crap. Wrong floor.

Avoiding elevators, she slipped into the nearest stairwell and counted each step as she climbed. Prepared to try again, she stopped two floors up and stepped out. The floor was carpeted, not polished.

But something drew her. *S*he continued down the long corridor. It felt empty here. Forbidden. She walked through the silence to the end of the hall, where she stood before a set of double doors.

Through a six-inch square window, she could see some kind of lounge. People were there. Some played cards. Two women were knitting. The couches looked old, but comfortable. A man sat on one end reading. A woman two seats over from him was holding her knees and crying. Carrie stared at the woman.

"Don't cry," she whispered.

She studied the people. They didn't look sick. She tried to go into the lounge but the door wouldn't open. When she pulled on it, it banged. The people inside looked up at the sound. She turned and ran. Catching her breath, she pushed a button for the elevator.

Carrie finally found Sassy's room, one floor below the inpatient psychiatric ward.

CHAPTER 16 – ENOUGH

Jerry went missing about a month after Sassy's surgery. Sassy was yelling at Carrie when Adam and Oliver got to the house. "Why would you leave the gate open, Care? All you had to do was pull it shut behind you. You know he likes to run."

"I'm so sorry." Carrie played with the zipper on her windbreaker. "I thought the latch clicked. I forgot to…"

"Which is it?" Sassy snapped. "You forgot, or the latch didn't click?" She heard the anger in her own tone, and she hated the fear in Carrie's face. She hadn't meant to be so harsh. All she could think about was the fact that her dog was gone.

Carrie eased herself closer to Adam, who blindly took her side.

"Sassy, it was an accident," he said.

Sassy twisted the leash in her hands. *Don't be a bitch, don't be a bitch,* she reminded herself. "Fine. I'm going to find him."

They split up to look for him, searching the neighborhood for hours. Sassy carried the empty leash, calling his name over and over, but there was no sign of him. It was long after sunset when they finally met back at home.

"Sorry, Sis," Oliver said. "Nobody's seen him."

Sassy glared at Carrie.

"Sometimes the latch sticks," Oliver said. "It's late. We'll look again tomorrow."

"Okay." Sassy hung her head. "But I'm sleeping out back in case he comes home."

Oliver took the leash from her hands. "That's stupid. You just had surgery. Besides, you'd freeze."

"The surgery was like a month ago and it's spring," Sassy said. "It's getting warmer. Lots of people go camping in April." She knew the idea was silly, but it was the best one she had.

"You don't have to sleep outside," David said. "I'll wait out for Jerry."

Sassy didn't know what she loved more, the gesture, or the look on Oliver's face when he handed David the leash.

#

Sassy slid the back door open and stepped outside. The late-night air was cool and damp. She could hear the tree frogs chirping in the woods. David shifted inside the sleeping bag. She knelt beside him and pulled the zipper open. Snuggling up against him, she kissed the back of his neck.

He rolled over and took her into his arms. His firm body was soft and cuddly in his heavy clothes. Her hands crawled into his sweatshirt and roamed. His skin warmed her fingers. Her lips found his. His mouth tasted like peppermint.

"Are you sure you're okay?" he asked, as she kissed her way down his neck. "I don't want to hurt you."

"Don't you worry." She traveled to his chest. "I'm all better."

His touch released her from the world around them. In that moment, being with him was everything.

"I love you," she whispered. The feeling had been building for a long time, but the words felt fresh and exhilarating.

His body tensed when she said it. "Sassy…"

Her mouth stopped. She wished she could take the words back, but she really did love him. "Don't," she said. "It's okay. If you don't love me, you don't love me. I'll go."

"No, wait. It's not that. Stay.. I do." David held her hands. "I love you. But…"

"No. No way. There can't be any buts," she said. "I don't play like that."

David let out a heavy breath. "You thought you were pregnant."

Carrie promised she wouldn't tell, Sassy thought. "Well, yeah. I kinda did," she said.

"You'll be an awesome mom," he said. "I want you to have that."

"Someday. But don't worry. We'll be more careful. I have a few more years of school first. And then I have…"

"I can't."

"Can't?"

He rebuttoned his jeans. "I can't be a father. I'm sorry. I can't give you that."

"Well, not now," she said. "Later, when we're ready."

"I'd be ready right now if you wanted me to be," he said. "But…"

"What do you mean? We've…"

"Yeah. And that's incredible. But there's something else. I should have told you a long time ago."

"Tell me now."

David scooted himself over in the sleeping bag to give her more room. She snuggled up next to him and he spoke into her hair. "I had this uncle. He said he was my dad's brother. Dad was long gone, but Jack came to live with us anyway. Mom took off when I was ten. Jack was pissed, but he had lots of other women."

"Oh my God." Sassy sat up in the tent. "She just left you with him? How awful."

David didn't move. She could barely see his face through the darkness. She reached down and put her hand on his chest. Then she settled herself back against him and rested her head over his beating heart.

"He started smacking me around after she left," David finally said.

Sassy gasped. "He hit you?"

"At first, it was only the back of his hand. Some days he'd punch, but he was usually too lazy to do much."

"And your mother. She never came back?"

"Nah. I can hardly blame her. Jack had a way with women." David paused. "He used them," he said with a heavy breath.

"He used women? What do you mean?"

David paused again, as if he wasn't sure he should say.

"It's okay," Sassy said. "You can tell me anything."

His voice lowered. "Money," he said. "He used them to make money."

Sassy listened in stunned silence as he continued.

"I was stuck with him," David said. "I had to stay... you know, pretend I had a guardian, and that he wasn't a pimp."

Sassy couldn't hold back her tears. David wiped her face with his sleeve. "I was fine," he said. "I earned my keep cutting grass and delivering newspapers. I played it safe then. Kept to myself."

Sassy thought about David's apartment. She used to feel sorry for the way he lived in that old building, with only a few pieces of second-hand furniture. Now, the sad little room was an awesome trophy, earned by the resilience of the boy who got away.

"I can't imagine. You were just a kid. Did he at least buy you food? Clothes?"

David made a noise that almost sounded like a laugh. "I was warm and dry and usually had enough to eat. I'm good at making scrambled eggs, remember?" He gently touched her recovering abdomen.

The thing he had said earlier still wasn't making sense. *I can't be a father.* She kept still and listened, waiting for the right moment to tell him how great he'd be.

"I didn't need parents hovering over me," he continued. "The landlady gave me some clothes after her husband died. That got me through high school."

"David, I didn't mean to rush you with the whole, 'I love you,' thing."

"No. I'm glad you said it." David kissed the top of her head. "I do love you," he said. "Before I knew you, I didn't know what love was. I mean, I thought I knew. My mother told me she loved me once. Uncle Jack said she loved her whiskey more. I guess I figured whatever love was, I wanted nothing to do with it."

Sassy hated his mother for leaving him like that, but he didn't realize how well he had raised himself. And she hated Jack for invading his childhood. No wonder David thought he couldn't be a father. He never had one.

A steady stream of tears flowed down Sassy's cheeks.

"I was okay," he repeated, again offering his sleeve for a tissue. "I was content, really. Focusing on my studies and not giving a damn. I knew once I was old enough to be on my own, I could start a real life. So, I did what I could to get ready. I didn't need anyone."

Her love for him felt more and more real as he spoke.

"I did fine, too," he continued. "Good grades and all. The counselor helped me apply for scholarships. That's when it happened. Jack intercepted my mail." His voice got faster. "I was doing it. Making a better life for myself. Better than he'd ever have, and he knew it. Bastard was so jealous he couldn't stand it."

He stopped. They lay there together, still in the moment, listening to the frogs.

David forced himself to finish the story he had started. "When Jack hit me that last time, it wasn't an overgrown bully beating on a scared little kid anymore," he said. "I was bigger and done cowering to his abuse. But I wasn't me."

With her head on his chest, Sassy could feel his heart racing as he wrestled with his own words.

"I was this rage, attacking another human being. I hated myself for being like him, some kind of monster, but I couldn't stop. He was bleeding and moaning and I couldn't make my fists stop. Even when he pulled a knife from his pocket, I couldn't walk away."

"No!" Sassy covered her mouth to stop the word.

"The knife fell, and I grabbed it." His tone deepened. "Sass, I held it to his neck. The bastard begged for mercy." With a big breath of relief, he said, "I couldn't do it. Thank God, I couldn't do it… I barely left a scratch."

But the anger returned as the purpose of his story became clear.

"That should have been the end," he said. "I could have lived with it. But Jack. He tripped me… knocked me on my ass. I was on the ground and…he kicked me. Really hard. Right in my… right in the crotch."

Sassy couldn't believe what she was hearing.

"Neighbors must've heard all the yelling," David continued. "Someone called the police. I was still on the floor… hurt so bad I couldn't get up. Cops sent for an ambulance. I turned eighteen in the hospital. Jack ended up in jail."

Sassy touched the outside of his pants as if she could heal him. "You can't? Because of Jack, you can't?"

"I'm sorry. I can't be a father," David said. "I'm sorry."

Sassy paused, digesting his pain. She didn't want him to be sorry. She thought about her parents and their warped idea of marriage. She didn't want that either.

"David, I love you," she said, meaning it even more than when she had said it earlier. "This is real. This is what love is supposed to be."

She leaned back so she could look at him as she spoke. "Whatever happened to you. Whatever happens to us. We're together. Be with me. Stay with me. You and I. Together. We'll always be enough."

CHAPTER 17 – GOOD BYE

A full month had passed, and Jerry still hadn't returned. When Oliver first told Sassy he wanted to go to Chippi's Park, her first thought was Jerry. A small part of her secretly hoped she'd somehow find the dog there again. She knew it was silly to think he would have made his way up the mountain and return to the park alone, even more so that he'd be there looking for her.

Oliver wanted to go the park. "Just us," he had said. That was good enough reason for her to wake up early to go for a ride. They hadn't done anything alone together since he had moved in with Adam. They hadn't talked about the hole in the wall either.

They got to their rock just before the sun came up. A hint of light broke through the night sky. The darkness slowly faded as the sun rose over the valley, bringing in the morning.

"It's been too long since we've been up here," she said. "I've missed it."

"Remember the Amish people that used to have those picnics over there?" Oliver pointed toward an open grassy area.

"How could I forget? The kids made you eat that pie!" She laughed. "You were so pissed at me."

"You put them up to it. Telling that little girl it was my favorite. She looked so sweet and innocent." Oliver laughed with Sassy as he imitated the young voice, "I brought you some shoefly pie. I helped Mama make it."

"I'll never forget the face you made when you took that first bite."

"The raisins really did look like flies."

"You kept eating it!"

"I couldn't hurt her feelings."

Sassy sighed. "They were nice people. Always helping each other. They seemed at peace with each other, you know?"

"Yeah," Oliver said. "I wonder what they were hiding."

"What do you mean?"

"Nothing." He rubbed his bald chin. "You never know what's really going on with people. Look at Adam. He took the old man's house off the market the day I moved in. Bought the damn thing himself. He thinks now that he's done with school he can earn enough to keep paying the loan when I leave."

"Maybe by then he will be able to afford it. He's already planning to substitute teach in the fall."

"I know. Mr. Perfect has it all. Blah, blah. I didn't bring you up here to talk about Adam."

"But, Oli…"

"I have to go," he said.

"What? It's still early. We can't go yet."

"No. I mean… I'm leaving. The Air Force. I joined. I have to go."

"What? You're going to enlist? I don't understand."

"I already did, Sis. I need you to be okay with this," he said.

"Are you okay with this?" she asked.

"It's the right thing to do. Maybe when I come back, things will be better. I need to make some changes. I need to be… different."

They sat quietly, looking out across the horizon. Sassy rested her head on his shoulder.-"When do you have to go?" she asked.

"May 7th," he said.

"Crap, Oli! That's in three days!"

#

The night before Oliver left, their mother prepared his favorite dinner. They all feasted on her famous honey mustard chicken, baked macaroni and cheese (with extra cheese), and corn on the cob. Sassy made her secret recipe apple dumplings for dessert.

"David couldn't join us?" Mrs. Lingle asked.

"He had to work. His boss has him painting some lake house." Sassy sighed. "The guy thinks David is his maintenance man, groundskeeper, personal assistant, everything. All of the other young money bubbers go home at five. I don't get why David has to do so much extra."

Adam laughed. "What's a 'bubber'?"

Carrie watched him and Sassy tease each other back and forth. Sassy touched Adam's arm when she talked.

"This chicken is awesome, Mom. Thank you for dinner," Oliver said.

Carrie smiled at him, grateful for the shift in conversation. He smiled back.

Oliver turned to Adam. "Adam, you should come downtown with me tonight. There's going to be a party at Bennie's."

"A bar?" Carrie asked.

"Let him loose for one night, Care," Sassy said. "Oli's leaving in the morning."

Carrie hid behind her glass of water. She felt like everyone was staring at her, judging. She took a long sip, then set the glass down.

"Go ahead, Adam. I don't mind," she said. "I'm starting to get a headache anyway. I think I'd better go home."

Carrie excused herself from the table and thanked Mrs. Lingle for dinner. She gave Oliver a big hug. "I'll miss you."

He held on. "Don't drown," he whispered in her ear.

Adam stood to go with her. "I'll walk you home."

"No. I'll be fine," she said. "Stay and have your dumpling."

Adam sat back down next to Sassy.

#

After dinner, Adam said he was going to check on Carrie and he'd meet Oliver later. Sassy kissed him on the cheek.

"Thanks for coming, Adam. Rough night," she said.

He touched her on the nose with his index finger. "I know," he said. And he wiped the tear she was trying not to let fall.

Once he was gone, Oliver asked, "Is there something going on between you two?"

"Of course not," she said. "Let's go for a walk," she said, changing the subject.

They trudged in the spring heat through the neighborhood that raised them. The old candy store they used to race their bikes to was boarded shut. The ball field where Oliver had hit his first homerun had no use for him now. The swings in the park had never looked so small. Sassy laughed as she sat at the top of the little slide.

"Catch me, Oli," she said. Her attempt at humor fell short. He sat at the bottom of the slide, looking down into the dirt.

"You'll be okay," he said.

Sassy slid toward him, hanging her legs over the sides of the slide. She put her chin on his shoulder and spoke the simple truth into his ear.

"Growing up doesn't only suck. There's good stuff, too."

"Do you love this David?"

"I really do."

"Does he love you?"

"Yeah, Oli. He does."

"He better not screw up." Oliver stood and extended a hand to help her off of the slide.

"I won't let him," she said. "You taught me well."

"Sassy, don't be like me. You hear that? Don't."

"But, Oli..."

"Sleep in tomorrow, okay? I can only say 'good bye' once."

Reaching into his pocket, he pulled out a tiny box. He hung a delicate chain around her neck. The golden cross sparkled an end to the discussion. They walked home in silence.

CHAPTER 18 – LETTING GO

Sassy woke the next morning to the sound of her father's voice. He was talking to someone downstairs. She hopped out of bed and looked out the window. A police car was parked in front of their house. She ran down the hall, then stopped at the top of the steps. Two uniformed officers stood at the door with her mother. Her father had his arms around her. Both of her parents were sobbing.

The older policeman looked up at her. "Miss," he said, tipping his hat. "I'm Officer Kane." He nodded toward the younger one, "This is my partner, O'Brian."

The guy was only about Oliver's age. He looked familiar. Maybe they were on the same baseball team.

"I'm very sorry," O'Brian said.

"What?" she asked them. "What happened?"

Her mother buried her head in her father's chest. He held onto her, kissing the top of her head. Sassy moved down the stairs.

"Oliver. Where's Oliver?"

Kane and O'Brian looked at each other. Finally, Kane spoke. "Miss, there's been an incident." He cleared his throat. "Mr. Lingle's body was found at the bottom of the ravine below the area of Chippi's Park."

"Body? He's…"

"I'm very sorry, Miss," O'Brian said again. "We found an empty vodka bottle in his car in the lot at Chippi's."

A sharp look from Kane admonished the rookie.

Her mother gasped, "How could he do this to me?"

With that one thoughtless question, the woman tainted her relationship with her daughter forever. Sassy felt the room move. Everything went bright, then dark. She collapsed into a puddle of nothingness.

#

Day turned to night as the rest of the world kept turning. David was in her room now. Sassy couldn't remember when he came or how she got into her bed. It was dark outside. Some kind of meat was cooking downstairs. Dinner. Onions. Oliver loved onions.

David couldn't convince her to go downstairs to eat. The thought of food annoyed her. But she wondered what her mother had done with the leftover honey mustard chicken from last night. Her father probably ate it.

Someone knocked. "Go away," she said flatly.

The door opened. Carrie and Adam came into her room. They were holding hands. Carrie's eyes were red and puffy and she sniffed a lot. The hugs and love they brought helped Sassy to cry some, making her feel better and worse at the same time.

"Come downstairs," Adam said.

"I can't. I'm not hungry," she said. "You all go. I'm sure Mom made a ridiculous feast."

"No. Outside," he said. "Sassy, you need to see this."

#

There were hundreds of them. Flowers surrounded the tree in the backyard. Their tree house hung above like a time capsule refusing to be buried. Some friends lingered. Most placed flowers and left. Mrs. Lingle fed anyone she could get into her kitchen.

David stood by her side as Sassy watched Adam gather roses from the piles. He handed her a bouquet and kissed her on the cheek. Then he sneezed, spraying her face with spittle. He wiped it off with his sleeve and backed away.

Sassy stepped toward him. "You spit on me," she said. "Adam, you know I'll have to kick your ass for that."

Carrie handed her a lacey pink handkerchief. Sassy smiled. She laughed a little, then a lot. The awful noise coming out of her grew out of control. Carrie put an arm around her.

"You guys get something to eat," Carrie said to Adam and David.

She eased Sassy back to her room and into bed, then crawled in next to her and held on.

"Remember the storms, Sassy?"

"Yeah, you'd sneak into my bed and snuggle next to me. Then you'd rub those fuzzy socks against my feet until I said you could stay."

"I was just letting you know I was there."

"I always knew, Care. But I waited for the socks anyway. They were so soft and warm."

Carrie rubbed her fuzzy feet against Sassy. Together, they slept.

#

The days and nights blurred past. There was a service, more flowers, and more food. Sassy could feel the change in the neighborhood. Some people looked away, others stared. Things were whispered, as if folks had a right to talk about her brother but she didn't deserve to hear it. It didn't matter what they were saying. They were wrong.

Sassy was the only one who understood why Oliver had gone to

Jerry Rock. He always went there to think, to figure things out. He'd look out at the bigger world and see something in himself. He was scared... or sad... or angry. Probably all three... and lost... so lost.

He definitely shouldn't have been drinking up there, and she was beyond pissed at him for driving like that. Anger didn't help ease the pain, however, or stop the questions. Maybe Oliver had fallen. It was an accident; that's what the official report stated. But maybe it wasn't. They couldn't prove that he hadn't jumped.

Either way, it was too late. Her brother was gone. He had planned to leave, wanting something to be different. Her heart ached for the answers he had never found, but his death had taken those too.

Now people were offering her the sympathy, not him. It didn't make sense. She got to stay safe in her home, not at the bottom of the ravine. Her boss had accepted her resignation, telling her to come back when she was ready. The kindness felt wrong. She wasn't the jar of ashes on the mantle. She could walk and breathe, live and be pitied.

Sassy left the house early to avoid contact with anyone who might feel sorry for her. In the dark morning silence, her running shoes smacked the pavement. Her even breaths followed the rhythm. Focused on the road ahead, she pushed forward. Past the playground, past their high school, past Adam's house, where her brother had lived just days ago, she ran.

Her eyes fixed on the mountains in the distance. A hint of daylight energized her. The run broke into a sprint. She ran fast and free. Her legs burned with the fire of an athlete, but she couldn't outrun the pain.

She couldn't get to David's fast enough. She needed to be with him, to share his touch, to feel his love.

#

Sassy and David were at the Lingles' house eating dinner with her parents when the doorbell rang. Her father wiped marinara sauce from his mouth and set his napkin on the table. Sassy followed him to the door.

"I talked to you about the car," the guy said. "I have the cash."

David entered behind her. He put his hand on her shoulder. Her mother hid in the kitchen, probably clearing the table or washing dishes.

"What car?" she asked, but she knew. "Dad, no! It's only been two weeks. You can't do this." Sassy pushed past her father. "My brother's car is not for sale."

"It's not sitting in my driveway forever," her father said, and he took the guy with the cash outside to Oliver's car.

David didn't try to stop her as she dug Oliver's wooden baseball bat out of the hall closet. She loved him for that. Their mother had once called Oli's favorite bat a toy. He had defended his homerun partner. Now Sassy stormed outside with it and marched over to his car.

She raised it above her head and brought it smack down on the windshield. The bounce back surprised her with a thud to her face. The windshield barely cracked. She could hear her father yelling as he came at her. David said something to him and he stopped. The cash guy ran away.

Blood dripped from her nose. Angrier and harder, she kept swinging the bat. "You can't do this!" she yelled over and over. The driver side window smashed into Oliver's seat. She slammed the bat against the door and it caved. The roof buckled with one whack. She kept swinging. Her hands stung, but she couldn't stop herself. Again, she struck the windshield. Oliver's bat cracked in her fingers. The pain brought her to her knees.

"You can't do this," she cried.

#

Sassy's words haunted David as he helped Adam carry Oliver's bed down the stairs. *You can't do this.* Yet here he was, just three days later, removing more of Oliver from her life. They eased the mattress through the front door and to the truck. Mrs. Lingle had arranged a donation to the thrift store. Adam and David had been chosen to haul the stuff. They'd be paid in beef stew with biscuits.

Oliver's clothes were boxed up and taken to the truck. His music collection had already gone to Sassy. Adam kept some of the sports stuff, but the rest was on the truck. David grabbed an empty box and reached to open the nightstand drawer.

"This is stuck," he said, trying to wiggle it free.

"Eh. Leave it," Adam said. "There can't be much in there."

But David was curious. "There's a crowbar in the truck." He heaved the nightstand down the stairs and to the street.

He didn't wait for Adam to come down. He pried the drawer open. It only took about a minute to discover the secret lock, which he'd broken. There was a wooden box inside the drawer, which was also locked. He lifted it out, studying the box like an unburied treasure. Then he jammed the crowbar into it and busted it open. The contents fell to the ground, as if it had been rescued.

David scooped up the pieces and put them back into the box. *That sick bastard.*

He hid the box in the *trunk* of his car before going back inside to help Adam.

CHAPTER 19 – A MAN WITH A PLAN

Mr. Logan's secretary opened David's office door. Startled, he turned. His hand swung with him and knocked a picture of Sassy off of his desk. He scrambled to pick up the pieces of shattered glass.

"Claire! You didn't even knock!"

She bent to help him. "Oh crap! I'm so sorry." Her perfume reminded him of his mother and citronella candles. She lifted the busted frame and gently removed the photograph. "Whew! Your young lady here is as lovely as ever. I'll pick up a new frame this afternoon. She'll be back on your desk as good as new by the end of the day."

David pulled the trash can closer. He sat on the floor and picked tiny slivers of glass out of the carpet. She stopped his hand. Her long orange fingernails crept inside his shirt sleeve and played on his wrist.

"I'll see to this, sweetie," she said.

David took the picture from her and inspected it. "It's a month ago today that her brother died," he said.

"Awh. You take such good care of that little girl. It's a shame all she's been through."

Claire's skirt bunched dangerously short. David noticed a small rosebud tattooed on her thigh. He stood and brushed off his pants. She held her hand out for help up. Standing on two-inch heels, her eyes leveled with his. Heavy mascara clumped her lashes like little tarantula legs.

"Can you keep a secret?" she asked grabbing onto his arm. Fresh off the floor and already another wrinkle hazard threatened his good suit.

"No, Claire," he said sarcastically. "I'm a terrible gossip. You can't tell me anything."

"I thought we were friends." The little tarantulas clapped around her eyes. "Can't you let a woman be nice to you?"

He stepped away from her grip. "I have lots of work to do. Did you need something?"

"He's leaving tomorrow," Claire said. She flashed a seductive smile. "He'll be gone all summer."

"Who? Logan?"

"Yep. I booked the flight myself. They're going to California. His wife's family is there."

"Why is that a secret?" David asked.

She closed in on him once again. Her padded boobs pressed against him as she spoke. "Well, that fancy lake house will be awfully empty..."

"That's perfect!"

His mind planned faster than he could speak. Sassy could spend the summer at the lake. She had told him she felt like the neighborhood didn't know how to handle her. She wasn't handling herself very well yet either, but he couldn't say that to her. He'd have to let her think she was doing him a favor. He'd figure out how later. First, he needed to talk to his boss.

He ignored the Claire drama and followed his feet to Mr. Logan's office.

"Sir, I understand your house on the lake is going to be empty this summer. I thought you might like to do a little business."

"Business is what I do best, son. What do you have in mind?"

#

"He'll give you each two hundred dollars," David fibbed.

"Stop with the money!" Sassy said. "I'm sorry, David. I know you're trying to help. I just can't think of money right now."

"They need someone to take care of their dog," he said, rather impressed with his own quick thinking. "You can stay at the lake house and look after him until school starts again."

"Poor fella. How could they up and leave him like that?"

"Sassy, the Logans aren't as bad as you think. Their house isn't just pretty, it's peaceful. It will be good for you. The lilacs I planted draw those little hover birds you like. You know, the ones that buzz."

"Humming birds?" She let herself smile.

"Yeah, and they have a boat. You and Carrie can go out on the lake."

"She might like that. If this place is so great, why are the Logans leaving?"

"They're going to visit fam…" The word froze on his lips.

"Family," Sassy said crisply.

"C'mon, honey. You and Carrie house sitting for the Logans would really help me out," David said, pulling her close. "The dog needs you."

Sassy sighed. "What's his name?"

David blinked away the image of Claire's awful rose tattoo.

"Daisy," he said.

#

Later David stopped at the pound and adopted the Logans' new pet. He bought a fifty-pound bag of kibble, and a shopping basket full of dog paraphernalia. Sassy and Carrie would be there in two days. Daisy had to look like she was at home.

"C'mon, Daisy," he said. "We're going for a ride."

When they arrived at the lake house, the giant dog was panting out the window of David's Volkswagen. David gripped the leash as he opened the car door to let Daisy out. Her strength caught him off guard as she tried to run. He fell to the ground, clunking his head on the road. David dropped the leash. Daisy ran wild around the Logans' yard. Unwilling to accept defeat, David lured her to his side with a handful of treats. He bent to grab her collar and the dog bolted with a mouthful of beef snacks. David turned to retrieve the kibble. As he opened his trunk, he could have sworn he heard the dog giggling at him.

Walking up the driveway with the heavy bag, he heard the sound again. Distracted by curiosity, he set the bag down and scanned the yard for the source. Instinct led him behind the shed. Huddled on the ground, no longer giggling, a scared little face looked back at him.

"I-I'm s-sorry," the boy said as he pulled his baseball cap over his eyebrows.

"Are you in trouble, bud?"

The boy shuffled his untied sneakers. His hands pulled at his oversized shirt.

"What's your name?" David asked.

"J-Joseph."

"How old are you?"

"T-t-ten."

"Where do you live, Joseph?"

Joseph pointed to the house next door. David looked into his eyes and saw reflections of himself.

"I haven't seen you around. Are you here for the summer?"

Joseph bobbed his head up and down. Daisy's barking made its way into the conversation. They both looked over to see her tangled around some patio furniture. David's exaggerated laugh allowed Joseph's giggle to return.

"I could really use your help, Joseph. You seem like a good man. I need a man like you working for me. Do you like dogs?"

Joseph answered with a wide grin. David handed him the leash. It took Daisy precisely three and a half minutes to knock Joseph over and break loose. She wreaked havoc in Mrs. Logan's flower beds and tracked mud all around the wraparound porch. Joseph hid his face in his hands to laugh when the dog tackled David into a bush.

Plan "B" took the giant Daisy, now "Vertigo," home to live with David. The one room apartment was at least bigger than the cage she had lived in before. David prepared a cozy nook for Vertigo to sleep in by turning a stack of old towels into a nest of sorts. He added a couple bed pillows and covered the nest with some of his old sweatshirts. "Go ahead, girl. Make yourself comfortable. This area is yours, okay?"

Vertigo looked from the doggie haven David had prepared to the pitiful layer of mattresses in the middle of the room. Without so much as a sniff at the fancy display, she jumped up and curled herself at the foot of her new master's bed.

"Sassy's going to love you," David said. "When she's ready."

In a second trip, to a second pound, David came upon a cuddly little lap dog who had fallen upon hard times when her spoiled owner married a guy with a Rottweiler. Little Daisy got a haircut, bath and pedicure before settling into her fluffy new bed at the lake house.

"She's a pr- pr-priss dog," Joseph complained.

"She's house trained," David said.

Mumbling complaints about the heat, David grabbed a shovel and a rake. Joseph followed him to the garden with little Daisy nested in his shirt. David stopped at the edge of the flower bed. Not a petunia was out of place. He looked at Joseph in amazement. The boy's proud grin answered every question but one.

"How…?" David asked.

"I'm g-g-good," Joseph said.

David rustled his hair. "How 'bout some pizza?"

Joseph nodded his approval.

"Run along and ask if you can go."

He hung his head and petted the dog.

"I can hold her," David said.

Joseph reluctantly handed the dog to David. He petted her again and looked over at the car in the driveway.

"Something wrong?" David asked.

Joseph shook his head, then bolted to his house, stopping dead at the front door. He looked back at David and hesitated before ringing the doorbell. He stepped back when a tall man wearing dress pants and an untucked t-shirt appeared. David moved closer so he could hear. Smoke from the man's cigarette assaulted the boy's words as he tried to speak.

"Nice boy you have there," David called out.

The man stood up straight at the sound of David's voice.

"You just have to know how to handle them."

"Uh. Anyway. If he's allowed to go…"

"Yeah. Whatever. As long as his chores are done."

"D-d-done," Joseph said.

The guy snickered. "Don't worry. I'll give you another list in the morning."

"Joseph does great work," David said. "Your place looks beautiful."

"His mother lives here by herself. If I didn't come over nothing would ever get done around here."

"Is his mother home now?"

"Oh, she's here," he said with a boastful wink. "She's a little… indisposed at the moment." He adjusted his pants. "Women can't resist a man who gets things done."

"Let's go, Joseph."

"Go ahead boy. Get your p-p-pizza."

David took a step toward the swine, his biceps flexed and ready to go. He was toe to toe with his new enemy, about to declare war when he noticed young Joseph from the corner of his eye. His little fists were curled like he was ready to make it a two-man army. He deserved better. David took a deep breath and pulled himself together. "Yeah, bud," David said. "Why don't you get Daisy into the car? I'll be right there."

Joseph scurried away, leaving David free to pounce. Instead, he chose his words carefully as he pulled a friend's business card from his wallet.

"Here's my card," he lied, holding it out. "I'll be around quite a bit this summer. We should talk someday."

The guy studied the card and looked back at him. David cocked his head and raised his eyebrows, further advising the bully of the intended tone of the conversation.

"Have fun!" he called to Joseph.

"Tell his mother he'll be back in an hour. I guess you'll be gone by then, huh?" David said.

"Actually, I planned to…"

"Is that your car?" David said gesturing toward the mid-life crisis in the driveway. "Wow. That must have set you back a bundle. A guy like you must keep pretty close track of his finances."

"Of course, I…"

"Yep. I'm sure you have everything in order. Who says nice guys can't win? It'd be a shame though- if you weren't such a nice guy. The slightest indiscretion could… anyway, guess you'd better get going. We'll be back in an hour."

David reclaimed the card and stuck his hands in his pockets to avoid the potential shake. He wondered how his buddy would feel about him passing his business card off as his own. The guy only gave them out to brag about his new auditing job with the IRS. David had never really liked the guy much anyway. People in that line of work tended to make

him nervous.

CHAPTER 20 – HEAL VS. HEEL

Sassy smelled a lie. This dog gig David had concocted may have fooled her mother, but her father was proof that wasn't difficult to do. The woman acted like she believed her husband really did go to the men's study group on Friday nights. *He leaves the house with his Bible, dear. Don't question your father.*

Sassy didn't have to question. To her, Daddy's lie was as obvious as his motive. David's story puzzled her though. He didn't have to lie. It pleased her to learn he sucked at it, but that wasn't the point. One of the things she loved most about him was that she could trust him. She wondered why he didn't trust her with the truth. David could have told her he wanted to play house. She needed him now more than ever. A summer at the lake sounded pretty good, despite Mrs. Logan's swank.

Entertaining denial however, tires the heart. A tired heart stumbles over bumps in its path. The morning they were due to leave for the lake house, a rather large bump stood in the middle of Sassy's bedroom, in the form of Oliver's suitcase.

Sassy was perched on her bed surrounded by piles of clothes when Carrie came in.

"I hate my father. He has no heart," Sassy said.

"That's…" Carrie pointed at the suitcase.

"Yep. Sure is. The suitcase Adam gave Oli last month. It's full, too. Isn't that sweet? He may as well have left it in the car when he sent it to the junkyard. Scrap everything! Pretend my brother never existed. He can have all the whores he wants, and he never has to share."

Carrie's finger was still pointing at the suitcase.

"I found it in the garage," Sassy continued. "Dad never even brought it into the house." She straightened one of the clothes piles. "Didn't seem fair. That poor suitcase didn't get to go anywhere. I thought I should use it…I thought I could."

Carrie touched the handle. "The red one. You used to have a red one. I bet it's in the hall closet. You can use this one next time." She awkwardly patted Sassy's shoulder and dragged the heavy suitcase out of the room.

Sassy heard her knock on Oliver's door. Habit, she supposed. The familiar sound brought her to tears.

#

Carrie opened the door to Oliver's old room and stepped into the emptiness. Her footsteps echoed across the bare floor. In the past, the only way she had ever dared to enter Oliver's room was with Sassy. Memories teased her now but didn't really come. All she could see were walls.

The room was empty. Oliver had taken everything when he went to live with Adam. But he didn't live anywhere anymore. The suitcase hit the floor with a loud thud.

Carrie's vision fogged. Her head felt like it was trying to escape through its own eyes. The lids went into lockdown. Light seemed to pour in through her nose. Pain pulled her under like a wave and drifted in and out with the tide.

She ducked into the bathroom and rummaged through the medicine cabinet for aspirin. A large white bottle donated two pills. She cupped her hands for water to swallow, then again to splash her face. She dried her hands on her jeans and her face on her shirt, looked in the mirror and took two more pills.

Forcing a smile, she returned to Sassy's room with the red suitcase she had found in the hall closet. Moments later, the girls were on their way.

David had told them it should take about fifty-seven minutes to get there. Carrie looked at the clock. *Forty-nine minutes to go…forty-eight. Keep driving.* She rubbed the back of her neck. *Just get there. Stupid headache. Forty-seven… Say something… Anything. Sassy needs you.*

A hateful voice disrupted her thoughts. "You have no right."

Blaming the radio, Carrie adjusted the dial.

"You're not worthy," the voice said. The man's disdainful tone made her shiver.

She clicked off the radio in protest. Still, she heard him ask, "How dare you?"

Sassy only stared out the window. Her hair blew in the wind. *"Didn't she hear it?"* Carrie tried to focus on the road. She couldn't stop thinking about the voice. She began to wonder if she could have accidentally grabbed something other than aspirin from the medicine cabinet.

"Uh, oh. Are we lost?" Sassy asked.

"What? I'm fine. We must be getting close, right?"

"I love ya' darlin.' Really, I do. But I think maybe you screwed up."

Carrie pulled the car onto the shoulder of the road and pretended to study David's directions. Sassy reached over the seat for the cooler her mother had insisted on packing for their lunch. The girls laughed when they opened it. It held the same kind of lunch she used to pack for all of their school field trips. They each had a chicken salad sandwich with no crust, an apple, a juice box, and a homemade cupcake. On top was the usual note reminding them to save the cupcake for dessert.

"Remember that field trip to the science museum in eighth grade?" Sassy asked.

"We missed the bus because you wanted to talk to those boys," Carrie said.

Sassy bit into her cupcake and laughed. "Yeah. Oliver had to steal Dad's car to come and get us. He and Adam didn't even have their licenses yet."

Carrie laughed with her. "Your mom grounded all of us! Even Adam!"

Tales of the foursome's antics carried them through the rest of the two- hour ride.

"Don't tell David we got lost," Sassy told Carrie.

But it was too late. He was sitting on the porch with Joseph and Daisy when they pulled up the driveway.

"Did you have any trouble finding the place?" Sassy teased him.

"I came to introduce you to my friends here."

"Nice to meet you, Daisy," she said shaking Joseph's hand. He blushed and held the dog out proudly for her to pet.

"It's a priss dog," Sassy said, taking it in her arms for a cuddle. Joseph beamed.

David showed them around his boss's house like it was his own. There were four bedrooms, each decorated with a different theme. The Nautical Room was blue and white with model boats and a bunch of lighthouses. The Beach Room had starfish and sand dollars. The Lavender Room smelled like fresh lilacs.

"There you go, Carrie," Sassy said. "Look at all the pillows, just like in a magazine."

Carrie didn't answer.

"Care?"

"What? Sorry. I didn't bring any magazines," Carrie said.

"Magazines? No, the room. Do you want to stay in this room?"

Carrie turned and ran to the bathroom. When she rejoined the group, they were in the Music Room. Sassy was admiring Mr. Logan's collection of record albums.

"Hey. Are you okay?" Sassy asked. "You look kind of pukey."

"I'm fine. Just a little headache."

"Again? Here, lie down for a bit." Sassy pulled back the comforter on the giant bed. The sheets were white, with tons of tiny black musical notes." She grinned and winked. "Looks like a great place for a rest."

Always a good sport, Carrie laughed at the corny joke.

David shook his head and smirked.

"How about some fresh air?" Sassy asked. "David, do you mind if we go down by the lake? I'd like to dip my toes. We can see the kitchen and stuff later."

"I better be getting back to work, anyway," David said. "Joseph, would you mind guiding the ladies to the dock?"

Joseph nodded happily.

#

Their quiet little tour guide proved to be quite a valuable asset over the next few days. Joseph's youthful energy offered a refreshing shift from grief. His bounce was contagious. They played games and threw baseballs. He knew the best places to swim, the right way to pitch horseshoes, and the perfect time of day to catch lightning bugs. He always heard the ice cream truck first, and the guy at the bakery gave him free "day olds."

#

Carrie stirred a big pot of sauce for the parmesan chicken they were making. David and Adam would be there soon, and dinner was almost ready. Mrs. Lingle would be proud of how well she fed them on all of their visits.

"I'm glad you're feeling better," Sassy said. "No more headaches?"

"Nope," Carrie said. She hadn't heard the voice since their ride to the lake. "You were right. Nothing a little sunshine couldn't fix." Without measuring, she sprinkled garlic and oregano into the sauce.

"You cook like Mom," Sassy said.

"I've hung around enough to pick up a thing or two."

"Well, picking up the cooking is fine. Skip the rest." Sassy dipped a breadstick into the pot of sauce.

"C'mon, Sass." Carrie blew on Sassy's breadstick and took the first bite. "She's not so bad."

"I guess. It's just not home without Oli."

"He wanted you to be happy with David, you know."

"Yeah," Sassy said. "He never even beat him up. I think Adam is the only other guy in town who can make that claim."

They heard a horn honking outside. Sassy went to the window.

"Oh my God!" she said. "They're here. Adam brought his grandfather's Mustang."

Carrie turned off the stove and put a lid on the pot. "He hasn't driven that since he graduated."

They went out to greet the guys and burst out laughing when they saw that Adam and David were wearing tie dyed t-shirts and little round sunglasses. The girls put on the long, straight wigs and brightly colored headbands the guys had brought. They all sang their favorite Beatles' songs and played sixties trivia as they cruised around, enjoying the blast from a past they had never really known.

#

Sassy carried Daisy as she and Carrie walked around the lake. "It's weird," she said. "Sometimes I feel guilty having fun. Oliver would hate that."

"I get it," Carrie said. "He would have told you to hold your head high and carry on. But it's not that easy."

"He couldn't stand it when I was sad. He thought he had to fix it or something. One time when I was upset, he even blurted out, 'Be a man.' I was so pissed I flashed him. Both boobs. Just for spite."

"You're kidding! That's hilarious. You never told me that."

"I think you were away that week. Anyway, he promised to remember I was a lady. I promised him I'd never remind him like that again." Sassy set Daisy on the ground and tried to get her to walk on her own. The little dog wouldn't move, so she picked her back up.

"Don't let what you don't have spoil what you do," Sassy said. "That was his less chauvinistic version. I was impressed when he came up with that one."

"I remember him saying that," Carrie said. "You were freaking out because you couldn't find any raisins for the oatmeal cookies you were making."

"They were for the bake sale. I didn't tell Oli, but I was trying to impress Jeremy Jones. They had to be perfect."

"He wouldn't have chopped up those maraschino cherries and walnuts if he had known that. Your cookies were a hit."

"Oatmeal Surprise," Sassy said. "Since that day, walnuts and cherries have always reminded me to count my blessings."

"Let's bake some when we get back. I bet Joseph would love to help."

"He'd love to lick the bowl."

#

Sassy had chosen the Music Room for her summer bedroom. It had a cool old record player that really worked. She flipped through Mr. Logan's records until she found something fun to dance to. Soon she was bopping about the room like she was trying to make it rain. The second song was slower. She took a pillow from the bed, hugged it and swayed. As she floated by the window, she glanced down and noticed Joseph in the yard with Daisy. He was staring up at her and had the silliest grin on his face.

She opened the window and yelled to him. "Hey, Joseph! Do you want to dance?"

He laughed and wiggled his hips. Then he enlisted Daisy for a quick Tango. The game ended when he spotted the red sports car. He set Daisy in the grass and bolted into the house. She barked as his mother's boyfriend pulled into the driveway.

"Get outta here, mutt," Sassy heard him yell. He got out of his car and walked toward the dog. "Go on. Git," he said. He kicked her and her little body flew. Sassy ran down the stairs.

Daisy was on the porch with Carrie when Sassy flung the front door open. She scooped her up and gave her kisses. "Okay, girl. Okay."

she said, stroking her fur. She looked at Carrie. "Did you see what that scumbag did to her?"

"All she did was bark," Carrie said. "He scared Joseph away, too."

Sassy set Daisy inside. She patted her head then shut the door. "I'm going over there."

"I'm coming with you," Carrie said. "What are you gonna do?"

"I don't know. Kick his ass or something."

As they approached the house, they could hear the boyfriend yelling inside.

"You stupid little punk!" he was shouting. "I told you I wanted that done before I got home."

"Th-this is n-not your h-h-home."

"You think you're going to talk back to me?"

The girls crept around to the side of the house and stood beneath the kitchen window, trying to hear what was going on. There was more yelling, then a crashing noise. They stretched onto their toes to see what was happening, but the window was too high up.

They ran to the door and stopped.

"Wait. We can't just bust in," Carrie said.

"The hell we can't," Sassy said with her hand on the doorknob. It was locked. "Damn him. He can't talk to Joseph like that." Sassy's hands shook with anger.

"We'll call the police," Carrie said.

"But we have to get him out of there right now."

Carrie rang the doorbell. "What do we say? He's not going to let us take him."

"Umm… Appendix!" Sassy said. "Pretend you're sick again… like last week when you had the flu."

"I can't fake that. He'll never buy it."

Sassy stomped on Carrie's foot.

"Ow!" Carrie yelled. "What are you doing?"

Sassy patted her tummy. "Appendix," she whispered, then she banged on the door.

Carrie looked her in the eyes and knew she had no choice. She doubled over, hugging her abdomen. "Owww," she moaned.

"So sorry, Care," Sassy said as she pounded on the door with both fists. "Help! Help! She's dying!"

The door swung open. "What's going on out here?"

"Ow, ow!"

"My friend is sick! I need to come in and use your phone," Sassy demanded.

"Please," Carrie groaned. "Ours is broken."

"C'mon. What are you girls up to?"

"Ohhh! Oww!" Carrie dropped to the ground.

"You gotta let me in," Sassy said.

"Alright. Hurry up. She looks kinda green."

"Watch her for a minute."

Carrie stayed on the porch and continued her performance while Sassy moved in to check on Joseph. Her rush of panic turned to heartache when she found him seated at the kitchen table with his head buried in his arms. His little body was shaking. Sassy put her arms around him.

"Joseph, honey. Are you okay?"

He picked up his head and looked into her eyes. A broad smile lit his face. "I'm f-f-fine."

"We want to help. You can trust us." Sassy took his hand in hers and walked him to the door.

"Doc says I should bring you in right away, Carrie. Joseph, I need you to show us the way to the clinic."

Leaving no time for argument or questions, the girls whisked Joseph away from his mother's dumbfounded boyfriend.

"Now what do we do?" Carrie asked as they drove off.

"Ice cream," Sassy said.

They didn't take Joseph back until the sports car was gone. The next morning, they baked a three-layer chocolate cake filled with sweet almond cream, iced it with a rich fudge frosting and walked across the lawn. Joseph's mother opened the door, half awake. The conversation started out pleasantly enough. She had a lovely home. Yes, they were friends of the Logans. Then it went right to the warning they better not let that dog bark all night. Her attitude was above small talk, which was fine. Sassy preferred to get right to the point.

"So, your boyfriend's giving Joseph a hard time."

"What business is it of yours?" she snapped.

"C'mon, lady. He's a good kid," Sassy said.

"Keep your nose out of my life, little girl—and stay away from my son. Isn't he a little young for you?"

"We brought you this cake." Carrie stepped in front of Sassy with the peace offering. She held it out, inches from the woman's face. A phony smile spread across her lips. She took a step back. Sassy jerked Carrie's elbow, knocking the cake from her hands. Chocolate and cream buried the bitch's feet up to her ankles.

"Oh dear. I'm so clumsy," Carrie said. "I'm terribly sorry."

"You idiot!"

Joseph's mother kicked off her slippers, trying to shake off the cake. Standing barefoot, she ranted until her feet slipped and she fell on her butt. A small mound of cake goop broke her fall. She stuck her nose in the air and crawled back into the house.

The girls watched from the bedroom window as Joseph hosed the cake mess off of his mother's front porch.

"A sweet lot of good we did there," Carrie said.

"I'm sorry I knocked it out of your hands, Care."

"I knew exactly what you'd do." Carrie winked.

"What a wicked way to keep your good girl hands clean! We make a perfect pair."

"I wouldn't hold a chocolate cake for just anyone."

A spray of hose water against the window startled them. Joseph raised his thumb up to the girls in approval.

"Next cake we bake, he gets to eat," Sassy said.

But at the end of the week, Joseph disappeared. He didn't come over when his mother left for work. They thought he might be sleeping late again. After a few hours, they knocked on the front door, but nobody answered. Daisy barked for him. They looked all over the yards and checked his favorite spots around the lake.

David left his office as soon as they called. He and Adam made it there in fifty minutes. They searched for hours. David tried to get into his house, but it was locked. He peered in the windows and saw no sign of Joseph.

"Maybe they took him back to his father," David said. "Joseph told me he was only here for the summer."

"He wouldn't go without telling us," Sassy said.

When his mother finally got home, David asked her if Joseph could come over and help him in the yard. She told him he was out for the evening. The shiny red sports car arrived around dinner time, but left an hour later.

Sassy rocked in the swing with Daisy late into the night. David walked the porch.

"Come sit with me. The sky is full of stars," she said.

"I'm more of a moon guy."

"Very funny, David. I've seen you create a romantic moment over a chocolate stain and you're going to try to tell me this sky isn't incredible?"

"Hey. You seduced me, remember?"

"My intentions are pure…this time. I just thought we could both use a shoulder."

David cuddled up next to her and took her hand in his. The swing moved back and forth to the tune of the crickets. He had almost fallen asleep when he smelled the smoke.

"Carrie isn't letting Adam cook in there, is she?" he asked.

"Nah. They went for a walk."

"Maybe someone's having a late-night bonfire?"

"Wait…did you hear something?"

The woman's screams for help became clear. Smoke filled the air around Joseph's house. His mother hung out of an upstairs window. David rushed to the garage for a ladder.

"Where is Joseph?" Sassy yelled.

"What? I don't know," the woman yelled back. "Help me. My house is burning!"

David slammed the ladder against the house and climbed up and through the window. "Where is he?" he demanded.

"He's not here," she said, coughing from the smoke.

"Where is he?! Where the hell is he?" David lifted her up and pinned her against the wall. "Lady, don't fuck with me."

Before she could speak, he heard a pounding thump-thump-thump coming from somewhere. He dropped her to the floor and she fumbled out the window, swearing at him the whole way down the ladder.

"What have you done?" Sassy screamed at her. "Where is Joseph? Where is David?"

The woman spit at her and Sassy attacked like a rabid dog. Joseph's mother punched her in the gut, then in the face. The two were rolling on the ground when Carrie and Adam returned. "Where are they?" Sassy kept yelling. Joseph's mother reached for her throat. Adam ran over and pulled her off Sassy. Her arms and legs flailed as he lifted her. She didn't even stop swinging when David yelled from the window.

"He's here!" he shouted. But he didn't know where. He turned back into the room. He could barely see through the thick smoke.

"JOSEPH!" David choked and coughed. Over the pops and crackles of the fire below, he heard another thump. Thump. THUMP. He got down on his hands and knees and crawled to the next room. The door was closed. He reached up to open it, but it was locked. Covering his mouth with his shirt, he yelled, "Joseph! Where are ya' bud?" A fire truck wailed in the distance. "Joe! Are you in there?" The thumps were muffled. "Get down on the floor! I'm coming in!"

He stood and kicked the door open, splintering the frame and tearing off the lock. Flames devoured the stairs behind him. Following the persistent thumps, he fumbled toward the noise. "JOSEPH! Help me find you!" The frightened whimper was barely audible. "D-D-David!" Another thud followed. David dropped to the floor and looked under the bed.

"D-D-D-D" The closet! David let out a gust of feelings with one sigh. "I'm here, Bud." A silver bolt held the door shut. He turned the lock and ripped it open. Joseph was on the floor in a ball.

His cap was twisted, his shirt soaked. His thirsty lips were pasted half shut. Clouded eyes blinked away hours of darkness; then beamed at the sight of David. His cramped legs wouldn't stand. David scooped him up, threw him over his shoulder, and carried him. He smashed the window with the closest thing he could find. He stuck his head out to yell and saw Adam already moving the ladder toward them. He kicked the rest of the glass away as he waited for Adam.

Sweat dripped down David's face as he assured Joseph everything would be fine. He raised him over the windowsill into Adam's arms. Sassy dropped to her knees and sobbed. Cheers came from the gathering crowd of neighbors as Joseph's feet touched the ground. Sirens drew closer as David started to make his own way down the ladder.

#

Safe inside the Logan's house, David sat with Joseph, trying to ease his nerves. He pretended to stay calm himself as the firefighters worked to get the fire next door under control. There was a police car in the Logan's driveway, and concerned neighbors lined the yard. David could see Adam leading Joseph's mother to an ambulance.

Good idea, David thought, grateful that Adam was keeping the bitch away from Joseph, and from Sassy, like he had promised.

Carrie and Sassy were on Mrs. Logan's swing, waiting for word it was okay to hug the boy again.

David needed to talk to Joseph, but the words were hard to come. He felt like he had failed him.

"Joseph," he said. "Can you tell me what happened?"

He didn't speak at first. David waited, then said, "You can trust me. I want to help you."

Joseph picked at his fingers. "I- I- I w-was b-b-bad."

Hearing what he had feared, David seethed. Fighting not to let his emotions show, he said, "No. You're a good man. This wasn't your fault. Please, tell me. How did you get in the closet?"

Joseph hung his head. "S-Steve."

"Your mom's boyfriend locked you in there? Did she know you were home?"

Joseph's head didn't move. Tears dripped onto his bare feet. He dried his face on his shirt. David put a finger under the boy's chin and gently raised his head. He looked into his eyes as he spoke.

"Joseph, this shouldn't have happened." But David listened as the same grueling words again struggled to leave Joseph's mouth.

"I-I-I was b-bad."

"No," David said again. "Believe me. I understand." He put a firm hand on his shoulder. "You don't deserve to be treated like that. This wasn't your fault. None of it. You didn't do anything wrong."

Joseph's head dropped again. David took a deep breath.

"You know, Bud, some people aren't so nice. Being a grown up doesn't make it right."

Joseph didn't look up.

"I understand how you feel. I had this uncle. He wasn't too nice either. Even put me in the hospital once." Joseph lifted his head and watched David's face. "He made me feel so small. I got away from him though. Now you got away too. You're going to be okay, Buddy. You're tough like me."

David held up his hand and Joseph returned the high five. They talked for a bit longer before David signaled the others it was okay to come inside. After the girls got their hugs in, Sassy filled a plate with peanut butter cookies. Carrie poured some milk. Joseph sat with Daisy in his lap, unable to look at their faces. The attempt at comfort remained on the counter untouched as David crossed the lawn below them.

A commotion of concern and curiosity charged the area. David contemplated slipping away, unnoticed. He could find the bastard himself. No rights needed to be read. He'd see to it the prick remained silent permanently.

As he opened his car door, he sensed Joseph watching him through the window. He looked up and saw the innocent young face pressed against the glass, both hands curled into fists. David shut the door and found a policeman.

"We need to talk," he said.

"You know something about this fire?" the officer asked.

"No sir. Worse. I know about the child that was locked inside of it. He almost didn't make it out of there."

"The boy? What are you saying? He panicked?"

"I'm saying they bolted him in a dark closet and left. He had no water, no food, nothing. It was a punishment. The boyfriend. His bitch mother was loaded or whatever. Didn't give a damn. We think he was trapped in there for about fifteen hours."

The policeman called a second officer over. David told them Joseph's mother had left in an ambulance. A patrol car was sent to the hospital.

"What do we know about this boyfriend?" the officer asked.

David shared everything he knew about Steve, including the claim from his vanity plate, "ShockDoc."

"And sir," David glanced up at his little friend, still watching him from the house. "Joseph, uh, says it wasn't the first time."

"Does the boy have a father?"

"He's out of town with his new wife. Joseph lives with them during the school year. His mother's house was supposed to be summer vacation. He wants to go home to his father."

"We'll have a chat with his mother." The officer sighed. "He'll have to go with social services for tonight. At least until we can reach his father."

David handed them a scrap of paper with the phone number for Joseph's father scratched on it. He managed to keep his cool enough to convince the officers that Joseph would be safe staying at the house with the girls for the night. It was late and he had been through so much.

Joseph's father agreed to allowing his son to stay with Sassy and Carrie for the night, assuring the officer he'd be there the next day. David didn't know that later Sassy would also make a call to Joseph's father.

When the time came for him to leave, Sassy kissed Joseph on the forehead and handed him a little white ball of fluff.

"Take care of yourself, sweetie. We'll keep in touch, I promise. Thank you for everything."

"G-good bye, P-priss dog," he said with tears in his eyes.

"He's yours now," Sassy said. "Your Dad says it's okay."

Joseph looked to his father, who nodded his approval. The simple exchange comforted David, who had been studying the man since he'd arrived. Convinced, for the time being, that Joseph would be in good hands, he smiled.

"I'll see you in a few days," David said. "We'll go to a ball game."

Joseph swung his little arms around him and squeezed with all his might. "Good-bye," he said. That simple phrase had never sounded so clear.

#

That night David tried to bring the romance back to the lake house. He didn't bother asking Sassy how she figured out about Daisy. It didn't matter. He loved that she never let on. He took her by the hand. Together they gazed up at the wonderful, starry sky. In spite of the mound of wet rubble behind them, it was still breathtaking.

The last couple of weeks at the lake were quiet and restful, the ending summer needed. Their time away had been such a medley of overlapping emotions. With help, the grief didn't get to stay on top. Sassy mourned the loss of her brother with a new sense of purpose. She could still play and love and laugh. Life remained.

She was able to refocus her thoughts from Oliver's transient existence to his everlasting spirit. Plans brewed in her mind. She would be his torch. Through her, his light would always shine.

CHAPTER 21 – SANE

Carrie looked over her shoulder as she slipped the package into her bag. She tucked it under some antacids and the research notes for the Lit paper she was supposed to have turned in yesterday. She groaned when she saw the roll of film, still waiting to be developed. She had been in this store several times since their recent return from the lake house, and again, she had forgotten to drop it off. Deciding she wasn't up to dealing with that right now, she left the store clutching the bag as if she was smuggling doughnuts into her aerobics class.

An early autumn breeze blew across the parking lot and brought a small green baseball cap to her feet. She bent to pick it up and heard a mother's scream. A driver slammed his brakes in front of her. The boy that had been running for his ball cap stood frozen, inches from the car's bumper. The mother breathlessly scooped up her son, planting kisses all over his face. Safe in her arms now, he cried. When the driver of the car got out and started yelling at them, the mother hugged her son a little tighter and walked away.

Carrie gripped the cap in her hand. "Wait!" she called after them.

The woman turned and looked back. Walking toward them, Carrie smiled nervously, waving the hat.

"Whore," she heard. "You irresponsible bitch."

She searched the faces around her, desperate for a source. The little boy was laughing now, his mother tickling his tummy. Carrie dropped his hat and ran.

As she hid beside her car vomiting, the strange voice continued. "You're junk," he said. "Look at this mess. That's all you are, a puddle of nasty junk." She wiped her mouth and climbed into her car. "You deserve to be spewed across the blacktop," she heard. She chewed some antacids and started for home.

Should she tell her doctor about the headaches? Or would they lock her away in an insane asylum for migraines. She thought about her father. What would he think about his baby girl now? She couldn't handle being an adult without cracking up.

"Your mother couldn't handle you," the voice said. "Your father hates you for that."

Carrie pulled over and hung her head out the door. Other cars whizzed by as more junk hit the side of the road. She sat up and searched for a mint. She found the cherry lip gloss Sassy had given her.

"That's a code beautiful people use when their ugly friends need make up," Carrie said out loud. She dabbed her lips and dropped the tube into her purse. One thing was sure: She wasn't going to say anything to Sassy. *She has enough going on. She doesn't need my drama.*

Her father was home when she got there. "I ordered pizza," he said. "Are you hungry?"

"No thanks, Daddy. I have a paper to write."

He felt her forehead. "You look pale. Are you feeling okay?"

"Little headache. I took some aspirin. I'll be fine."

He scrunched his eyebrows. "Maybe you shouldn't have so many classes. You're overwhelmed already."

"I only have two this semester," she said. "I'm already behind everyone else. If I keep cutting back, I'll never finish."

"But…"

"Don't worry, Daddy. It's only a headache."

She pretended not to hear the stranger calling her a liar as she went upstairs to the bathroom.

"Incompetent slut," the voice said.

Denying the man in her head wasn't enough. Wounds of his words still bled. Confused and afraid, his anger caged her. Shame turned the lock. The stranger created a division within Carrie as her body fought its betraying mind.

Headaches could be a safe place to hide. The pain was socially acceptable. People wouldn't whisper or stare about that. Nobody had to "keep an eye" on her. She didn't scare anyone. Adam could love her just fine.

Her body again expressed its objection to the arrangement via the digestive system, as a wave of nausea passed through her. Her chest burned with acid.

"You know I'm right," the stranger said. "I could run your life better than you ever did."

The idea tempted her. Surrender it all to him. Let the man inside her mind deal with this mess. It might improve her grades. She had no idea what her professors had been droning on about anyway. This man... this stranger...this crazy voice pushed everyone else into the background.

Carrie locked the door and opened the package. If her suspicions were correct, there would be no choice. The results of the test she was about to take could change her life forever. The man's voice scornfully ridiculed her as she read through the little booklet.

"You stupid whore," the stranger said. "You can't hide from me."

Her future would be determined in three minutes by a few drops of urine on a stick.

She thought a baby was the last thing she needed. She could barely take care of herself. She had failed to keep her body the temple God had intended it to be. The man's invasion wreaked havoc on her health. He disrupted her sleep and her energy dwindled.

"You weak coward," the voice said. "I will destroy you."

Stress had steered her diet toward chocolates and potato chips and her pants were starting to notice. She wasn't exactly an ideal incubator for a healthy baby. She wasn't ready to welcome another unplanned visitor.

One by one, the seconds ticked. The headaches were a tangible obstacle that could be alleviated with aspirin and a nap. They'd go away. Sleep. That's all she needed, a little sleep. She sat on the bathroom floor and closed her eyes.

The man would not be put to rest. "Selfish bitch," he said.

She prayed through the minutes. When the third mercifully ended, she reached out to view her fate. She looked at the test strip in awe. An unexpected sense of meaning and hope filled her as she welcomed a newfound love. Fresh strength overpowered the weakness. Her baby needed her.

#

Carrie thought about Adam and their first kiss on New Year's Eve. She remembered the way he had held her face in his hands and made her feel special.

"You're pathetic," said the voice. "He'll never look at you like that now."

"Adam, I love you," she whispered into her empty hands.

"Adam knows what you are. You're not fooling anyone," she heard.

Maybe Adam never did understand the movie style romance Carrie had felt with that first kiss under the fireworks.

She forced a more pleasant thought to the front of her mind, one the strange voice could never take away. Cuddled on a blanket under the stars, looking out at the moonlit lake, Adam had loved her like a man is supposed to love a woman. And she loved him back. It wasn't dirty or ugly or wrong.

Carrie turned out the light and squeezed her eyes shut. Nothing could hide her from herself. The man devoured her weakness.

"Adam deserves a nice girl," the voice said. "Worthless tramp. He knows what you are."

It was too real to be only in her mind. She went to her room and crawled into bed, covering her belly with a pillow. But she couldn't shield the life inside her. She held a second pillow over her head. Again, the cover did no good.

"You can't hide," the man said. "He knows."

She threw the pillows against the wall. Taking her mother's embroidery cloth from her nightstand, she laid it across her chest. For a brief moment, she felt peace. Her stomach growled. Her thoughts jumbled. The stranger wasn't going away, and now he had a hostage.

Reasoning with her fear, she struggled to accept the notion the voice had no power without her actions. As long as she kept control, this stranger was nothing more than noise. Control. Without it she would lose.

Their baby needed a strong mother, body and soul. As she climbed to her feet, she held onto the fabric resting on her chest; and she fought the only real way she knew how.

"Dear God," she prayed. "I'm afraid I'm going crazy. Please allow me the strength I took from my mother. Help me to be sane enough to live for her. For Daddy and Adam. For our child."

Amen. So be it.

CHAPTER 22 – A FRIEND IN NEED

Adam watched Mrs. Antonio's ninth grade history class reluctantly file into the room. He could see their moods lighten as they realized she wouldn't be joining them. Their relief was unwarranted. He was there to inform them that class would go on. He would try not to take the inevitable groans too personally. He knew from experience a teacher's absence was like a license to party. As a rooky substitute, he was the host. His job was to disappoint his guests by carrying out the regular teacher's lesson plan.

He recognized a few faces, maybe even knew a name or two. The guys that did basketball drills so eagerly for him in gym class didn't seem as interested in what he had to say about the United States Constitution. He guessed the girl hiding behind her book putting on lipstick didn't even notice she was holding up her Algebra book.

Adam understood. Not all that many years ago, he had been a student here himself. Heck, his grandfather had been bringing him to Wayne Valley High since he was a little kid. His role had evolved, but his alma mater hadn't changed. He had thought that was what he wanted.

"I'm Mr. Jenkins," he told the students. "Mrs. Antonio is out today, but she would like us to review chapter three for your exam on Friday."

Ugh. Another chapter review. If this was his class, he'd have the kids work together to write a classroom version of the Constitution. Once they put to pen the rights they felt they should have, he'd compare it with the rights written by their forefathers. But this wasn't his class. For all he knew, tomorrow he could be stuck in home economics hoping he wouldn't need to extinguish any fires.

"Would anyone like to volunteer to read?" The only hand raised was that of a girl in the front row. He thought she looked familiar. Oh yeah. On the second day of school he had helped her open her locker. She smiled at him kind of goofy when he called on her to begin. He looked down at Mrs. Antonio's notes, pretending to listen.

His mind wandered back to the offer he had received from Marshall High School. On the surface, it appeared flawless. He had been invited to fill a permanent teaching vacancy in their physical education department. The possibility of being named as an assistant football coach made the hundreds of miles between Pennsylvania and Iowa seem almost incidental. New guys never get offers like this.

He wouldn't have applied for the position if Oliver hadn't talked him into it. Adam had hoped to earn his grandfather's old job at Wayne Valley. But Oliver had made a good point; the guy the school had hired wasn't going anywhere for a long time.

When he contacted Marshall six months ago, Adam hadn't really believed he'd get an offer, much less, consider one. He didn't even tell anyone he had sent them his resume. It was one of many schools he had applied to. By July, however, it was the only one that called him for an interview.

Secretly leaving town in his best suit hadn't felt like a lie when he'd done it two months ago. The girls were at the lake house then. He'd told himself there was no need to cause a stir over something that would probably never happen anyway.

Now, with only a month into the school year, Marshall had a sudden opening. He had accepted the job without thought, knowing that he might hang around Wayne Valley for another twenty years and still not have as good of an opportunity.

He only had a few weeks before he'd have to leave. As his dream job waited for his arrival, the reality of geography chomped a gaping hole in his future. Marshall had everything he wanted, except Carrie. He didn't know how to tell her. She'd been acting especially strange lately.

After school, he went home to the insatiable house that ate his paychecks. He'd never have been able to keep the place without steady work. Soon, he was out in the garage, sitting in the Mustang. He had only driven it a few times since his grandfather died. It still didn't feel like it belonged to him.

It was supposed to be his. There were supposed to be lots of fun rides like the one around the lake. That day with Carrie had felt so right. He'd needed her beside him then, and he needed her now.

The beige leather seat beside him looked too empty. The old whistle dangled from the rearview mirror instead of resting on Pop's chest. He managed to avoid hitting the trash cans as he backed out of the garage, even without the warning the old man used to issue. Pop wasn't there to point toward the football stadium and grunt anymore, but Adam drove there anyway.

He stared out into the field thinking of his grandfather, his favorite coach. Whenever Pop blew his whistle, his team stopped and looked to him for direction. Their leader spoke out loud and clear, without hesitation. Standing on the sidelines beside his grandfather, the game had always made sense.

He reached up and flicked the whistle hanging from the rearview mirror. It swung back and forth without a sound. Damn. He tried to hold on to images of stadiums full of cheering fans, but his thoughts fell to his own backyard and a game of blitz with Oliver. The guy didn't even play football, but he could stop Adam in his tracks better than any defenseman ever had.

"Keep moving forward," Pop would shout. "Keep moving forward."

All the way to Iowa.

Pop and Oliver were both gone now.

The Mustang was soon on its way to Carrie. Adam stopped at the bakery to buy her a muffin. She hadn't been eating well lately. While scarfing doughnuts at a red light, he happened to notice a layer of powdered sugar covering his lap. "Pig," he said, laughing at himself. But the familiar sentiment touched a nerve. Taking Carrie away was only half of the story. Leaving Sassy behind was a moral debate he had been trying to ignore. He licked the sugar from his fingers, made a u-turn, and headed to see David.

In the parking lot for the offices of Logan and Reed, Adam saw David's Volkswagen parked between a Mercedes and a Hummer. He drove to the other side of the lot and settled into a spot where he felt Pop's car would be safer. When he noticed Mr. Logan walking toward him, he figured the guy was going to ask him to move it.

"Uh, hey. I won't be here long."

"That's quite a set of wheels you have there," Mr. Logan said.

"Oh." Adam rolled his shoulders back and stood a little straighter. "It was my father's car. My grandfather rebuilt it. Took it apart in his own garage, put her back good as stock. Didn't even change the color."

Mr. Logan nodded his head in approval. Together they examined the car.

"Pop said he cussed my father out pretty good for bringing it home."

"Mmm hmm."

"After Dad died, he..."

"Mind if I take a look?"

Adam popped the hood open, stood back and tolerated Mr. Logan for another thirty seconds.

"Well, it was nice seeing you again, Sir. Guess you have to be getting back inside."

Mr. Logan pulled out a handkerchief and wiped his hands. Then he blurted out the question that always made Adam's teeth clench.

"What's your price?"

"Sir, you may not have heard me," he said as civilly as he could muster. "This car was my father's, then my grandfather's, now it's mine."

"I'm leaving in two days. I'm sure we can come to some kind of agreement before then." Mr. Logan pushed a business card into Adam's shirt pocket. "Think it over."

Adam didn't have time to be pissed. He shook his head and hurried in to see David. The office was buzzing with gossip and speculation. Some kind of bombshell had been dropped. Lacking any details, he decided not to care. His pace quickened toward David's abnormally closed door.

A knock went unnoticed. Adam let himself in. David was sitting at his desk, deep in thought. A calculator danced at his fingertips. He had been presented with an offer of his own. He looked up at the sound of Adam's voice.

"What's up David? I hear your boss is skipping town."

"Word spreads, huh? Mr. Logan stopped in to announce his retirement. He and his wife are moving to California."

"California?" Adam asked. "Didn't they just get back from there?"

"Yeah. Well, he did. She wasn't with him."

"Maybe they struck gold." Adam plucked a bite sized candy bar from a dish set out for clients.

"Whatever's going on, he's leaving for good," David said. "Their house sold first week out."

"For a money bubber, he's awfully quick with personal investments."

"Adam, he offered me first shot at buying the lake house." David straightened Sassy's picture on his desk. "It's perfect."

"No offense, Bud, but that house is a little out of your league, isn't it?"

"He offered me an unbelievable deal. He said something about his wife's father being sick."

"The lake is an hour away," Adam said, louder than intended. "What about Sassy?"

"Her school is only twenty minutes from the lake. The diner is right across the street from here. We could ride to work together."

Together. Adam grinned at the word. The answer he had come to hear from David didn't even need a question. Of course Sassy wouldn't be alone.

David slapped his hand down on his calculator. "All I need is ten thousand dollars and I can take over Logan's mortgage."

"How much do you have saved?" Adam asked.

"Ha. My most recent savings went into the vending machine at lunch."

"Dude, people trust you with their money?"

David stopped and looked up at him. Then he motioned for him to shut the door.

"Remember what I told you this summer?" David asked. "About my uncle racking up a bunch of bogus debt in my name?

"Yeah."

"Well, because of Jack my credit is crap. I can't get a decent loan. Logan can't know my numbers suck. I'm supposed to be good with investments. He trusts me enough to let me buy his house."

David shook his head. His calculator was not cooperating. "Adam, Sassy needs this. She has a plan. She wants to start a group home for troubled girls. The lake house would work. We could live there until she's ready."

"She doesn't even have her degree yet and she knows exactly how she is going to use it," Adam said. "That's Sassy alright."

"It'll take a while, but she can do it." David paused. "She thinks helping girls in trouble will be a great tribute to Oliver. Rough as he was, he always looked out for her."

Adam thought of Carrie and wondered if she'd ever finish school. She had mounds of crumpled paper in her trash can, but she never seemed to produce a complete assignment. Maybe she should see someone about those headaches. Her face looked so pale lately. He had never seen her eyes so dark.

"...lake house... money...Sassy..." David was still talking.

"The lump up front is all you need, huh? You sure you could take it from there?"

"I know I could. It'd be tough, but we could do it—once I find a way to get it started. I'd do anything to make her happy. You understand what I mean. You'd do anything for Carrie, wouldn't you?"

"Absolutely."

Money seemed to be the answer. Ten thousand could get them started. David would handle the rest. Adam did a mental inventory of his most valuable possessions, but he already knew. One item stood out above all. He left David alone with his arithmetic.

\#

Memories of his grandfather filled him. He thought of the time Grandpa made him share his trick or treat candy with a strange kid from school who had the chicken pox and couldn't go out. Having already suffered the dreadful itch, he sympathized with the guy. Still, he had been horrified at the thought of giving up half of his candy.

"Sharing rarely leaves you with less," Pop had said. "In fact, it often gives back better than you thought you wanted."

His grandfather had been right. His friendship with Oliver had started with a plastic pumpkin full of bite sized chocolate bars, some candy corn and a bunch of peanut butter cups. Adam never admitted to hiding a few packages of licorice in his pocket.

He also remembered his grandfather's words of wisdom when he had gotten an "F" on his math test. Pop had lectured him on the importance of understanding numbers saying, "Sometimes you'll need dollars to make sense." Math still wasn't his favorite subject, but life had taught him the lesson was true.

Adam realized he already knew what his grandfather would have told him to do now. He had to make some sense for all of them.

With a couple of phone calls, and the pretense of the flu, a romantic dinner with Carrie was postponed. Instead, he headed across town to a restaurant she would have loved. He sat at the bar watching a ball game on an overhead television, oblivious to the live piano music fifty feet away. With a gulp of soda, he washed down a handful of complimentary nuts. He was pleased with himself for remembering to cover his mouth as he belched. He figured Sassy would also have been impressed. She was always reminding him not to be a pig. "Carrie deserves a gentleman," she would say.

His interest in the game had taken over when a firm hand on his shoulder reminded him he was there on business. Mr. Logan was grinning at Adam's change of heart. His grandfather's pride was about to reunite with its truest recipient. The car had been the old man's pleasure. His grandson was his treasure.

With a mere nod the two men were escorted to the finest table. Without ordering, they were brought the house's best New York Strip steaks, accompanied by the biggest, weirdest, french fries that Adam had ever seen. Their platters were also adorned by something green that almost made his fictitious stomach ailment come true.

The older man was on his third scotch and water by the time Adam had enough nerve to make his proposal. Placing the keys to Pop's Mustang on the table, he looked Mr. Logan right in the eye and forfeited material pride.

"Twenty thousand, one condition," Adam said. His tone was barely audible. Mr. Logan raised his eyebrows.

"It stays between us. Take it away. Keep it away. Nobody has to know."

They each sipped at their drinks. Adam suddenly wished his glass contained more than ice and cola. He faked an interest in his overcooked steak as his prospective customer briefly considered the proposal.

Mr. Logan phoned his notary. An hour later, Adam walked home with a cashier's check for twenty thousand dollars and an old silver whistle in his pocket. He was ready to share his candy.

#

Having done so many homework assignments for Oliver, it was easy to forge his friend's handwriting. Adam slipped a carefully worded note into an envelope along with one hundred large bills and went to David's apartment.

"Ten thousand dollars. That will get you started," he said. "Give the note to Sassy. Tell her Oliver asked you to invest his savings."

David looked into the envelope amazed. "How could...?"

"Don't worry, it's legit," Adam said. "Don't screw it up."

Adam stopped David's questions before he could ask. They all had the same answer. "It's for Sassy."

"You are an excellent broker," Adam said as he turned and walked away. No explanation. No regrets.

CHAPTER 23 – ROMANCE DELAYED

There would have been candlelight. It wasn't going to be their usual dining out experience unwrapping sandwiches on their laps and eating fries off the dashboard. Last week Carrie and Adam had reservations. They had planned a fancy date inside one of the finest restaurants in town. It was the kind of place with plates and silverware. There would have been linen tablecloths and napkins too crisp and white to use for things like wiping spaghetti sauce from her mouth. They probably would have even gotten free rolls with butter you don't have to open.

Carrie had pictured a man at a piano. She would drop a tip in his giant glass and ask him to play a special lullaby. Then she would give Adam the tiny shirt bearing the title "Daddy's Little Rookie." He would be surprised at first; then he would realize his joy. Everyone in the restaurant would applaud as the happy couple clinked glasses in a grape juice toast. It would have been wonderful. Unfortunately, Adam had been sick that night.

Carrie lay in bed wishing her stomach could rebound as quickly as Adam's had. She had never expected to develop a relationship with saltine crackers, but lately they were her new best friends. She kept a box hidden under her bed to tame the morning nausea. Nibbling a few crackers usually made the difference between a little queasiness and outright intestinal hysteria. There were, however, days that even the crisp white squares couldn't help.

When Adam opened her bedroom door, Carrie was hanging over the side of the bed with her head in a bucket. She was in no condition to pretend she was delighted by his surprise visit. She pulled a sheet over herself to hide her current lack of dignity. She tried to claim she'd caught his flu.

She hoped she didn't stink as he tucked her back into bed. He leaned in to kiss her forehead. When he stood back up, she realized he had in his hand the "Little Rookie" shirt that she had hidden under her pillow. He held it up like a giant question mark.

"I look awful," she groaned. "You weren't supposed to find out like this. I wanted it to be special."

"Special? You can't be serious." Adam looked scared.

Carrie nervously repeated the words she had practiced in front of the mirror a hundred times, "We're having a baby, Adam."

She waited, but Adam didn't say anything. So she said the thing she wanted him to say to her, "Everything is going to be okay."

He didn't even smile. "Are you sure?" he asked. "This can't be happening. It's crazy."

Carrie wanted to cry, but she was trying so hard to be a good adult. "Of course I'm sure! I'm not crazy. How could you say that?"

But Adam stared at her like she had three heads. The stranger was laughing. She couldn't fight with both of them.

"Will you lay with me?" she asked Adam. "I couldn't sleep last night. I was worried about you. I'm glad you're feeling better."

"Oh. Yeah. I was sick. I didn't sleep either." Adam laid down next to her. "Carrie, are you sure you're okay?"

"I'm fine," she said. "Morning sickness is normal. This is fine. Normal."

"But this baby thing," Adam said, getting off the bed, "you're not freaked?"

Carrie sat up. "Honey, don't be scared. You'll be a great father."

"But..."

"Adam, I love you so much."

"I love you, too." He brushed her hair away from her eyes with his fingers and kissed her forehead.

He sat with her on the edge of her unmade bed and suggested they get married. She squirmed in her ragged pajamas. Fantasies of reliving their first beginning under midnight fireworks on New Year's Eve fell away. She expected the stranger would say she didn't deserve a proposal at all, but he was silent.

Instead, it was Adam who spoke. He told her he had been offered a job at Marshall High School, a thousand miles away. He wanted to take it, and he asked her to move with him. He said they could be a family. A real family.

She felt a strange sense of victory over the stranger. Still, Carrie was conflicted. Marshall High was so far away, so wonderfully, but horribly far away. Adam had been part of her life for so long. Of course she loved him. But when she played with her dolls, thoughts of leaving home never came up during the romantic proposals. Carrie rubbed her hands across her belly. The doll never got to have a little baby bump either. That poor skinny bitch.

It was a shame none of the dolls in her bench had heads anymore. Carrie wondered if Adam would still want to marry her if he knew that.

"But... Sassy," she said. "I can't leave her now."

"Sassy is a strong lady," Adam said a little too quickly. "She'll be okay. David says she's doing great in school."

"I'm trying! My classes are harder this year."

"I didn't mean that. I know you've not been feeling well. This all has been hard on you."

"I should be here for her." Carrie started to make her bed. "I'm sorry, Adam. I can't go."

"Carrie, I'm trying to take care of you. Now there's a baby. It needs you to be healthy."

She stopped and held his hands. "Our baby needs both of us."

"I promise. I'm going to take care of you. Please come to Iowa with me."

"Adam, we'll be a family. I love the idea of that. But, everything is changing."

"We need change now more than ever," he said. "Trust me. We can do this. Sassy will be fine."

"Mind if I go talk to her?" She left her unmade bed and went downstairs.

Adam helped her to the door like she was a fine china cup full of hot tea. She promised him she wouldn't break. As she crossed the street, she promised herself the same thing.

For the first time, she walked into Sassy's house feeling like a woman. The little girl that had grown up here was immediately pulled into the argument already in progress.

"Talk to her Carrie. Tell her it's not right," Mrs. Lingle demanded.

"Mother, I'm not your pure little virgin daughter. I'm sorry, I'm not Carrie."

Carrie steadied herself against the wall and crossed her legs, trying to look proper.

"It's a sin, Elizabeth Lingle." Sassy's mom was still holding a spoon in her right hand. "What would your brother say?"

"He'd say, 'Sassy, don't be a puppet like our mother,' and he would be right! He could see David loves me. Why can't you?"

"It's not a question of love." She waved her spoon like a magic wand. "Doesn't he respect you enough to marry you first?"

"This is my dream. He gets that. He has more faith in me than you ever did." Sassy paused, took the spoon from her mother's hand and stuck it into the pocket of her apron. "Mom, this is a once in a lifetime chance. David and I are going to buy the lake house together. Someday Oliver's name will hang proudly over the mail box."

"What's going on?" Carrie asked.

"You tell her, dear," she said, her eyes pleading with Carrie. "You're a good girl. Tell her," Mrs. Lingle begged.

"Yeah, Carrie," said the stranger. "Tell her what a nice little whore you've been."

Ignoring the voice, Carrie looked at Sassy's perfectly fit jeans. Her stomach was so flat.

"I know, I know. I'm a sinner." Sassy threw her hands in the air. "I should wait for my wedding night. Tra, la freakin' la. Well I have news for you, Mother…"

"I'm pregnant," Carrie said. Her entrance into the conversation ended it with stunned silence.

Mrs. Lingle gasped, then frantically made the Sign of the Cross. Through mumbled prayers, she left in a huff. She banged her pots and pans about the kitchen as if she were in search of some baking miracle to solve everything. Sassy took Carrie's hand and pulled her upstairs.

"Sweet honey!" she said, shutting her bedroom door. "I knew Adam couldn't resist you forever. When did this happen? I can't believe you didn't tell me."

Carrie shrugged her shoulders, embarrassed. "I'm sorry. I tried. It's just kind of weird to talk about."

Sassy laughed. "I always tell you."

Carrie wouldn't allow herself to ask if that was completely true. She'd forgiven Sassy and Adam for kissing a long time ago.

Before she could say anything, Sassy plopped down on her bed and asked, "How're you feeling? You look like crap."

Carrie sat next to her. "I'm fine. Are you're really moving into the lake house with David? How'd he pull that off?"

"I'm not sure yet. Mr. Logan gave him some kind of deal. He said he'll explain everything when he gets here. He has something he has to give me first."

"A diamond ring, perhaps?" Carrie asked.

"Nah. It's some kind of envelope. By the way, your finger is looking kind of bare. Has Adam found the cure for a romantic like you?"

Carrie folded her hands together and rested them on her lap. She needed some crackers. Mrs. Lingle entered with a banana cake. The sweet smell sent her running to the bathroom. Sassy followed with a hair tie. She ran cool water, wiping Carrie's pale face between groans.

"And don't you worry, Care. I won't be too far."

Carrie sunk her face into the towel. Her body drooped into the comfort of her best friend's arms.

"He wants me to leave, Sass. He got a job. It's a million miles away… Iowa! Do they even have mountains there?"

Sassy couldn't speak.

"I don't want to leave you," Carrie said.

#

Sassy sat up straight as Carrie rambled the details that would take her away.

No, Carrie, she wanted to say. *Please don't go.* The thoughts continued. *But she's really leaving… They're both leaving. Carrie will be gone. And she'll be with Adam… That's good… Adam will take care of her. They'll be together… A family… with a baby…good… I love David. Carrie loves Adam. It's all good.*

"Carrie, everything is going to be okay," she said.

"Come have some peppermint tea," Mrs. Lingle called up the stairs. "It'll make you feel better, dear."

"Not now," Sassy started to say, but stopped. She couldn't ignore the whim. "C'mon, Care. Let's party." She slid under her bed and pulled out an old box.

"I can't believe you still have that!" Carrie said.

"Don't tell David," Sassy said as she wrapped a lavender boa around her neck.

The girls presented themselves for the tea party wearing big floppy hats and tight white gloves. The high heels wobbled less, this time actually fitting their feet. The long strands of colorful beads dangling on their chests had a little more to rest on.

Sassy handed her mother a fake mink stole. Sighing, she covered her shoulders with the fur and eased herself into the chair. She filled the girls' cups, and one for herself. They lifted their mugs with raised pinky fingers and sipped.

#

Carrie felt better with Sassy's blessing when she went back to Adam and answered his proposal with a hearty "Okay." The moment she told him, she knew it was right. Soon they would be a family. All grown up. Up, up, up... and away.

Two weeks later, she stood in front of a mirror wearing her mother's wedding dress. Sassy pinned tiny ivory flowers in her long auburn hair. When the father of the bride stopped in the doorway, he stood there, admiring his daughter.

"You are the most beautiful bride in the whole wide world," he said, taking her on his arm. "Like your Mom."

"Daddy, that's the greatest compliment I've ever had."

Rose petals lined the way as her dad walked her down the aisle. The sweet floral aroma filled the church with a fairy tale scent. A merry flute sang out in delightful agreement to the joy in the air.

#

"Stop," Adam said as Carrie approached the front of the church. "There's something I have to do."

The music stopped. Everyone held a collective breath. Sassy held her bouquet to her mouth to cover a giant grin. Carrie stepped to the side of the aisle to allow room for Adam to run past. But he didn't.

"Carrie, before we do this, there's something I want to say to you."

Adam glanced at Sassy, who nodded her approval. *Do it how I told you, Adam,* she thought, *Carrie's been dreaming of this for years.*

At the front of the church, he bent on one knee and held out the pretty little blue box Carrie's father had given him.

"Open the box," Sassy whispered into her bouquet.

"Carrie, you are the sweetness and beauty in my life. I love you like crazy and I want to be with you forever."

He looked around the room as if he needed assurance he was doing it right. Carrie stood before him with tears dripping on her veil.

"Oh!" he said. "And you look really pretty in that dress."

"Open the box," Sassy whispered a little louder.

Adam lifted the lid and removed the ring. Carrie held her hand out and he slipped it on her finger, like Sassy had showed him to do when they'd practiced it.

"Carrie, will you marry me?" he asked.

A sanctuary full of family and friends, the minister, the photographer and the organist waited for the bride to reply.

"Oh, Adam. Yes!" she said from behind the moist veil.

Adam jumped to his feet and wrapped his arms around her. He ducked into her veil and kissed her.

Perfect.

#

Sassy and Carrie walked together through Littleston Station, hand in hand, fuzzy mitten in leather glove.

"Adam will be waiting for you at the train station in Iowa, right? I think it's colder there," Sassy said. "Did he check to see if there's somewhere warm you can wait? I'll call him when I get home."

"He'll be there," Carrie said.

"I could drive you to Iowa! I'll stay for a few days and help you set things up. That way I'll know exactly what it looks like. I need a mental picture."

Carrie wiped her eyes with her mitten. "Adam said it's supposed to snow there tonight. That's why my father insisted I take the train. He even bought my ticket."

"Okay." Sassy squeezed her hand. "I'll see you in April when I bring your car. As soon as the baby is born."

"And I'll be back when you're ready to open Oli's House," Carrie promised.

Sassy plopped onto a bench. "This can be our spot. Every time you come to visit we can meet right here, on this bench." She gestured toward the newsstand. "I'll get you some tea just before the train pulls in, so it'll be nice and hot."

Carrie sat beside her. The cold seat made her shiver. Sassy leaned up against her and rested her head on her shoulder. "This is a good spot," she said. They sat on the bench together until Carrie's train was called.

They got up and hugged like they were never going to see each other again. Then Carrie kissed Sassy on the cheek. "I'll meet you right here. On our bench," she said.

Sassy watched her walk away. Carrie turned to wave as she stepped onto the train. From her seat, she looked out the window and saw Sassy, still waving, standing in front of the empty bench.

CHAPTER 24 – MISSION

Joseph was sitting on the front steps waiting when David came to pick him up at his father's house. David could see his breath in the cold as his little buddy ran to greet him. Joseph was wearing a knit hat and a warm coat that seemed to fit well. Handing David a paper, he pointed to the giant red "A" at the top.

"Wow, Joseph. Great job!" David looked over the math problems they had studied together, confirming in his head the answers on the test were right. "I'm so proud of you."

"My f-first 'A!' Th- th- thanks."

"I knew you could do it. Can we bring this to show Sassy? She started her job back at the diner tonight. I thought we could have dinner there."

Joseph nodded happily as he folded the paper and tucked it inside his coat.

"Mind if we swing by my place first?" David asked. "I caught Vertigo trying to eat a bar of soap when I stopped home at lunchtime. Crazy dog. I want to make sure he isn't sick."

Joseph laughed. "S-sassy know about him y-y-yet?"

"Ha! They're best friends," David said. "She laughed when I told her about him. Couldn't wait to meet him. I guess it was kind of dumb to try to fool her like that."

It had been four months since their summer at the lake, and with all of their weekly visits, Joseph had still never seen David's apartment. They rode through the quiet streets of Joseph's neighborhood, past Wayne Valley High, to the other side of town.

"How's the paper route going?" David asked. "Getting the hang of it?"

Joseph pulled a handful of dollar bills out of his pocket and smiled. "B-b- burgers my treat."

"Impressive. Keep saving. When you're a little older I'll teach you about investing."

#

Vertigo jumped up on David as soon as he opened the door. "Easy, girl," David said. He petted her as he scanned the apartment for any soap-eating related messes. "I better take her for a walk," he said to Joseph.

Joseph had already spotted a stack of comic books on the table and was inching closer, trying to get a better look.

"Oh, hey. Adam left those for you when he moved," David said. "I meant to bring them for you. Go ahead and check them out. We'll be right back."

Joseph was thumbing through pages of superheroes when there was a knock at the door. He figured it was David, so he opened it, still holding one of the books. The man on the other side had a hairy face and a fat nose. It looked like a Halloween mask, but Halloween was over. He smiled with yellow teeth.

"Who the hell are you?" he asked, sounding like an ogre.

Joseph was too frightened to speak.

"Don't ignore me, boy. I asked ya' a question."

"I- I-I…"

"Shit. You some kinda freak, ain't cha? Where's Davey?"

Joseph shook his head back and forth. He swallowed hard, forcing his words to be clear, "Not here."

The guy pushed past him into David's apartment. "You here by yourself?"

As Joseph struggled to answer, David appeared in the doorway. He grabbed the guy and pinned him against the wall. Vertigo sat beside Joseph and barked.

"You looking for me, Jack?" David demanded.

"Well, there, Davey. Look who growed up."

"You okay, Bud?" David asked over his shoulder.

"Yes, yes," Joseph said, dropping to Vertigo's side and trying to hug him quiet.

"Jack here is leaving now." He released his grip and Jack brushed himself off.

"You're not going to introduce me to your kid?" Jack asked. David didn't correct him. "I'm offended. Didn't that fancy-ass college teach ya' no manners?" Walking around, checking things out, he gestured toward David's little apartment. "They sure as hell didn't get ya' no job."

David moved in front of Joseph, but the boy spoke loud enough to be heard. "He has a j-j-job," he said, petting the dog's head.

"Really, now? Ain't that super." Jack scratched his chin. "Ya' send me up the river, an' y'all are livin' it up." He picked up a comic book and looked through it. Then he tore it apart and threw the pages on the floor. "That there's a load of shit. There ain't no good guys."

"I don't imagine you met many in prison," David said. "But they do exist."

Jack moved closer. "I taught you better than that, boy. You remember." He pushed his shoulder. "Shove enough, ya' can make any man fall."

"Get out," David said.

"I'll get when I'm ready to get."

Jack was dirty and smelly. Joseph wanted David to hit him. Instead, David picked up the phone and dialed someone's number. He listened for a moment, then spoke into it, "I'd like to speak with Officer Samuel O'Brian please."

Jack stepped back.

"You have thirty seconds," David said to him. "Unless you'd rather wait for the police to get here. I'm sure they'd be happy to see you again."

"Ungrateful punk," Jack mumbled as he left.

David held the phone and waited. "Hey, Sammy," he finally said to someone on the other end. "Any news on that matter we discussed?"

Joseph watched David's face as he listened for an answer. *His face relaxed and he looked relieved.*

"Great," David said. "Yeah. He's gone."

CHAPTER 25 – TWELVE HUNGRY MEN

Mrs. Adam Jenkins was in a whole new world. The newlyweds'
house not only sheltered them in two stories of old-fashioned charm, but it
did so with the mixed familiarity of Adam's bachelor pad misfits and
Carrie's girlie bedroom furniture. His king-sized bed sort of matched her
mother's rocking chair, once she bought the new bedspread. He didn't
complain about the pink curtains and she didn't mind his wall full of hats.

The brown and blue plaid sofa they had found for the living room
hid a convenient pull out bed. She appreciated its stiffness. Those
cushiony new couches would have been too hard for a growing-bellied
pregnant lady to get out of when she was alone. She had never seen it
opened, but figured it would be nice to have if anyone from back home
ever came for a visit.

The folding table in their kitchen wouldn't have been her first
choice, but it looked pretty when she covered it with a gingham tablecloth.
As long as she was careful not to wiggle the legs, she had a nice place to
sit with her tea. She could stay inside, safe from the chilly November air.

Despite the seasonal dreariness, the kitchen was bright and
cheerful with delicate yellow rosebud wallpaper and creamy white

cabinets. Citrus scented candles filled the room with memories of childhood summers.

On occasion, she would jot down a few words. Carrie liked to write rhyme and verse. It gave her a sense of order, otherwise difficult to find. Seeing it on paper was proof that she still knew what order was. She may have had scraps of papers tucked all over the house, but at least each one briefly demonstrated the small, but huge, accomplishment of getting her thoughts together.

It takes snow to build a snowman,
Cold weather is great,
For the pond to freeze over,
So children can skate.
When the rain falls,
Flowers grow.
The ground is nourished,
Rivers flow.
Good can come from bad,
In nature and in life.
I pray that good will come to you,
And end your time of strife.

Pen and paper made good company. Since her new neighbors were a vacant field and a pond waiting to freeze, stationery was the next best thing to having a friend with her when she didn't want to go outside.

She watched from her kitchen window for the kids up the road to get off the school bus. She imagined they'd come in bundled layers with ice skates and hockey sticks when it got a little colder. She'd bring out hot chocolate and freshly baked cookies. They'd want to stay for dinner sometimes. She should probably keep stocked up with extra food. She expected they would have fishing poles and baseball games come spring.

They lived across from a quaint little farm with seven cows. Carrie counted them every time she looked out, for fear of being caught off guard by one peering into her kitchen window. Adam teased they were ghosts of hamburgers past waiting to catch her at her hungriest and make a vegetarian out of her. Hoping for an ally, she sent Sassy pictures of them lurking by the fence, staring. Sassy dubbed the animals "The Dubious Beef Cult" and insisted Carrie name each member.

Carrie complied, writing back, "T-Bone is their leader, Roquefort has an odor offensive to the others, and Milkshake moos jokes about me when I pass by. KaBobby tends to be a bit snobbish but Stewart seems to get along well with the rest of the guys. I have yet to form opinions regarding Stroganoff and Asiago."

Beef or dairy, she really didn't know or care. The long-distance communication was more fun if she wrote about cows than, "I miss you. I miss you. I miss you." Now, she could also see the cows and laugh. She didn't have to be afraid.

She could be normal. Even better. She could be an awesome mommy. She would. She'd bake cupcakes and make costumes. She'd read every article, try every healthy recipe, and use every coupon Mrs. Lingle sent. Maybe someday she'd even go back to school.

Carrie focused on housework, baby preparations and meal planning. Letters to and from her father brought a level of closeness and comfort that living together had never seemed to reach. She tried to keep all contact with him positive.

"Iowa is beautiful. I've never seen so much corn!"

"Mrs. Lingle brought you another cake?"

"The baby's been kicking a lot. Adam's already recruiting for his team…"

"Maybe you should try dating…"

"She sounds great! Definitely ask her to dinner."

"I'm excited for you, Daddy! Wear that blue sweater… I can't wait to hear all about it…"

Carrie felt like a real grown up. Yes. She would be okay. With seven bovinely wonderful new friends across the street, she could do normal. She'd make it work. Sassy would approve.

Her illusion of reality suited her new life fine until the man found her again.

"You can't hide from me you little slut. I'm part of you," the stranger said. "Look at you. Adam deserves better."

Carrie turned up the volume on the radio and sang with Bon Jovi. Her broom handle was a microphone and she swayed as she swept, pretending not to hear the voice. She cleaned the small kitchen floor all morning, never noticing the time. Still, the stranger persisted.

"I have him," he said. "I have your child."

The claim halted her breath as her worst fear was put to words. No. It couldn't be true. She wanted to tell him she knew better. He should leave her alone. But that would mean giving him the satisfaction of an answer. Once she crossed that line, there would be no turning back. Rustlings in her tummy begged her to be strong. Her body needed to protect its precious cargo.

It was time to get rid of the little plastic bodies. She went to the attic and found the suitcase. It was heavier than she remembered. She popped the lock and it sprung open. The dolls fell out. Scattered on the floor, lay a mini party of slender females, still in their ball gowns and tiny shoes. Carrie still had no idea what had happened to their heads. She'd found them like this the night she was going to tell Adam about the baby.

What did I do? she thought. She couldn't think about that now. She had to make it all go away. She gathered the bodies and stuffed them back into the suitcase. They'd have to go.

She stood the suitcase at the top of the stairs and pushed. It bumped its way down to the second floor and crashed at the bottom. *They'll think I'm crazy.*

The trip to the first floor was easier as she slid it, step by step, down the carpet. *No mermaid. Where was the mermaid?* It was as if her mind had just finished the role call and she realized the mermaid was missing.

Crisp dead leaves announced her presence as she walked the suitcase through her quiet yard to the pond. She tossed some rocks into the water. Plunk. Plunk. A turtle retreated into its shell. A frog croaked. Another rock plunked. The suitcase splashed. It floated across the pond.

"Sink," she said. "Sink!"

It didn't. Carrie rubbed her hand across her belly. She faintly heard a distant moo as she waded into the water. The shocking cold held her feet, her knees, and her grip on the moment. Mud squished through her toes. She inhaled the brisk autumn air. She bit the palm of her hand hard enough to leave a mark. At last, she pulled the suitcase from the water and hid it behind a bush.

After Adam left for work on trash day, she slipped out back and dragged the frozen case out of the bush. She stood it with their garbage at the end of the driveway and looked across the street. A cow standing by the fence stared back at her.

"Our secret, Milkshake," she said to it.

She went inside and watched from the window. An hour later the truck came. The dolls left with it. She could forget them now. But she looked over and saw Milkshake talking to his friends. She went to the freezer and pulled out a package of ground beef. Adam would be having meatloaf for dinner.

#

In the weeks to follow, Carrie rediscovered the four food groups. The guys in the produce section of the local grocery store got to know her by name. She avoided the junk food aisles and made sure to visit Fred in dairy. The butcher knew she would only buy the leanest cuts.

Energized by the balancing of her diet, she used the added oomph to exercise. With one month to go, her pregnancy was progressing nicely. Her crusade against this strange evil neared an end. Soon, the man would know who ruled. Soon, she could be sure herself.

Until then, she faked being content playing house with Adam. She'd send him off to work each day with a kiss and a thoughtfully prepared lunch. When he returned home, she'd serve a hot dinner and listen as best she could to stories about his day. He often promised to bring home some of his players to meet her. He said he wanted to show her off.

She hadn't expected it would be on Valentine's Day. She was all gussied up in a sweetheart red dress, setting the table for a romantic lasagna dinner, when Adam and eleven rather large high school athletes popped in to surprise her. The men inhaled the lasagna before she had the garlic bread out of the oven.

As she scrambled for a second course, the uneasiness she had been feeling all day escalated to intense pain. Clutching the sides of her stomach, she took a deep breath.

"Adam, the baby!" she said with a panic.

"You said it wouldn't be here until March."

Adam wasn't trying to sound like an idiot. It just happened. He quickly rebounded as he called his team into action. He helped Carrie to her feet and started walking her to the car. The running back wanted to carry her, but the quarterback thought he should take her himself. Fueled by nervous adrenaline, Adam scooped her up and one of the guys grabbed an afghan from the sofa to cover her. Her bag made it to the back seat and the doctor got word she was on her way.

Floating in her husband's arms, a pack of burly men clumsily escorted her to Adam's running car. Their kicker drove and Adam held Carrie's hand for comfort. A four-car procession raced to the hospital. Luckily, they made it on time for the doctor to play receiver.

Adam thought he was ready for this. Since the day Carrie had told him she was pregnant, he knew ready was what he needed to be. So, he had rubbed her swollen feet, made midnight ice cream runs, and even went with her to a few doctor appointments. He'd helped prepare a nursery and put a crib together.

He could feel how much his wife loved this child, this stranger. She did everything she could to take care of it. He did everything he could to take care of her. For months, she'd spoken about their "little family" with such pleasure. He loved being on her team.

The ride to the hospital rushed his adrenaline like a touchdown in a bowl game. He had expected to hear his players cheering from the waiting room, which he did. He had expected Carrie to cry happy tears, which she did. But when she handed him that baby, he felt something he had never imagined he could feel.

With his son in his arms, Adam wept. He was a dad. He gently petted the fuzz on their child's sweet head. The little guy was so ugly and so beautiful. Red faced and wrinkled, he squirmed until he let out the cutest fart they had ever heard. Finally comfortable, he nestled himself on his daddy's chest and slept peacefully.

"He needs a name," Adam said.

Carrie's smile shone brighter than he had ever seen. "Let's name him Daniel," she said.

CHAPTER 26 – CARRIE'S DARKEST DAY

The heat of his flesh woke her. Carrie had snuggled Daniel into their bed because she was concerned about the fever he had earlier. A chesty cough racked his little body. Adam rushed downstairs to fetch the medicine the pediatrician had prescribed. The wheezing continued to get worse.

The usually chatty two-year-old lay helplessly in his mother's arms. His listless figure barely had time to recover between gasps. Daniel looked up at her, his face trusting, yet frightened. His dark eyes were sunken and watery. His pale cheeks were on fire.

She released him from his favorite blanket and stripped off his warm footy jammies. Adam returned with the medicine dropper and a damp cloth. Daniel didn't have the strength to resist as Carrie held his head and squirted the nasty liquid through his crimson lips. She gently rubbed his hot skin with the cloth, desperate to bring the fever down.

He gasped, kicked his legs, and batted his arms. His body sunk into her lap and lay panting. Carrie hummed softly and rubbed his chest as Adam called for an ambulance.

"They'll be here soon," he said.

"How soon? The hospital is so far."

"A few minutes. They'll be here soon."

Carrie wrapped Daniel up in his blanket. "It's okay, sweetie. Daddy's here," she said.

She and Adam were standing outside with Daniel when the ambulance arrived. They both moved to get in with him.

"Sorry, folks," the paramedic said. "Only one parent allowed."

"But…" Carrie started.

"Don't worry." Adam kissed her cheek. "I'll be right behind you."

The door closed between them. She could see herself with her baby in the back of the ambulance. A giant hand held a smoking mask over his little face. Daniel's head tried to move away. She pressed him still against her chest and hummed. Lights flashed around them as they sat on the outside of the world. Daniel needed her to be brave.

"He needs a real mother," the stranger said.

Sirens agreed with him. She kept humming. The driver spoke into the radio. The radio spoke back. She couldn't understand the words. Someone else was there. He was asking questions. Her mouth was answering. The headlights of Adam's car followed behind them. She kissed Daniel's forehead. Still hot.

"He's not a doll," the stranger said.

The ambulance stopped outside of the hospital. Medics ripped her baby from her arms and took him into a bright white room filled with people and machines. Carrie reached out for him, but he was surrounded. A nurse pinned him to a stretcher while the doctor examined his helpless body. Monitors beeped as another mask took over his tiny mouth and nose. Needles violated his delicate skin. Daniel didn't even cry.

"What did you do to him?" The voice in her head sounded angrier than ever.

Carrie hummed in the corner. At last, they finished. The pack disappeared. A kind nurse called out to her, "Mrs. Jenkins, you can hold your son now." She tried to go to him but couldn't walk. Her feet weren't on the floor. She was on her knees.

"You thought you had control," the stranger said. "Stupid bitch."

#

Outside the door, Adam heard Carrie's familiar hum. She sat on the bed with Daniel, stroking his hair. He watched her look, willing their child to breathe. Two days ago, he had watched them splashing and giggling their way through a bubble bath. Now, here he was. Adam stepped into the room and put his hand on her shoulder.

#

An orderly came to take Daniel for an x-ray.

"He can't go right now," Carrie said. "He just got to sleep."

"Doctor's orders, miss," the orderly said.

"He needs his rest."

"Carrie, it's okay." Adam stood. "They'll take good care of him."

"I'm going with him," she insisted.

"Let me go. I'll make sure he's okay," Adam said.

"He knows you're crazy," the stranger said. "He doesn't trust you to handle this."

"Adam, he needs me."

"He does need you," Adam said. "Honey, you're trembling and exhausted. Close your eyes and rest a bit. We'll be right back."

"Idiot. You're no mother," the stranger said.

"I'm a good mother." Carrie hugged her arms around herself to hide the shaking.

"Of course you are, sweetie," Adam said. "Don't worry. Daddies can comfort, too. We'll only be gone a few minutes. You can rock him back to sleep as soon as he's done." He lifted Daniel from his bed and went with the orderly down the long hallway. Carrie followed behind him, softly humming the Sesame Street theme song.

#

By the time the doctor came to talk to his parents, Daniel was enjoying a game of patty cake with Carrie. His hearty belly laugh filled the room. The solemn old man with the stethoscope instantly deflated it.

Daniel slobbered on Carrie's shoulder as she tried to understand what the doctor was saying.

"The child does not have pneumonia."

"Oh, thank God."

"But…"

No. No buts. Please no buts.

"The x-ray showed a rib had been broken and healed."

She rocked Daniel back and forth in her arms. *What does that mean? Did he have some kind of bone disease? Did he need to drink more milk?*

Annoyed by her presence, the doctor looked to Adam for help. Her husband shushed her as the men discussed her baby. *Our baby,* she reminded herself.

The doctor wasn't answering anything. Daniel was starting to fuss. She never saw the doctor's next question coming.

"Is somebody hurting this child?"

She clung to her baby. How dare he!? Her eye started to twitch. Adam stepped between her and the doctor, as if he was banning her from the conversation.

"They're going to take him away," the stranger said. "You'll never see him again."

"Maybe it happened when you fell, Care," Adam said. "You see, Doc, a few months ago there was a little accident. My wife was bringing Daniel downstairs…"

"For breakfast," Carrie said. "He likes oatmeal and bananas."

"Anyway. She slipped on the steps."

"My feet get cold. I had those fuzzy socks on."

"She was carrying the baby and…"

"I twisted. I was afraid I'd land on him. I didn't drop him! His foot got caught on the banister. We fell. It was an accident."

"All. Your. Fault," the stranger said.

"We took Daniel to the pediatrician…"

"He was limping. He usually bounces." Carrie was bouncing a little herself now.

"His leg had a hairline fracture," Adam continued. "They put a cast on it, but it was off in two weeks."

"He was bouncing again by the end of the first day."

"He doesn't believe you," the voice said. "They're going to take him."

The doctor listened to the couple ramble, shaking his head as if he understood. He spoke into his notes like Carrie and Adam weren't standing right in front of him. He removed a pen from his shirt pocket, jotted something on a prescription pad and handed it to the nurse. She rolled her eyes. Before the nurse left the room, Carrie stretched her neck to see what the doctor had written. "Turkey on whole wheat," she said out loud.

"Can we please discuss how we can help the little guy breathe?" Adam asked.

Yes! Help him, Adam! she thought.

The doctor returned to Daniel's chart.

"Is the child in day care?"

"He'd be better off with someone else," the stranger said.

"No. My wife stays home with him."

"She's the primary caregiver?" The doctor looked at Carrie, adding further insult to his tone.

"He blames you. It's your fault," she heard the voice say.

"I take care of him! I'm his mother."

She felt Adam's hand on her shoulder. "Doctor, it's been a difficult night," Adam said. "Please tell us what's wrong with our son."

"We're waiting for the results of his blood tests. The doctor on the morning shift will be in to see him. But you need to know that we are obligated to report anything suspicious to Social Services."

"Suspicious," Stranger said. "Suspicious. Suspicious. Suspicious."

Carrie felt like she was going to throw up.

"You are not a real mother," screamed the voice inside her head. "They know you're incompetent. They're going to take him."

Suspicious. Carrie sunk into Adam's arms, crippled by the very word. The doctor left. Probably to find his sandwich.

"Adam! We have to get out of here." She walked back and forth across the room like a caged animal. "They're going to take him away."

"They're going to make him feel better, Care. We're right here with him."

"No! They're going to take him. You heard what he said. They think I did this! We have to go!"

"Calm down." Adam stopped her pacing and held her. "They have to ask those things. It's procedure, a precaution. Everything is going to be alright."

"You think this is my fault too! Don't you! Don't you?"

"Carrie."

"Is it, Adam?" she cried. "Is it my fault?"

"Of course not." He petted her head. "Don't worry. It's going to be fine."

"You aren't fooling anyone," Stranger said. "Adam knows you're not a real mother."

Daniel started to cough again. Another breathing struggle loomed. Adam picked him up and touched his forehead. The fever was returning.

"He needs to be here for now," Adam said. "But we will go home together."

"I love you, Adam," she said. She knew that Adam already knew. She wanted Stranger to know too.

He can't hurt you, she told herself. *He can't hurt you.*

Carrie looked out into the hallway for a nurse. Instead, she saw two men in suits lurking outside their room, whispering.

They're here to take Daniel away, she thought. She didn't have to hear what they were saying. Stranger said it for them.

"You did this," she heard him say. "You're not a mother. You clumsy oaf, you hurt your own child."

No! her mind screamed back. *My baby, my baby. I won't let them take you.* She tried to reason against the battle within her. *It's only noise. It's not me. He can't be me. It's noise… a voice…a man… a stranger.*

"You did it," Stranger said.

"It was an accident!" she answered the voice out loud for the first time.

The men in suits turned to her in judgment. She stood, shackled by their stares.

"My baby is ill," she said before fainting.

When she opened her eyes, Adam was kneeling beside her, holding baby Daniel. She could see the suits hovering above them. She reached out and touched Daniel's cheek. His warm little hand found hers.

"Mommy," he said.

"I love you, baby." Carrie closed her eyes as blood seeped from her body.

#

The men in suits wore white coats now. They had introduced themselves when they helped her off of the floor earlier, but she couldn't remember their names. Adam kept telling her they were doctors. He promised they weren't going to take Daniel.

"Please," she said. "I'm fine now. I need to hold my son."

"Honey, he's sleeping," Adam said. "The nurses are looking after him until I get back."

"But Adam…"

Adam put a finger to Carrie's lips. "Dr. Jones, my wife is exhausted. She's worried about the baby."

Doctor Jones nodded sympathetically. "Mrs. Jenkins," he said. "I'm afraid you've miscarried."

"It was an accident!" Carrie cried. "I slipped. Fuzzy slippers! I didn't drop him!"

"Daniel is fine," Adam said. "His doctor said he has an upper respiratory infection."

"Adam, I didn't drop him. I'll never wear those stupid slippers again! Please take us home."

"M'am, your son is fine," the doctor said. "Did you know you were pregnant again?"

"What?" She looked from the doctor to her husband. "Adam, what is he talking about?"

Adam couldn't save her. The man had gotten to their child before she even knew it existed.

"This is your fault," Stranger said. "The damage is beyond repair."

His power had been proven.

"Adam, I'm so sorry," she said.

Adam moved closer. He gently held her face in his hands. She looked up at him, unable to say anything more. In that moment, she felt his pain, greater than any pain she'd ever felt. She had lost their child. Her husband didn't say a word.

"Kook," she heard from the man inside her head.

She wanted to comfort Adam; and for him to comfort her. The men in suits stood, waiting for a moment of weakness. They knew she didn't deserve to be a mother or a wife.

The fear of being stripped of her children would forever be branded on her soul. Carrie's decision not to reveal the man's presence had been validated. Daniel needed her to be sane. Her secret had to stay hidden. The man would not claim another child.

"Adam," she said. "Please go check on Daniel. I'll be over as soon as I get dressed."

#

Adam reached for the whistle that was usually hanging on his chest, but it wasn't there. He walked through the halls of the hospital's emergency department, from Carrie's room to Daniel's.

"How's he doing?" he asked the nurse.

"Sleeping like an angel, poor little fella. His fever is down. How's your wife?"

Adam reached over the bars of the hospital crib and fixed Daniel's blanket.

"She's…okay," he said. "Thanks for all of your help."

"If you need anything, hit the call button."

Her words echoed inside his head. *If I need anything…I need to go back in time.*

And he needed to talk to someone who would understand. He picked up the phone and dialed.

#

"Collect call from Adam Jenkins," the operator said. "Will you accept the charges."

"Adam! What's wrong?" Sassy answered.

"Will you accept the charges?" the operator asked again.

"Yes. Yes, of course!"

Click.

"Sassy, it's me. We're at the hospital. Daniel's sick. Carrie's freaking out. She thought they were going to take him away."

"Whoa, whoa. Slow down. Is Daniel okay?"

"Yes. He's going to be fine. Upper respiratory infection. They gave him antibiotics. She was taking such good care of him."

"Of course she was. Why would they take him? That's crazy."

"They're not taking him," Adam said. He slowed himself, trying to speak more clearly so she could understand. "He had a chest x-ray. It showed a fractured rib that had healed. Remember that broken leg he had a few months back? Must've happened then, right? I mean, he was limping, so we had his leg checked. Nobody thought to check anything else. Anyway, they asked a few questions. Standard stuff. The guy was kind of an ass, but that was it. A few questions. She thought they were accusing her. She panicked."

"Oh, Carrie. She must feel awful."

"Sass, she takes really good care of him."

"I know she does, Adam. He's a lucky little boy. Want me to talk to her?"

"I knew I could count on you," he said. He tried to keep his voice steady, but he broke down sobbing.

"Adam, you must be exhausted. It's going to be okay."

"No. There's more …it's…she… she was pregnant again." He sniffed. "She lost the baby."

CHAPTER 27 – THE TOKEN DANCING BEAR

Carrie plugged in her crockpot and set in on low. She put in the roast and added vegetables. Lots of vegetables. Adam would be pleased. He liked carrots. Since the miscarriage a few months ago, she had been trying so hard to do everything right. Adam didn't need to worry.

She couldn't find her journal. The doctor had promised to call yesterday. He was a liar. She told herself to wait until ten o'clock. If the phone didn't ring by then, she'd find a new doctor. He had three hours. She had to keep busy. She thought about waking Daniel. No. The article Mrs. Lingle had sent claimed he needed a schedule. Where did she put that article? It was in that magazine with the skinny blond chick on the cover.

Shuffling through a pile on the kitchen table, she fumbled for a distraction. The skinny blond chick showed up halfway through. Carrie eyed the cover girl. The tiny waist annoyed her. As she picked up the magazine to throw it away, her journal fell out of it.

She took a sip of coffee. Oh good, it was still hot. Her pen and journal reunited.

The Right Direction
Every day is a fresh start. Yesterday is no longer.
With faith and courage you can be, little by little, stronger.

Each step need not be big, just in the right direction.
It's okay to make mistakes. Heal with the correction.
Look up when you want to look down. Try to see the light.
Believe it or not, it really is there, waiting to make things right.

She reread the words she had written and scribbled the date at the top. Retrieving the magazine from the trash, she leafed through the pages and ripped out the article. The tiny waist returned to the can. Her journal found a home in the drawer.

Daniel bellowed for his mother. His crib wouldn't hold him for long. She reached his room just as a leg flung over the side. She lifted him out of bed and indulged in the day's first snuggle. He latched onto her ear and rubbed it like a silk blanket. They sang one of his favorite silly songs. Tickling his belly, she laughed with him. After giving him a warm bath, they proceeded to breakfast.

The phone interrupted their morning around eleven. The call lasted less than thirty seconds. She and Daniel celebrated the news with a giddy dance. They jumped and cheered around the living room until both were ready to plop on the couch for a rest.

Elated to learn of her third pregnancy, she spent hours fantasizing over how she could best tell Adam. Her favorite idea involved soft music and rose petals. She figured Adam would probably prefer his own style of celebration. Since dumping ice water over his head didn't seem appropriate, she settled on a compromise.

When he came home wearing his cap and whistle, she was ready. Daniel had gone to bed early. Their bedroom glowed with a dozen burning candles. A six pack of blue Gatorade chilled in a crystal punch bowl while Queen softly performed "We Are the Champions" in the background. She stretched out on the bed, barely dressed in the lacy black wedding present Sassy had given her.

"Adam, I have some wonderful news!" she said.

"I love your jammies," he said.

#

For weeks the boost raised her from an extended health hiatus. It didn't take long, however, to be reminded of some of the normal pregnancy challenges. Waddling through months of waiting, while chasing a rambunctious toddler, tested her inspiration.

Her stamina dwindled as her waistline stretched. She was running out of lap for Daniel to sit in for his stories. She had nightmares featuring her bathroom scale cowering in the corner, begging for mercy, as she plowed through a maze of hot fudge sundaes. She'd then have the nerve to wake up hungry. She'd sit at the table with her breakfast, wondering how

the cows across the street could stand all day on those skinny legs.

A PREGNANT PAUSE
With swollen ankles, I bide my time.
These thirty pounds cannot "look fine."
How can he look at me, so fat and bloated?
My stretch marks have stretch marks, my waistline's exploded!
My horizon has broadened, in more ways than one.
I hope he remembers, he started this fun.

Carrie's emotions, and her doctors, bounced from one to another

through the first seven months. Then she met a handsome, young resident.

About six foot two, with piercing dark eyes and a smile worthy of

toothpaste commercials, he was the kind of guy Sassy would have called a

"gourmet male." His voice soothed her nerves as he discussed her

progress. His confident tone kept her at ease as he explained the

ultrasound he wanted to perform.

She blushed when she caught herself in the middle of an innocent

flirt. His caring interest, alone in the darkened room, briefly swept the

reality of the situation aside. For just a second she had forgotten

everything but the fact he'd noticed her.

Real life came crashing back as he lifted her shirt, exposing the

silly bear tattoo Daniel had rubbed on her giant tummy earlier. The

surprise from his cereal box had pacified him while she cut the tangled marshmallow goop from his hair. She had forgotten all about it until "Dr. Stud" allowed himself a little chuckle. Too humiliated to speak, all she could do was give a little wiggle and make it dance.

By her eighth month, the lack of hormonal harmony tipped her off balance physically and mentally. The voice was mercifully quiet, but her personalities defied propriety. She could laugh over spilt milk; then be angry with poor Adam for not cleaning it up correctly. Story hour at the library made her cry. Well-intentioned fools patting her tummy could inspire emotions she didn't even know she had. Adam became a master of dance. He swayed gracefully through every mood swing, catching her on every turn.

One day at the park, Daniel persuaded his father to take him down the sliding board. Carrie took the opportunity to give her swollen ankles a rest. She enjoyed her view from the bench as her boys played. But it wasn't long before she was interrupted by the cramping and pains familiar from once before. Playtime ended with a family rush to the hospital where they were eventually rewarded with an exquisite little girl.

Carrie called Sassy from the hospital. "Little Miss Elizabeth Jenkins is a living doll," she said.

"Elizabeth? Really, Care? You named her after me?" Sassy sniffed. "I'm honored." Then she laughed a little. "You may want to avoid the nickname, though. It's a lot to live up to."

Carrie laughed. "You certainly had no problem, Sassy."

"I do what I can."

"I can hardly wait for you to see her."

"Soon."

#

When Carrie held Beth in her arms, she wondered how she could possibly be worthy. Their family was complete. She felt like the luckiest, least worthy woman in the world.

But with her dolls, she played. Daniel and Beth made her feel real. They counted on her for food and comfort. She gave them all the love she had dreamt her mother would have given her. Loving them gave Carrie a strength she didn't know she had.

She thought she pulled off normalcy just fine. It seemed okay to be awake at three o'clock in the morning writing letters to Sassy and her father. She had to stay awake anyway to make sure the kids were breathing.

The twelve dozen, double-chocolate mint cookies she made for Adam's team didn't go to waste. Making and delivering them left no time to pay the electric bill, but the kids enjoyed eating pizza by candlelight. Her family never went hungry. The dishes usually got washed and all teeth got brushed. Carrie could handle things. Nobody would take her babies.

"It's going to be okay," she'd tell herself.

"They know. That smile mask isn't fooling anyone," Stranger said.

Still, she wore it like a shield. Smiling didn't scare people away and required no explanation. Smiling made sense. She had a wonderful family, a happy home. She had no right to despair. She was grateful for her life. Grateful. She didn't have to make anyone understand emotions she didn't understand herself. Instead, she played the role of a happy mommy—happy, grateful and sane.

But no smile could shelter her from Stranger. Hidden or not, the man invaded her presence. Her emotions were clear to him. He could hear her every thought. He knew it all.

Damn it, she thought to him. *You're not going to see me cry.*

#

Her strength grew with her children, but they were growing faster. She stood at the end of the driveway clinging to Beth as the big yellow bus carried Daniel off to his first day of kindergarten. She could see his little hand still waving wildly as they turned the corner. She gave her daughter an extra squeeze. Time was so fickle. Endless hours were dissolved and forgotten by the fleeting years.

"What should we sing, Mommy?" Beth's happy question cut into the sadness.

"How about, 'Don't Say Good Bye, Say Hello'?"

Their latest remix became an instant tradition. At the tender age of three, Beth was already a Beatle's fan. The real lyrics could wait. Beth's love of music didn't require accuracy until much later. Until they both learned the right words, the tailored to the moment tributes to the classics would do. All they had to do was sing.

"Children grow up," Stranger said. Over and over. Again and again.

CHAPTER 28 – OLI'S HOUSE

Sassy and David were finally ready. Oli's House was about to become real. After years of working together, Sassy's dream was coming true.

"Oliver would have been impressed," Sassy yelled from the bathroom as she put on her makeup.

"I knew you could do it, Sass," David called back from his new home office.

"I feel kind of bad leaving the hospital. Wayne Valley's Psychiatric Department really is understaffed."

"You were there as long as you needed to be. They were lucky for the time they had you."

Sassy walked into David's office. "I'm so glad you are home. I'm getting spoiled now that you're partners with Reed. Are you sure you don't have to go in this week?"

"Yep. I'm all yours," he said. "Of course, I still have to work."

"Me too! She'll be here in an hour. Can I have the package from Carrie now?"

"I can't believe you waited this long." David opened the bottom drawer of his desk and pulled out the gift Carrie had sent earlier that month. "I'd have opened it the day it came."

Sassy ran a letter opener down the side of the box. "I didn't want to jinx anything," she said. "It's to celebrate our first day. That's today."

"You're not upset she didn't come?"

"I'm fine. I mean, she understood when I couldn't get out there to see Daniel… or Beth."

Foam peanuts spilled onto David's desk as she pulled out the bronze frame. She brushed white bits from the glass. "Oh, Carrie," she cried. "It's perfect."

She held the picture up to show David. "I made that for him," she said, pointing to the small wooden sign in the photo. She had given it to Oliver for his birthday that year. "He hung it right over the entrance."

Sassy had never seen this picture of her and Oliver, up in his tree house. He was wearing his favorite green polo shirt. Sitting in the entrance with his feet hanging over the side, his feet looked giant in his high-top sneakers. She was standing behind him with her chin on his shoulder.

"Oli's House," read the sign hanging over their heads.

She took the picture downstairs and hung it in the foyer, only thirty minutes before young Alice Myers was scheduled to arrive. Their first client, an abused teen, would be given more than a safe place away from her father. Sassy had met her at the hospital and was well-prepared to provide a deeper level of counseling.

Double-checking every last-minute detail, she got ready for Alice's arrival with a hint of deserved confidence. The degree with her name on it had been hard earned, but this place was special. She and David made it happen together. Sassy straightened the throw pillows on their cushy red sofa. Their home was about to be shared.

Sassy pulled a wooden box from the closet shelf. She looked to the little bit of nostalgia when she needed inspiration. She opened it often, visiting the reminders. Oliver's letter, his travel orders and the newspaper clippings had faded some, but the memory of her brother remained. She unconsciously touched the golden cross that hung on a chain around her neck. Then she squeezed the small stone in her pocket. Satisfied everything was in place, she read the letter yet again:

Dear Sassy,
    There's so much I want to say to you, and so much that I can't. I wanted to leave you with a little something in case I don't come back. You are now the proud owner of twelve years' accumulation of loose change and lucky poker hands. Your David promised he could turn it into something. I guess he knows about money. The rest can come from you.
    I'm sorry I have to go. Please trust me when I say this has to be. There were mistakes. That can't be changed. The best I can

do now is keep them from reaching you. I hope it's not too late. I love you, Sis. Look forward and don't worry.

Love,
Oli

Time had eased her past the anger. She had no choice but to accept his need to protect her. Only because it was too late to help him, she also chose to honor his request. The nagging curiosity and concern was buried under the dream of Oli's House.

Whether she liked it or not, Oliver had been her self-appointed gatekeeper ever since her first crush. He took the role very seriously. David was the only guy who'd even come close to earning his approval. Oliver had refused to let his sister be hurt the way their mother had been.

#

As the time drew near for her first session, she could almost feel her brother's presence. She took the stone from her pocket. It was six years since she'd been to their spot. That trip was prompted by his letter. When David had given it to her, she felt as though she'd been visited by an angel.

The letter had sent her to Jerry Rock, where she said a final goodbye. Sassy remembered with mixed emotions. She'd sat alone on the cold ground, running her fingers through the moist dirt. The stone found her hand. She had dug it out and wiped it on her jeans. It didn't need her to pick it up and keep it safe. It could have withstood the natural course of time without her protection, but it didn't have to. The lint in her pocket had warmth to share.

#

The doorbell rang.

"She's here," Sassy said. She kissed David on the cheek. "Remember, Alice is shy. I want her to meet you, but then say you have work or something and give us some time, okay?"

"Yes, ma'am." David said with a laugh. "I do have work, remember?"

"And when Joseph gets here, tell him not to do anything right outside of my office window. I don't want her to feel like she's being spied on."

"He's only trimming the front hedges today."

"Good. Tell him there are cookies in the jar."

"Sass, you're ready. Everything will be fine."

"I know," she said, mostly believing it. She smiled nervously as she opened the door.

"Alice…"

Her mouth dropped open in surprise. It wasn't Alice at the door.

"Well, ain't you pretty," Jack said. Then he turned to David. "Hey, Davey. You gonna introduce Wifey here to your favorite uncle?"

#

Joseph parked in front of the vacant lot next to Oli's House. He stepped out of his car and inhaled the fresh air. He walked along the field of daisies he and David had planted after the remains of his mother's house were cleared away. Taking a dog biscuit from his pocket, he stopped beside a large rock near the edge of the property and bent down to place the treat on the usual spot.

"M-m-miss you, g-girl," he said. The little white dog had been buried there for nearly a year.

As he made his way toward David's shed, Joseph saw an older man standing alone in the driveway. He looked familiar. The man was staring up at the bedroom window, like Joseph used to do when he was ten. This creep didn't belong here. As Joseph moved closer, the man turned toward him. In an instant he knew. This was the man he'd met at David's apartment years ago. Here in the driveway, leering up at Sassy's bedroom, stood David's Uncle Jack.

A rush of anger surged through his body. He charged at Jack, knocked him to the ground, and started punching. He only got a chance to land a few good blows before David stopped him.

Joseph squirmed in his grip. David held onto him as he yelled at Jack. "I told you to leave! Get the hell out of here!"

Jack brushed himself off and chuckled. "I see you been settin' a fine example for the next generation o' punks there, Davey. Shame you can't breed yourself a real kid."

Joseph struggled harder to free himself, but David had a firm hold on him.

"I'll be back," Jack said with a laugh.

They watched him as he walked away. He stopped at Daisy's rock, picked up the dog biscuit and ate it.

David released Joseph and straightened his collar. "He's not worth it."

Joseph grunted.

"You're a good man," David said. He turned to go back to the house. "C'mon, Sassy has cookies."

Joseph told him he'd be in after he finished the yard work. But when David went inside he followed Jack instead.

#

Sassy called up the stairs for Alice. "Dinnertime. Six o'clock." The gentle reminder didn't help. For the third night in a row, Alice didn't come to eat.

"Should we wait?" David asked.

"No. Six o'clock. It's a rule," Sassy said, putting a hot pot full of beef stew in front of him.

David ladled some stew into his bowl.

Sassy sat down and put a biscuit on her plate. Passing the basket to him, she looked at the clock. It was already ten after six. "Damn," she said, getting up from the table. "Go ahead and start while it's hot. I'll be right back."

She walked up to Alice's room and knocked on the door. There was no answer. She tried again and waited. "Alice, are you okay? It's time for dinner." Still no answer, so she entered the room. "Alice?" She looked around, checked the closet and underneath the bed. Alice wasn't there, but Sassy found the pillowcase she had given her. She pulled it out and peeked inside.

Food. Some wrapped in paper napkins, some loose, the stash hit Sassy with a hard truth. On Alice's chart at the hospital, she had read how horribly malnourished Alice had been when she was admitted. Initially, an eating disorder had been suspected, but the theory didn't fit.

She had been eating well, even without imposed requirements. Her weight had progressed normally, and though their sessions only lasted an hour, she didn't seem to be preoccupied with the numbers of it or body image.

"That's not mine," Alice said, standing in the doorway.

Sassy jumped, startled. "Alice, we were worried about you. Why didn't you come down for dinner?"

"I'm not hungry." She stared at the pillowcase in Sassy's hand. "Am I in trouble?"

Sassy handed the case back to her, "No, you're not in trouble. But I'd like to talk about this. There's a lot of food in here."

"I won't do it again."

"I appreciate that. But I'm more concerned about why you felt the need to hide all of this."

Alice stood with her hands in her pockets.

"You don't have to worry about being hungry here, but I want you to feel secure. Later, we can discuss some better options than hiding food."

"Yes, ma'am."

"No more secrets, okay?"

Alice nodded.

"Now, let's go downstairs for dinner. Together. I made beef stew and biscuits. It's my mother's recipe. I think you'll like it."

The girl didn't move. Sassy put a gentle hand on her shoulder. "Please, try it. At least come sit with us. Mr. Martin will make a mess if I leave him down there alone too long."

Alice laughed a little, then she cried. Sassy hugged her and could feel the emotions shaking through the poor, terrified, child.

"You couldn't eat at home, could you, sweetie?"

"I…he…didn't." She sniffed. "My father…I wasn't allowed."

"You weren't allowed to eat dinner?" Sassy wanted to cry with her. Instead, she took her to the bathroom and dampened a washcloth. She smiled at her, hoping she'd feel the sincerity. "You're safe here," she said as she patted the girl's face. "We'd really like for you to eat with us."

CHAPTER 29 – HEART

Alice ran away from Oli's House a month after she'd arrived. The social worker called to let Sassy know that Alice and her sister had been found at the bus station downtown. She wouldn't be coming back. Her father was in jail, partly due to the report Sassy had filed. The girls would be going to live with an aunt, from out of state. Unready to face David, Sassy sought comfort in the arms of her mother.

"You did your best, dear."

"But, Mom. I really thought I could help her. We were making progress."

"Progress is good," her mother said. "Alice left with more strength than she had before. She'll have a better life."

"I don't know if I can do it again. How can I?"

"How can you not? Elizabeth, this is your calling, your gift."

Sassy rubbed her temples. "Maybe I should go back to the hospital. At least working there was safe."

"But it's not what you wanted. It's not your dream. You need to do what you set out to do."

"What if I can't?"

"I'll not allow it."

"Allow it?"

"I won't let you settle," her mother said. "You can't abandon your dream just because it got hard. Or because you've been hurt. There's more to it than that. Hold your head high and claim your life. There will be bad, and there will be good, but it will be yours. It will be real."

"Mom…"

"Learn from my mistakes, Sassy. Don't settle. It doesn't do anyone any good."

Sassy went back to Oli's House and got ready for a new client. Progress continued, building slowly over the years. Riding the drama at Oli's House became their normal way of life.

#

David watched Sassy file away another picture album. Carrie and Adam seemed to be so happy. He wondered if Sassy ever regretted not having children.

She would have been an incredible mother, he thought. *If she'd had the chance.*

Sassy stood and smiled at him. "You were checking out my butt when I bent over, weren't you?"

"It's a good butt," he said.

She wiggled a little and laughed. He wiggled back. The ringing telephone ended their game.

"Hello." Sassy pushed the button to speaker as she answered.

"Sassy, Sassy it's your mother," her father said, breathlessly. "You need to come. Please come."

"What happened, Dad? Did she fall again? Does she need an ambulance?"

"No, she's … it already…"

"Is she okay?" Sassy interrupted. "Let me talk to her."

"Sassy. Please, come home."

"Won't she talk? What did I do now?"

"She can't talk." His sad, final tone said too much. "She collapsed while she was making breakfast."

"What? What is it?" Sassy demanded. "Is it her heart?"

"Honey…"

Sassy started shaking. "No. No! Feel her neck, Dad! Use two fingers by her throat. Can you feel her pulse? Raise her legs, damn it. Raise her legs!"

David held her against himself, trying to comfort her and keep her grounded.

"They tried, Elizabeth," her father said. "They tried. Your mother is gone."

#

Eerie organ music mocked the goodness of her mother's life. A rhythm of rebellious fights, helpless denial and shameful jealousy echoed through her mind, as Sassy stood with David, the man with whom she lived in sin. Unholy. Unmarried.

Her cheating father sat in a red velvet chair, showing more emotion for his wife than Sassy had ever seen when she was alive. The good daughter wasn't even there.

Sassy watched people trickle into the room. "I thought Carrie would have come," she whispered to David."

"You told her not to. Daniel's sick."

"She could've left him with Adam. He can handle it."

"Think so?" David asked.

"I know I told her not to come. I guess I thought she would be here anyway."

Carrie's father came up and knelt beside the casket. "Thank you, Mrs. Margaret Lingle," Sassy heard him say. He touched her father's shoulder as he walked past, then stopped to hug Sassy. "Your mother was a good woman," he said. "Thank you for sharing her with my daughter."

Sassy felt guilty for talking Carrie out of coming, though it hadn't been hard to do. "Mom loved Carrie," she replied. "I'm sorry she couldn't come."

"Me too," he said. He hugged her again and moved away. A line had formed behind him.

Half an hour, and a few dozen hugs later, Sassy whispered to David, "I need to get out of here."

They went out to the parking lot and sat against the hood of David's latest Volkswagen. "Isn't that Carrie's father?" David asked, pointing toward a man hunched over in a Black Lincoln.

"Yeah. It is," Sassy said. "I thought he left." She went over and knocked on the window. "Hey, you okay?"

He looked embarrassed as he dried his eyes. Then he opened the door and handed Sassy a Tupperware cake holder. "This belonged to your mother," he said.

Sassy could see he had a story that he wanted to share. "Mom loved to feed people," she said. "I hope she made you something good."

"Chocolate cake," he said with a sly grin. "My wife didn't know I ate it."

The timeline threw Sassy. "This container must be older than I am," she said.

"Your mother brought the cake over to welcome us to the neighborhood, I think. I found it on my porch when I came home for lunch one day. Best cake I ever had. It was chocolate…but had peanut butter I think? I didn't mean to…but I ate the whole darn thing."

Sassy smiled. Chocolate with peanut butter was her mother's specialty.

"Anyway," he continued. "When my wife got home she was upset it was gone. Apparently, she had seen the cake sitting there earlier in the day, but left it sitting out there intentionally. I guess there was some kind of fight. Donna was a little paranoid. Very private. She had bad days. She had a whole story about how the cake had been left by a busy body neighbor…" He stopped short and made an apologetic face at Sassy.

"It's okay," she said with a laugh. "I'd have guessed it was Mom too."

"I couldn't tell her I ate it, so I hid the dish in my workbench and let her think your mother took it back. So many times, I meant to return it."

Sassy held up the empty container. "You know," she said with a wink. "I still have Mom's recipe."

#

After her mother had been laid to rest, Sassy grieved in silence. She continued to work, plowing ahead with life as usual, only quieter, and unable to bring herself to talk to Carrie. She avoided her calls and unopened letters piled on her desk. David sat back, hoping she'd come around, but the strong will he had always loved wouldn't budge.

Sassy was busy in her office the day the package came. She didn't come out when the doorbell rang. David brought the box inside. He smiled at the return address. Carrie hadn't given up. Then he noticed this package wasn't addressed to Sassy. It was addressed to him. He took it into his office and locked the door.

He wore the gift to bed that night, just as Carrie had requested in the note she had enclosed. Sassy didn't notice his new fuzzy socks until he rubbed them against her bare feet. She sat up in bed.

"What are you wearing?"

"I got a package from Carrie today."

"She sent *you* a package?"

"Weird, huh?" He tickled her leg with his foot. "They're all fuzzy. She said I should put them on at bedtime."

"Please tell me you aren't wearing pink socks."

"Well, mine are black. Yours are pink."

"Mine?"

David reached under the bed and pulled out the pink booties Carrie had sent. Sassy laughed.

"She's such a girlie girl." She slipped the booties on her hands and held her face.

"She said she wants you to know she's there," David said.

"I do know. I really do. Maybe tomorrow I will send her some cookies. Oatmeal."

"I still have those letters you told me to throw away."

#

Together that night, two months after Sassy's mother had died, they opened Carrie's letters, filling Sassy's picture books with page after page of Adam proudly taking care of his family. A hint of jealousy teased David. But he knew better. Something was hiding under all that perfect happiness.

David thought about the night Adam had given him that money.

"It's for Sassy. Don't screw it up," the guy had said.

David had to take it. He should have listened and not asked questions. Now he knew too much. Covering for Adam's crime had been easy. But David was still haunted by the things he couldn't answer.

For the first time in his life, David himself heeded a lesson from Sassy's book of Oliver. She often said he had told her she should count her blessings. One of his favorite blessings happened to be sitting right next to him, ready to be counted. He lifted his beautiful lady away from the pictures of Carrie's and Adam's children and whisked her back upstairs to the bedroom. They spent a blissful night; free from the worry of fussing babies and curious toddlers.

"David," Sassy said. "Will you marry me?"

#

On a warm Sunday afternoon, in their very own backyard, Sassy and David exchanged their vows. It was a simple ceremony, with only a handful of guests. Carrie, with the help of an extension cord and a telephone, served as a long-distance matron of honor, and Joseph was best man.

Sassy wore a red dress. Her energy and passion could not be veiled by the simplicity of white. In her hair, she wore a single flower, and her feet were bare. She was comfortable with David. He enjoyed her free spirit. In honor of it, he added his own secret touch of rebellion.

Handsome in his neat grey suit, polished shoes and straight tie, he was painfully proper. Sassy could hardly wait to claim her husband. When the pastor gave David the instruction to kiss the bride, he turned to her and puckered up with a small diamond stud in his earlobe. The piercing was delightfully shocking. She found his attempt at boldness adorable. The two made a perfect one.

Her mother would have been pleased.

#

Adam watched Carrie hang up the phone after the ceremony. She looked beautiful in her new dress. The cut was a bit lower than she'd normally wear and the hem was above her knees. He wasn't used to seeing her in black. He thought it was cute how she had insisted she dress the way Sassy would have wanted her to if she had actually gone. He handed her a tissue.

"Don't cry, honey," he said.

"She's my best friend. I should be there."

"Sassy understands. Seriously, a week's notice? She gets it. She's busy too. She didn't even take the day off of work for her own wedding."

"I could have gone," Carrie said. "She finally forgave me for not being there for the memorial. And this was her wedding! I should have tried."

"By yourself? That's cra... I mean... it wouldn't be safe. You get those headaches."

"Crazy. You were going to say crazy."

"It's only a word. I didn't mean anything by it."

"Adam, are we ever going back?"

"It's been a long time."

"When we left, I didn't know it was forever. I thought I'd get to see her again." Carrie picked at a loose string on her dress.

"Of course you'll see her again," Adam said. "Maybe she and David can come here."

"I want to see her. I really miss her. Is it crazy to be afraid?"

"Care," Adam said. "It's not crazy. You're not crazy." He wanted to tell her he understood, but at the same time, he wasn't sure she could handle it all. He hated that she had missed Sassy's wedding, but he had to keep her away. Things had happened that were better left in the past. He allowed himself to continue believing he was protecting

her.

"Thank you, Adam," Carrie said. "You always make me feel safe."

Adam couldn't look her in the eye.

CHAPTER 30 – PACED

Rumors spread throughout Marshall Junior High School. Students gathered at the windows between classes. A few eighth graders tried to persuade the sixth and seventh graders to change their bets. The senior high football coach would be here to discipline his kids soon. This visit could break the record.

For the third time this year, Daniel and Beth were in the principal's office, and Adam was on his way.

"They're not bad kids," he reminded himself. "They just need some coaching."

As per his arrangement with Principal Motts, Carrie hadn't been called. Though, judging by the number of faces peering out the windows when he pulled into the school's parking lot, she'd likely find out about this one.

"Coach Jenkins! He's here!" a student yelled.

"Get to class," a chemistry teacher warned.

"But we'll miss it."

"Move along or you'll be sent to see Principal Motts, too."

Adam walked into his children's school and greeted the secretary. "Hi, Christy. Sorry for the trouble. Has Mrs. Jenkins been called?"

"No, Coach. Thanks for coming."

The gelatin covered boy sitting on the bench by her desk avoided eye contact with Adam. Adam put a hand on his shoulder.

"You okay, Peter?"

Peter Douglas sat up straight. He looked surprised that Coach Jenkins knew his name. "You gonna make 'em run laps?" he asked.

Adam looked through the wall of windows into a hallway filled with students who were likely wondering the same thing. This was Daniel's last year at Marshall Junior High. So far, Adam had been called down from the high school nine times. Each time, he made Daniel run laps around the track. The number of laps depended on the offense he had committed.

Adam dismissed Peter's question. Though he had warned Daniel and Beth to be extra good, he had been expecting something to happen ever since Carrie had gotten fired from her job in the school's cafeteria a few weeks ago.

Everything had been going so well. Having her right there at the Middle School when he was at work had been comforting until Principal Motts called to tell him he was about to fire her for repeated offenses of sneaking in baked goods for children other than her own. Adam probably could have persuaded his friend to keep Carrie on staff, but Peter's mother had called the superintendent. It was only a matter of time before her kids

would have to step up and defend her.

Daniel and Beth sat side-by-side in the principal's office, enduring

another endless lecture. Principal Motts ranted on about the importance of

respecting others, or something like that. They pretended to listen, but

Daniel accidentally noticed Principal Mott's ears contained an

unprecedented amount of hair. A revelation such as this could not be

ignored. He had to wonder how the man could possibly hear. Didn't that

itch? He couldn't help it when his hand reached for Beth's ponytail. He

was about to test her hair in his own ear when they heard their father

outside the door.

Both children stood as Adam entered the principal's office. Beth

twisted her curls in defense of her father's angry glare. Daniel pursed his

lips, holding back the proud smile he knew would earn him extra laps.

"What do you have to say for yourselves?" Adam asked. He

looked pissed.

Daniel and Beth lowered their heads and stared at their shoes. Beth

poked her brother, but Daniel had promised his father he'd look out for his mom. He couldn't repeat the names Peter had called her in front of his principal.

"I'm sorry," Daniel said to the floor. "But I didn't hit him. I swear."

Adam shook his head. "Bill, could we have a minute?"

"Sure, Coach," the principal answered. He slapped him on the back. "Thanks for coming over."

"No need to disturb Mrs. Jenkins, right?" Adam asked.

"Whatever you say." Their principal winked at their father. "How's the team looking for Friday night?"

"They're pumped."

"Great. See you at the game."

Principal Motts shut the door behind him as he left.

#

"Guys," Adam said. "What happened?"

"Dad, I had to do it. But I was good. I didn't hit him," Daniel said.

"You should have," Beth said.

"Enough!" Adam said. "Daniel, tell me what happened."

Daniel looked up at his father. "See, Dad. We were at lunch. You know me. I normally love a good joke. I'm the guy that can burp on command or blow milk through my nose." His shoulders eased as he spoke.

"Anyway, I was entertaining the kids at my lunch table with an epic story about mutant jelly fish—or, wait—maybe it was rebellious nose hairs…"

"Daniel," Adam said sternly.

"So, Peter starts cracking wise…"

"He called Mommy a kook," Beth interrupted. "You said we should never let people call her names."

"She was trying to be nice," Daniel said. "Those kids didn't have money for lunch. She doesn't let people be hungry."

Adam wished that Carrie could hear the pride in her son's voice right now.

"It's crap, Dad," Daniel continued. "Peter can't go 'round talking about her. He said she's crazy 'cause her socks don't match and she gets the change wrong sometimes. So, I told him to shut his stupid hole."

"Yeah, that's crap." Beth said. "I heard Daniel getting mad. And Peter is such a butt. He always makes fun of people. I had to go over there."

"Watch your mouth, young lady," Adam said. "There's no excuse for either one of you to dump gelatin down a boy's pants."

"Daddy, Peter Douglas had it coming. He's a jerk. We only wanted to teach him a lesson."

Adam sat on the principal's desk, unsure how to proceed. Defending their mother's honor hardly seemed just cause for punishment. He probably would have done the same thing himself. Well, not exactly the same. He expected his approach would have been a little more dignified or, at least, subtle. Still, they needed to know he couldn't support their behavior.

"Look, I get it," he said. "Believe me, I'm proud of you for looking out for Mom. But guys, really? You can't go around filling people's pants with gelatin."

"Even Peter Douglas?" Beth asked.

"Even him."

"How about tapioca?" Daniel teased.

"C'mon, kids. There are better ways of handling bullies."

"Can you make him run some laps?" Beth suggested.

"Trust me, honey. If that kid makes it into my class when he gets to high school, he'll be running plenty of laps. For now, I'm afraid he's out of my jurisdiction."

#

Dozens of amused eyes peered out at the track waiting to count as Daniel and Beth began their run. Given the circumstances, Adam had reduced his children's punishment to only one lap.

Adam straightened his cap. *Fair is fair,* he thought as he slipped off his jacket and started running behind them. They began with a sprint; then eased into a jog.

CHAPTER 31 – HEARTS GROW FONDER

Sassy dialed Carrie's number, anxious to hear how Beth's tryouts for the high school musical had gone. She counted five rings before she heard Daniel's voice on the other end of the line.

"Hello? Jenkins Jigs," he said. "Where all the foxes come to trot."

"Daniel?" Sassy smiled. "Is that you?"

"Hey, Aunt Sassy. Mom was just showing me her dance moves."

"I think I may have the wrong number," Sassy teased.

"Actually, she's not too bad. She didn't even get mad when I broke the lamp."

"Sounds like you inherited your father's grace."

"Dad says I have grace on the field," Daniel said. "Unfortunately, they don't allow cleats on the gym floor. I'm in training for the school dance."

"Oh? Is there a young lady out there with your stamp of approval on her forehead?"

"They all deserve a chance…hang on, my mom is getting grabby."

"Okay then, Casanova. Take care."

"Hello," Carrie said, grabbing at the phone.

"So, your little prince is quite the dancer," Sassy said.

"He's trying…he may have to let his date lead though."

Sassy heard Daniel shout, "I heard that!" in the background.

"I'm avoiding the lines. Someday, all the girls will want a turn to whirl you around the dance floor. You won't have time to dance with your tired old Mom," Carrie called back to him.

Sassy could hear the sting in Carrie's words.

"You should she see him," Carrie said to her. "He's been practicing to Tango with the vacuum cleaner. Best I can show him is a waltz."

"Ah, Carrie, always the romantic. Next you'll be teaching him the art of chivalry."

"Just doing my part for society."

Daniel picked up the other line in mock hysterics. "Aunt Sassy, help! Mom is making me hold doors open! She threw my coat in a puddle! I can't even fart in public! What kind of man will I be?"

"Sweet honey!" Sassy said. "If your father can come around, so can you."

"Yeah," Daniel said with a chuckle. "Dad is pretty smooth."

#

Sassy opened the mailbox and peered inside. Still empty. She looked up the road for the mailman and saw no sign of him. She went to call Carrie.

"Are you sure you sent them?" she asked.

"Five days ago!" Carrie said. "Not yet?"

"Did you put enough postage this time?"

Sassy picked out an album from the seven on her shelf. It was the first of her collection. Starting with Carrie's best posed shots of her babies in their sweetest outfits, Beth's first pickle, and Daniel sleeping in the dog's bed, the pictures helped them stay connected. From hundreds of miles away, the books had let Sassy watch them grow up, and gave Carrie something to share.

Sassy flipped through the pages, unconsciously smiling. Carrie was rambling about forgetting her purse at the post office.

"What could be cuter than a kid hanging upside down from the monkey bars or flying on a swing?" she asked.

"Oh, you're looking at the pink one, aren't you?" Carrie instinctively looked for the red paint Daniel had gotten on the chair the day they had made that book. The handprints she used to decorate the cover had led to fingerprints on her furniture.

Sassy heard footsteps on her porch. She met the mailman at the door. "Thanks, Ed," she said to him.

"They're here!" she said to Carrie.

She dropped the rest of the mail on the floor and tore open the package, spilling the pictures onto her desk. With the first photograph, she could see the moment. Daniel, donning his pin striped suit, was posed with the vacuum cleaner.

Sassy doodled Daniel's quote on the envelope as she spoke into the phone, "What kind of man will I be?" She laughed out loud. "Thanks for the pictures, Care. They're awesome. Talk to you soon." She hung up and called the florist.

"Hi. This is Mrs. Martin. I'd like to order an arrangement of pink orchids and calla lilies, please. Send to Carrie Jenkins. I believe you have her address on file. On the card please write, 'Keep up the good work, society needs you'."

"Are you sure you don't want to deliver those flowers yourself?" David asked.

Sassy looked up and saw him standing in the doorway. His question knocked the nostalgia out of her. He had offered to take her to see Carrie countless times over the years. They never went. Not when the children were born, not for any of Beth's plays or Daniel's big games.

"We have a new girl coming on Monday. Two, in fact. I can't go," she said.

With that, she had pronounced the conversation, "over." Still, there'd be more calls from Carrie, more letters, and more packages. Her husband would ask her again if she wanted to go visit. Maybe next time she wouldn't be so busy.

CHAPTER 32 -- FAMILY

Sassy answered her phone on the first ring.

"I asked him, Aunt Sassy! He's taking me to prom," Beth said.

"I told you he would! You'll have a great time."

"Mom's taking me shopping this weekend."

Sassy opened her closet door and pulled out a dress. "Beth, I have something that would look perfect on you. How do you like green?"

"That emerald green one you're wearing in the New Year's pictures? Aunt Sassy, could I really? That would be awesome!"

"You'll have a great time," Sassy said again. She grabbed the matching shoes from the shelf. She'd put the package in the mail the next morning.

#

When Carrie brought the mail in, she was too excited by the return address to stop and notice the package wasn't for her. She opened the box and dug through some tissue paper. Recognizing the extravagant dress from Sassy's pictures, she ran like a wounded deer.

The dress was still in the box on their kitchen table when Adam got home. He followed Carrie's trail—shoes, socks, her favorite hooded sweatshirt—into the backyard and down to the pond. He found her standing in the mud at the edge of the water.

"Tomorrow," she said as she threw a rock into the pond. "I was supposed to take Beth shopping tomorrow."

"Care? You okay, hun?" Adam walked toward her with her sweatshirt.

"Beth has her dress for the prom," Carrie answered.

"I saw it. It looks nice." Adam slipped the sweatshirt over her head. "It's chilly out. Want to come inside?"

"It's perfect. Sassy sent it." She threw another rock.

"Beth is all grown up," Stranger said. "Sassy wore that dress five months ago."

Carrie's toes squished deeper in the mud. Adam stood with her and held her hand.

"Thank you, Adam," she said.

"I love you," he said.

#

On prom night, Carrie was ready with her camera. Beth posed at the bottom of the stairs for the first picture. She stood with Adam, then with Daniel. Carrie happily snapped as many shots as she could. Then Beth and her date left in his father's car. Carrie went inside to bake.

Sassy called, but she didn't answer. She had brownie batter on her fingers. *I'll send her pictures tomorrow,* she thought. The phone rang again half an hour later. Carrie plopped cream cheese into a mixing bowl and added butter. She scooped in powdered sugar and a few spoonfuls of cocoa.

#

Sassy listened to Carrie's message three times.

"Hey, Sassy. Sorry I missed you. I forgot you had that meeting today. I'm at the post office. Prom pictures are on their way. Love ya."

Sassy dialed Carrie's number, but hung up. She doodled a picture of a rose with petals dropping around it.

Underneath it she wrote, "GEOGRAPHY BLOWS."

She called Carrie when the pictures came. "Beth has your beautiful amber curls!" she said. "And those eyes. Care, it's like I'm looking right at you."

"You flatter me."

"You know I was always jealous of your hair," Sassy said.

"I had no idea." Carrie unconsciously played with her pony tail.

Sassy laughed. "Remember the time I tried to dye mine and it turned purple? Mom was so pissed."

"Omigosh! You had to use that horse shampoo. It smelled like the inside of your Dad's car."

#

By that summer, Daniel had a job and an active social life. Carrie often fell asleep on the couch waiting for him to come home. One night, he was especially late. He came in and patted her cheek.

"Mom, go to bed. I'm home," he said.

"Everything okay?" she asked in a froggy whisper.

"Everything is spectacular," he said.

Carrie sat up and rubbed her eyes, ready to receive good news. She looked at her son and she knew.

"You met someone," she said.

"Mom, she's not like other girls. This one is special," he told her.

Carrie started a pot of coffee and sat with him at the kitchen table. The tale captivated her. His face glowed as he told her how he met Abby that hot July afternoon.

"Look at me, Mom. We were planting trees all day at work. It was like a hundred degrees out. I'm filthy and stinky. She didn't even care."

Carrie laughed. "You were right. All those showers for nothing."

"Anyway. I was driving home from work and The Stones came on the radio. So, you know, I'm singin' along."

Carrie filled his cup with coffee.

"Then I see a car up ahead on the side of the road. This little Ford has a flat tire." He bit into a blueberry muffin. "And she's crying."

"Who? Who was crying?" Carrie asked.

"Ohhh. This girl," he said with his touchdown smile. "She was sitting against her car. All slumped over. Spare's on the ground next to her. The jack too. Remind me to teach Beth how to change a tire…"

"Daniel! The girl?"

"Yeah. Abby." He stopped and repeated her name. "Abby. Cute, huh? Anyway, I'm walking up to her. She's crying and all. So, I figure I'll lighten the mood a little, ya know?" He stood and straightened his dirty t-shirt. "So I sang."

"You what?!"

"Well, Mick Jagger was still in my head, so I let loose with my best rock and roll voice."

"You didn't! Omigosh! What did she do?"

"She looked up, startled. But then she did the only thing she really could do. She sang back."

Carrie laughed as she warmed another blueberry muffin.

"Mom, her nose was running. Her eyes were all swollen and red. She was as dirty and sweaty as I was. It was epic!"

"Oh, my."

"Yeah. So, I changed her tire and she bought me ice cream."

"Sprinkles?" Carrie asked.

"Of course," he said. "You know me well."

"Yes, I do." Carrie brushed a mini rainbow of sprinkles from his chest. "By the way, your sister knows how to change a tire. I taught her like I taught you." She happily accepted a stinky hug. "Now get upstairs and shower."

Before he went, he gestured to the telephone. "Go ahead, Mom. It's cool," he said.

"I love you, sweetie," she said, dialing Sassy's number. She could hardly wait to take Abby's picture.

CHAPTER 33 – GROWING UP MOMMY

Sometimes you don't realize how fast you are driving until you see the flashing red lights in your rearview mirror. Then, it's too late to slow down. Carrie felt like she had raced through the past eighteen years and was about to be pulled over. Although she had enjoyed the ride, too much time had been wasted trying to stay ahead of the man. His voice was always there.

The challenge of chasing her sanity sucked away her concentration. Jobs had been lost and the idea of her returning to school had long since passed. She couldn't even find matching socks.

"You're not qualified for the human race," Stranger reminded her.

She tried to compensate for her shortcomings with spurts of extraordinary cooking or cleaning. Daniel and Beth got homemade cookies in their lunches. Adam requested his favorite dinners, while he had the chance. Moving furniture and sorting drawers, presented opportunities to find remote controls, books of stamps and lost phone numbers. Sometimes she had even gotten ambitious and threw her efforts into some charitable activity.

None of it lasted very long. Soon, frozen dinners returned to the microwave. Clutter started to build. The couches again took hostages beneath its cushions. She had three different blankets waiting for her to finish knitting. Her attention wandered elsewhere, often leaving things half done.

"They deserve better," Stranger said.

Mothering was her fortress. Daniel and Beth could always hold her mind. Anything going wrong in her life could somehow be made better by what was right. Her family didn't make her life perfect, but they did keep her somewhat grounded. The children had grown so quickly though, she couldn't help but wonder if she had again just been distracted.

"They don't need you anymore," Stranger told her. She was starting to doubt if they ever had.

As her son put on his cap and gown, she snapped a picture to preserve his final moments of youth. The picture would later be preserved in a scrapbook with the words she had written.

Daniel

It's more than a diploma,
It's not just in the grades,
It's not just winning football games,
Or in the way he plays.

It is about who he is,
The character he shows,
Decisions he makes from day to day,
The directions that he chose.

This boy who has made us so very proud,
With all that he has done,
We celebrate, as he graduates,
The man he has become.

She had one hour left. Daniel's graduation was about to become real. He sat beside his mother as if he was bracing himself for some kind of speech. She couldn't speak. Looking into his eyes she wanted to say, "I'm so proud of you, son." Her smile tried to tell him she knew he could do this. He would be fine. The hug she gave him meant she loved him and she was always there for him.

"Avoid regret," was all she could finally say.

She heard his cell phone vibrate in his pocket. He hesitated. Both of them knew Abby was out there. Carrie paused to hang on to the little boy for one more second. She gazed upon her son. He was indeed a man. His young lady was waiting for his attention. She gestured her approval toward his cell phone, relinquishing the moment to technology.

"Go ahead. It's cool," she said. His future was out of her hands now. She prayed that he was ready, and that she would get to be part of it.

She and Adam rose to their feet and cheered when "Daniel Jenkins" was called. Her father and his girlfriend, Jane, cheered along with them. Carrie loved when they came to visit, especially when it involved a chance to show off her children.

By the time the last name was announced, the crowd was getting restless. Speeches and well-wishes had gotten tiresome. Parties were waiting. When the final soloist was introduced, people were already trying to plan their routes of escape. Then Beth took the stage.

As the enchanting melody filled the auditorium, her sweet voice wafted through the crowd. The lyrics hung in the air like a rainbow, promising a bright new day. She sang softly at first, almost a tease. It then blossomed into a confident and powerful performance. The evening couldn't have ended on a more perfect note.

Beth and Daniel each made an appearance at home before stepping out to more pressing social engagements. The adults were content to stay in and share a pot of coffee. Visits with her father now were so different from the relationship Carrie had with him when she was young. She liked when he talked to her like an adult. He listened to her opinions, even asked her for advice.   He probably wouldn't have asked Jane for a first date if Carrie hadn't been on the sidelines coaching him.

Before leaving at the end of the week, Grandpa and Jane had a surprising announcement.

"We're getting married in August!" Carrie's father was almost giddy.

"Daddy, that's wonderful!" The contagious excitement sparked an outpouring of ideas.

"You can have it here! We could set up a floral arbor in the backyard! I'll make your favorite meatballs, Daddy. The bakery downtown does beautiful cakes. I have a huge punchbowl. I got it at a yard sale, but nobody will ever know. We'll get fancy tablecloths and matching napkins. What color would you like, Jane? Beth could sing…"

"Carrie, wait." Her father halted her rambling.

"No meatballs?" She wasn't getting it.

"We appreciate the offer, honey. But we already have a place arranged," Jane said, trying to help.

Inexplicable panic started to brew. Not there. Please don't say it's there. Carrie unconsciously dissected her napkin. The sudden possibility of going home jumped her from the darkest alley of her mind. Her father was counting on her for support. She couldn't let him down.

"Really? Terrific. Where?" More pieces of napkin fluttered to the floor as she tried to fake enthusiasm.

"Sassy's lake house!" her father said as if she'd be thrilled.

Her head was starting to ache. The man inside bounced about. His springs were coiled with the subtle ouch that her father had told Sassy first, the disappointment of her rejected ideas, and her fear of the trip. She felt selfish and afraid. She couldn't spoil their moment. She stuck a peanut butter cookie in her mouth to prevent an over the top phony "yippee!" from slipping out.

"Carrie, I would really love it if you could come in July to help with the arrangements," Jane said. "Will you be my matron of honor?"

"You can spend the month with us," her father said hopefully.

Carrie couldn't keep up with her emotions. Excuses escaped her. Maybe she let them. She didn't know what she wanted. Going to the wedding with her family would be one thing. A weekend might be fun, maybe. Going home alone, just her and Stranger, felt like certain disaster.

Adam took a deep breath. He stepped closer to his wife as if he could save her from going on the trip.

She can't go! Carrie thought to Adam. *Say I can't go!* But she knew there was no reason he could possibly give.

Her father had done the trip at least every year. Once in return was not too much to ask, especially for his wedding.

She listened as Adam tried. There were reasons. There had to be reasons. He spouted off a few. He was committed to football camp all summer. He'd be lucky to get away for a week to attend the wedding. Beth had a Little Theater play through July, and Daniel had work and Abby.

Nothing he came up with would keep her from going. She could be gone for an entire month and it wouldn't matter to her family.

Carrie wasn't sure if it was the fact that nobody here needed her, or the lack of excuses to stay put, that caused her stomach to tighten. Her father had asked so little of her throughout her life. Time didn't seem too great of a request. She couldn't imagine how it would feel if her own children denied her that.

The room waited for an answer. She needed to hear one herself. Anxiety tried to keep her away. Stranger provided plenty. She wrapped her arms around her Daddy's neck the way she used to do when she was a little girl. Here, she was safe.

"Of course I'll come," she promised.

Her father and Jane went home happy. The plan was set for Carrie to come at the end of the month. Adam and the kids would come later for the wedding.

"I can't believe we're finally going to meet Aunt Sassy," Daniel said.

"This is awesome!" Beth said. "I thought I'd have to wait until I was out of college and go see her on my own. Dad, do you really think Mom will be okay?"

"What?" Carrie asked. "I'm fine. It'll be okay."

Carrie wanted to be ecstatic. She thought she should at least be glad.

"Nothing's definite," Adam said. But she had already promised her father she'd come. There was a plan. She and Stranger would be going home. To her father's wedding. At Sassy's lake house. Without Adam. Without her babies.

"It's fine," she said. "Everything is fine."

The next morning, she sat alone with her tea, allowing her pen to do the feeling for her.

Secret Me

The darkness is overwhelming,
Fear invades my soul.
The silence that surrounds me,
Loudly takes its toll.

War rages in my head,
Serenity is hard to find.
Spirits try to guide me,
This can't just be my mind.

Tranquility is possible,
Peace will come someday.
If only they could understand,
Life gets in the way.

CHAPTER 34 – UNCLE JACK

After years without contact, one evening David left his downtown office and found Jack sitting on the hood of his Volkswagen. Hard as he tried, he couldn't let go of the old feelings of guilt and anguish. He had come to terms with the abuse, but this creature represented the sacrifice his wife had made for him, and the children they couldn't have. Old, dirty, and pathetic, Jack smirked at David.

Years of simmering venom boiled within him. David stuck his hands in his pockets. *Behave*, he thought. He tried to sound calm. "What the hell are you doing here?"

"Ain't you gonna give your uncle a big ol' smooch?"

"Out of jail again, Jack?" he asked.

"You gonna send your kid after me again? Ain'tcha man enough to fight for yourself?"

"I don't know what you're talking about," David said. It made him sick to think about the beating Joseph had taken. By the time he'd realized he had left Oli's that day, it was too late to stop it. "Get off my car."

"You thought that little freak could take me? He's lucky I only busted his face."

David's hands came out of his pockets. "That was years ago. He was just a kid."

"That kid tried to rob me."

"We all know that's bullshit, Jack."

Joseph had insisted that he'd only followed Jack to threaten him. Things didn't get out of hand until David's watch fell out of Jack's pocket.

"Davey, Davey, Davey." Jack sipped at the beer he was holding. "He took my watch. You gave me that watch outta the goodness of your heart." He snorted. "As I recall, it was just a down payment."

"I gave you my watch so you'd leave Oli's House," David said. "You would have gotten the money too."

"Yeah, yeah. Oli's Place. Wifey's little project. Save the little girls! In the name of the great Oliver Lingle." He spat on the ground between them. "That son of a bitch was one of my best customers. Someone ought to tell Wifey that. Big brother liked to keep the working girls busy."

"What do you want, Jack?"

Jack slid off the car and gulped down the last of his beer. "Well, now. I'm a fair man. I'll settle for the money you snaked out on last time." He crushed the can in his hand and tossed it aside. "You can have the freak deliver it. Surely he ain't a minor no more."

David locked eyes with his uncle. "You need to leave. You need to leave right now."

"Check you out. Who do you think you are—tellin' me what to do?" He took a long drag on his cigarette and exhaled. "You. There in your swanky clothes, with your designer shoes. You forget I knew ya when all ya wore was hand me downs from a dead guy."

David stepped away from the smoke. "I didn't forget anything."

"And that house!" Jack shook his head. "You think livin' in that house means you're better than your own people?"

David squirmed. His fists curled. Warnings were going off in his head. *Back off,* he told himself. *Keep your mouth shut. You are better.*

Jack nodded at David's crotch. "Pity, really. Fancy pants like that don't mean there's a man in 'em."

David grimaced.

"C'mon, boy. That was an accident. You're over it by now. You done okay, all that money and all. And ya never even invite me to dinner."

"We've worked hard for everything we have."

"Is that so?" Jack stepped closer. The stench of stale cigarettes and body odor crept up David's nose. "Financial Investor. That what ya call it?

How fancy. To me, it looks like ya' prissed around with other people's money while your woman was slinging burgers."

Sassy had left the diner years ago, but David didn't have the breath, nor the desire, to debate.

"Wifey ever needs a real man, give her my number. She's one hot lady, alright. I'll have a go at her."

#

David was entitled to one phone call. As he sat in the jail cell waiting for the guard to lead him to the telephone, he only regretted two things; the blood on his lapel, and not killing Jack when he was sixteen.

When the guard opened David's cell door, Jack was still whining about his busted face. He clamored for his free lawyer, claiming David had started the whole fight.

"I innocently asked how my nephew's lovely wife was doing. It was the boy who went berserk."

To the guard, Jack was a monkey, swinging about his cage in search of a banana. David stood and shook the officer's hand before following him to his desk.

"You can use this phone, Mr. Martin," the guard said to David.

"Thanks, Mike. How's your daughter?" David asked.

"Much better, thanks to Mrs. Martin. Got rid of that loser. She hasn't been in any trouble since she left Oli's House. She's with a new guy, now. Has his own business. They're getting married in the fall."

"Hard to believe it's been so long. I'm happy for all of you."

Mike walked past Jack making monkey noises. David dialed Sassy's number. As the phone rang, he straightened his collar. There was a picture of Mike's daughter on his desk, posing with her fiancé.

David was proud of Sassy. She really did make a difference for so many families. He hung up the phone before she could answer. Mike was too busy with Jack to notice a second phone call.

"Hello. Pierce Detective Agency, may I help you?"

"Hi Linda. It's David. Could I talk to your husband, please?"

The voice he wanted to hear was there in seconds. "D-David! G-good to hear from you."

"Joseph, I need your help."

CHAPTER 35- MURKY WATER COLORED MEMORIES

Bail had been posted and David was home with his wife. Joseph returned from the lake house with a plateful of his favorite cookies.

Sassy hadn't lost her touch, or her figure.

Embers of a boyhood crush were swiftly dampened by the task at hand. He bit into another cookie and locked his office door.

Sliding a picture of the New York skyline off the wall, he uncovered the safe. He pulled a handkerchief from his pocket and wiped a layer of dust from the picture frame. A cookie or two later, he turned the dial. The safe clicked open. There with his family records, the deed to his home, and the stocks and bonds David had helped him buy, rested the file.

He pulled the folder out and opened it one last time, ashamed of the very label, "Martin, David J."

Rationalizing the information he had secretly gathered on his closest friend, Joseph reminded himself that David was the one who had taught him to question everyone. The lesson hadn't excluded the teacher. Still, when he was ten, the idea of questioning his hero had never crossed Joseph's mind. When David had his Uncle Jack pinned against the wall of his apartment, he'd looked like the same guy that pulled kids from burning buildings and took them to baseball games.

When he was a kid, Joseph had been impressed that David had a friend on the police force that he could call to protect them from Jack. He'd even filed the name, "Officer Samuel O'Brian," to memory, in case they ever needed him again.

Years later, when the police came to question Joseph about the fight between him and Jack, he gave David's business card to Officer O'Brian, wanting to point out the fact they had a mutual friend. O'Brian showed it to his partner, Officer Kane, and asked, "Hey, isn't this Martin guy the one who kept calling for information on the Lingle case?"

The name had hit Joseph like a rock to the head. *Lingle. As in Sassy and her brother, Oliver.*

"What kind of information?" he asked. "David said Oliver got drunk and fell."

"That case has been closed for years," Officer Kane barked at O'Brian. "Stop picking at it." Kane left the room without another word.

O'Brian had more questions for Joseph.

"How long have you known David Martin?"

#

There was a tiny crack in the pedestal Joseph had kept David on, but he'd never fallen. Still, he'd felt a duty to protect his friend from trouble. He studied the pages of the file he had put together. It started with a copy of Oliver's letter to Sassy. At the top, Joseph had written a note questioning the ten thousand dollars that had come with the letter. There was information on Adam's car that had been sold to David's boss for twenty thousand, days before David miraculously came up with enough money to secure his purchase of the lake house. The file also contained every scrap Joseph could find relating to Oliver's death. Despite his personal feelings, his gut told him these facts were all related.

As time went on, Joseph had stopped digging. Oli's House had become Sassy's rainbow following a twisted storm. Nobody involved needed more rain.

Now, Jack was out of jail and threatening Sassy. He was the bad guy, not David. Joseph needed to protect his friends. Of course, Jack had to be stopped. He stuffed the file into his briefcase and went to bed.

His wife snuggled up next to him, laying her head on his chest. "I didn't hear you come in," she said. "Did you just get home?"

Her hair smelled like sweet strawberries. "Mmhmm," he answered. He closed his eyes and inhaled. "I love you."

#

In the morning, Joseph returned to Oli's House with his briefcase. He was relieved to see that Sassy's office door was closed. David greeted him with his usual warmth.

"Hey, bud. I didn't expect to see you so soon. Everything okay?"

Joseph couldn't answer. He didn't know. *How do you tell your best friend you've been investigating him for years?*

David put a hand on his shoulder. "Geeze. Linda wasn't upset with you for being out so late, was she? I'm sorry. Want me to call her and explain?"

Joseph lifted his head. David was staring at him with those "dad eyes." He'd seen the concerned look countless times over the years. The look meant the guy was on his side. He learned that the night David rescued him from the fire. Since that summer, being on David's side was the only place he ever wanted to be.

"Let's go into my office," David said.

Joseph followed with his briefcase.

#

That night David sat at his desk, in the office one floor below his sleeping wife. He wrote the words again, as if he had a fresh thought. The quote from the back of the picture he'd found in Oliver's nightstand treasure chest still made him cringe.

He reviewed the file Joseph had given him. The kid was thorough. Still, the haunting doubt remained unsettled. *Was Oliver's death an accident?*

A ringing phone interrupted his thoughts but stopped before he could grab it. He looked at his watch. It was three o'clock in the morning.

Damn it, Jack! he thought as he went to check on his wife.

The Bible reference he had scribbled on his notepad whispered sentiments to the dark.

For love is strong as death;
Jealousy is cruel as the grave.

CHAPTER 36 – LET ME BE YOUR CHOCOLATE

"Let me out," Stranger said.

"No. I won't let you hurt them," Carrie said out loud. But thoughts followed, *He has no power. Get rid of him. Cut him out.*

"Let me out!" he said again.

The battle swept her under. She was lost in her own kitchen. She fumbled about for an answer. Anything. She couldn't find her journal. She couldn't find a recipe. The milk container was empty again. She opened a drawer hoping to find a new one. A long, serrated knife lifted with her hand. It felt alive.

"Let me out," he kept saying.

The knife agreed. Pulling her hand from the drawer, it stopped at her forehead. The blade slid back and forth until blood dripped into her eyes making them burn. She stopped. The knife fell to the floor.

"I don't want to be crazy!" she cried. Only he heard. She was alone with her demon. No person could save her. Her heart fought to pray, but her mind wouldn't let her. She wanted to scream, "God, please take me." Words would not cooperate.

She stared in the mirror over the bathroom sink, a washcloth soaked in broken sanity. He wasn't leaving without her. She cleaned herself off with cold water and pulled her bangs over the wound. Grabbing one of Adam's ball caps from a hook, she left the house.

"You can't go back," the man said.

All her father wanted was for her to come home for a visit. He deserved a nice wedding. He needed her help. So much time had passed since she had left. She didn't know why the idea of going back frightened her so much. She didn't feel strong enough to help anyone. Maybe her father and Jane would be better off without her. She mindlessly rolled through the countryside in quest of comfort.

"I own you," Stranger said.

Defeated, she ended her search at the grocery store. She took a deep breath and walked inside. She crept past produce and the organic aisles, hoping nobody would notice she wasn't interested in participating in the latest health food craze. She paused at the candy aisle, then moved on. That was kids' stuff. Carrie needed the bakery. Looking over her shoulder, she felt like a criminal stealing the creamiest, gooiest, chocolate covered loot she could find. She boldly paid cash at the self-service counter and walked out.

"Look at you," Stranger said. "You can't even talk to your own husband."

She slumped hidden in her car and unwrapped the pastry. One bite made her sick. Her love of dessert was one sided.

"Do it. Feed your guilt," he said.

The hollow pleasure touched her lips. Guilt pummeled the promise of oral gratification. A rational thought flickered like a small candle in a cave of darkness. *This won't ease my fears or explain them.* She set the pastry down.

"Damn you! What are you waiting for, a hug?" The man would not be silenced.

He cheered her on when she again reached for the empty calories. Chocolate dripped onto the wrapper. Her fingers were sticky. Her own eyes glared at her through the rearview mirror. She felt disgusting.

She stuffed the pastry back into its bag and opened her car door, dropping the bag on the ground. She stomped on it with all of her might. Over and over she stomped. Chocolate and cream oozed into an ugly blob.

Her new sneakers were a mess. She couldn't look up as she scraped the blob off the asphalt and threw it into the trash. When she got back into her car, her hands were sticky, and her cell phone was ringing.

"I beat the cream out of a chocolate éclair," she answered.

"I'm sure it had it coming," Sassy said with a laugh.

"Sassy, what's wrong with me? I'm such a freak. It's my father's wedding. He needs me. Why am I such a freak?"

"Slow down, Care." Sassy turned on her professional voice. "What's going on?"

"I don't know. My Dad. I'm coming home. I'm scared."

"You're flying?"

"No. Please don't hate me. I want to see you. I really do."

"You're afraid to come home?"

Afraid to come home. The idea sounded pathetic, ridiculous, and completely true. She wiped a tear from her eye and noticed chocolate on her fingers. "It's been so long."

"Carrie, don't be silly. You'll be fine."

"But the kids…"

"They're old enough to take care of themselves for a few weeks. Daniel's a high school graduate. He's not a kid anymore."

Carrie wiped her hands on a fast food napkin she found between the seats. "He has work. I have to make his lunches."

"He can handle it."

Carrie noticed a small hole in her shirt. "Beth has rehearsals. I have to sew her costume."

"You taught her well. She can do her own hemming."

"Yeah, I guess."

"Adam is a wonderful father," Sassy said. "You say so yourself, all of the time. Stop with the excuses. You're coming. We'll have a great time."

"They really don't need me, do they?"

"Honey, you've prepared them for this. Their needs are changing. They'll always love you. Isn't that better?"

"I'm not ready to let go."

"Don't ever let go. Adjust your grip."

"Sassy, it's so hard."

"Let the people you love enhance your life, not be your life. Love them with all your heart. Let them see you love yourself."

Carrie licked chocolate from underneath her fingernails. She wondered if that kind of talk worked on Sassy's clients. She didn't have the heart to tell her how ridiculous it sounded. Loving herself was preposterous as long as Stranger was part of her. She could love her family outside of him. They were safely separated. That's how it had to stay.

Sassy was saying something about a shower for Jane. Sales everywhere. Shopping together.

"It'll be like old times," she said.

"Old times?"

"Even better. We'll have credit cards this time."

Carrie wanted to tell Sassy the man was listening. She's a professional, she would understand. Maybe she would know what to do. He didn't like their conversation. His territory had been violated. An attack was rumbling. His voice got louder. The noise grew into a thought shattering blast.

"She's your best friend!" he shrieked.

The significance of his exclamation was lost on her. The tone issued warning, not comfort. The conflict made her head throb. She stifled her hunger for disclosure and heeded his call. But what did he mean? She tried to remind herself that he had no power without her. Or did he? A deep sense of doubt introduced itself.

Or did he?

At last, with one simple question, the power within her shifted. Control disguised itself with new strategy. She couldn't allow Sassy to be exposed to him any longer. She thanked her for her help and bid her what she expected would be their last good bye. He wasn't going to hurt anyone anymore.

As she prepared herself, she wasn't sure if she or the man was winning. An unclaimed energy took over. By the next evening, Carrie had washed every stitch of laundry she could find. The dishes were done, the windows were clean, and the carpet had been vacuumed. She balanced her checkbook and fed the dog. It was the most organized day she had ever spent. It was all part of his plan.

She kissed her family as she told them she was leaving to visit a friend. She hated the lie. He was no friend. She drove toward the train station with a solid mission. It was going to end.

#

But then, it didn't end. The train had come and gone. "God I am Yours, not his," she had said. The truth kept her safe for another moment. Relief teased when the train had passed. But it took nothing with it. Stranger was quiet, yet the secret of the man remained. She could take it home with Adam's pretzels or find another train. The station had plenty. Maybe one did have her name on it. The answer was so close. This time, doubt was silent.

She left her car. The freedom it had given her had brought her here. Bold spite would take her away. She walked up the tracks with renewed purpose. She smirked a bit, enjoying one of those rare instances in which crazy felt wonderful.

"What time is the next train leaving for Pennsylvania?" She asked the man at the ticket window.

"Twenty minutes, ma'am. Headin' straight through to Littleston Station."

"Terrific. One ticket please."

.

CHAPTER 37 –TIME FLIES, OR, AT LEAST, TAKES THE TRAIN

Adam couldn't let her go. He had to let her go. When they left Wayne Valley, he'd hoped through some miracle they'd never go back. He and Carrie never talked about it out loud, but they held an unspoken agreement that returning to Pennsylvania was a bad idea. There had been a few close calls over the years, but with the exception of Mrs. Lingle's funeral, they'd had good enough reasons to stay in Iowa.

But Carrie couldn't miss her father's wedding. If only it were somewhere else. It had been nearly twenty years. Now, it was finally going to happen. Carrie and Sassy would be together again. Distance had been a merciful protector, but the cloak was wearing thin. Would time be as kind?

Adam needed to talk to his wife. If she had to go back, he'd drive her there himself. First, he had to tell her about Oliver. Finding out on her own would only make things worse. Cursing himself for asking her to stop for his pretzels, he heated the kettle for tea. A car pulled into the driveway. The door shut. Beth's heals clicked along the sidewalk. Carrie's comfortable white sneakers only squeaked.

A quick consult with Beth informed him that Carrie used one sugar in her cup, and a splash of milk. He poured the boiling water into her favorite mug. The tea got darker, then cold. He dumped it out and refilled the kettle. It whistled again. Adam looked outside. Her empty parking spot scolded him.

History was bearing down on him. She deserved to know. Maybe she already did. He walked to the end of the road. Still no sign of her. He had waited too long.

Guilt is a powerful beast. Adam wasn't sure if it was friend or foe. He could only hope the alliance wouldn't sour. It had kept Carrie safe all these years. At least, that was what he had let himself believe.

When Adam returned to the kitchen, Daniel and Beth were sitting at the table eating pretzels.

"Where the hell did those come from?" Adam shouted.

"My room. I was watching the game last night," Daniel said defensively.

"Damn it, Daniel! Why can't you put things back where they belong?"

"But Dad..."

"No! No excuses. Be responsible. Don't act like you don't notice your mother needs a little help!"

"But Dad, there's more in the pantry."

"What?" Adam's tone softened. He hadn't seen them. He hadn't looked hard enough. He had no idea. "I'm sorry, Son. I'm a little worried about your mother."

"Mom just called," Beth said. "We need to pick up her car near the train station."

"What?! Why…?"

"She said she had to go to Pop's early. She was rambling again. I could barely make out what she was saying. It was so loud in the background. Something about Aunt Sassy. She said she told you she was going."

Adam's thoughts flew back to the call from Carrie. All she had said was that she was on her way home. *She was on her way home!* An image of his high school sweetheart sitting on her father's stoop flashed in his mind.

"Damn it!" he yelled.

When she'd left the house, she'd said she was going to see a friend. She couldn't have meant Sassy. She didn't even take a suitcase. Something must have happened. He dialed Sassy's number, then hung up.

Carrie was already on her way. He had to be there for her. She had a head start, but he had a wicked new Mustang that deserved to do more than tote him back and forth to work. Adam reached for his keys.

"Daddy, what's going on? Is Mom okay?" Beth asked.

Adam regarded his daughter. Her sweet face looked so much like her mother's. She looked at him with those same eyes, begging him to make it okay. Both of his children waited for his answer. He took out his wallet and handed Daniel a credit card.

"Be good, kids. I'll be back in a few days. Everything is going to be fine."

The words soured on his lips and his voice cracked. He tried again. "Everything is fine."

He wasn't even sure what "fine" was. Carrie used the word so many times it almost felt sarcastic. How could she say she was fine after she thrashed in bed all night? Was she fine when she forgot what she was talking about in the middle of a conversation? Or when she got lost on her way home from the grocery store? If he called her right this minute, as she sped away from him into a dark past, would she say she was fine? Maybe he deserved to be shut out.

"Don't worry, Daddy. She'll be with Aunt Sassy," Beth said.

"I'm not worried," he lied.

His children waited for some truth. "I need to be with her," he said.

"It's a long ride. At least let me make some sandwiches for you to take. Wait five minutes." In spite of her father's protests, Beth started a pot of coffee. "Daniel, throw some clean underwear and socks in a bag. Pack his blue shirt and his beige pants. Don't forget to throw in his tooth brush and some deodorant." She made half a dozen sandwiches, then filled a thermos with the hot coffee.

Daniel worked on filling a bag with the items he was sent to gather. "Okay, now socks," he rattled from his mental checklist. He opened the top drawer of Carrie's dresser.

"Oops. These aren't Dad's," he said out loud to himself. As he went to shut the drawer, the corner of a CD caught his eye. He pulled it out. It was the Beatles. Digging for more, he found an envelope. Thinking about how strange his father was acting, and how he was trying, and failing, to let them see how worried he was, Daniel opened the envelope. Just in case it had some sort of clue. He read the poem his mother had written.

Secret Me

The darkness is overwhelming,
Fear invades my soul,
The silence that surround me,
Loudly takes a toll.
War rages in my head,
Serenity is hard to find,
Spirits try to guide me,
This can't just be my mind.
Tranquility is possible,
Peace will come someday,
If only they could understand,
Life gets in the way.

Daniel folded the paper and put it in the pocket of his jeans. "Oh,

Mom," he whispered.

"Danny! Did you find everything? Dad's leaving," Beth called.

Daniel threw a few more things into the bag and brought it to the

car. Adam again reminded them to be good and gave them each a hug. "I

love you guys," he said.

\#

Adam's children humored him with a dramatic wave as he backed

out of the driveway. Silly kids. Glancing at the care package Beth had

insisted he'd need, it occurred to him how very grown up they really were.

He paused to look at them one more time before he drove away.

They are so innocent, he thought. Next time he saw them everything would be different. *I hope they can forgive me.*

#

As they rode to the train station to get their mother's car, Daniel and Beth again discussed their parents' imperfections.

"Well, this is weird," Beth said. "Even for Mom."

Daniel was quiet at first, thinking about the poem he'd found. All their lives they'd been told to protect their mother. Now she was gone. Their father was freaking out, and obviously hiding something big. "Yeah," he finally said. "Weird."

Carrie's babies rode along in silence. Daniel heard his sister sniffle. She was trying not to cry. He reached into his pocket, pulled out a pack of gum, and gave it to her. Then he forced a playful tone to his voice.

"I wonder what Dad did to get Mom pissed enough to leave Iowa," he said.

Beth flashed a knowing smile and did her best to play along.

"It couldn't be another forgotten anniversary," she said. "That's not for a couple months."

Daniel helped himself to another piece of gum. "Maybe he left his underwear on the bathroom floor again."

"Nah, she's used to that."

"Company could've seen it," he said, blowing a bubble. "She really hates that."

"Those were yours, Danny, and the preacher hasn't been back since. You guys can be such pigs sometimes."

"It was an accident. I didn't know he was coming over."

Beth laughed. "I guess washin' all your whites with her new red scarf taught you a lesson."

"Locker rooms can be tough on a guy in pink boxers." He yanked his up a little to reveal he kept wearing them anyway.

"You should pay attention when you get dressed in the morning."

"I have, ever since Mom started taking laundry advice from Aunt Sassy."

"I can imagine what it will be like when they both get their hands on Dad." Beth's voice cracked a little. She bit down on her pinky finger.

Daniel reached over and lowered her hand from her mouth. With a gentle squeeze, he brought it to rest on the seat beside her. Then he tried again to lighten the mood.

"Poor guy was sweatin' something. I haven't seen him so unraveled since the night before district championship. Bad time for your front line to get the trotts."

Beth smiled at his effort. "Mom had to be pretty freaked to up and leave like that," she said.

"Not enough to make her fly."

"Guess a fear of heights isn't the worst flaw a mom could have."

"How 'bout a fear of cows?"

Beth didn't say anything when Daniel passed the train station. He drove for a while, then pulled into a gas station and filled the tank. She went inside and bought a map, though she knew Daniel had been studying the route to Pennsylvania since before he'd even gotten his driver's license.

"Don't worry, Beth," Daniel said when she handed him the map. "I never get lost." Then he grinned and held up his father's credit card. "We can even sleep in a hotel halfway."

CHAPTER 38 – THY WILL BE DONE

Sassy had been distracted when Carrie called. She answered the phone hoping for some funny anecdote about the kids, or anything happy, really. Her underlying worries about David had not allowed her to hear the terror in Carrie's voice.

"Sass, I did it. I'm on my way. I'm coming home."

"What! You're coming? Here? Now?" Sassy opened her appointment book. "I'll pick you up! When's your flight due?"

"I'm about to get on the train right now. I should be there by ten tomorrow morning."

"Wow. Long ride… Okay, great. We can meet at our spot! You know, the bench by the newsstand. They put a new one in, but it looks the same. Carrie! I can't believe you're finally coming."

Sassy was so excited to hear that her friend was coming home, she didn't notice Carrie had forgotten to factor in the hour time difference between them.

#

Sassy left Oli's House at eight o'clock, planning a quick stop to check on her father before going to the station. She had plenty of time before Carrie's train arrived.

Thank God for happy diversions, she thought. *Carrie's finally...*

Something ran in front of her car. *A cat?* Sassy's foot fumbled for the brake. *A squirrel.* The pickup truck swerved from her path just before impact. The massive oak tree didn't budge. She heard the screams but couldn't tell if they were her own. Her head snapped back with a jolt of pain, then bounced forward. Through a puff of cloud, angels smacked her in the face and lifted her. The car hissed and spit as its mangled body accepted its fate.

"Get her out! Get her out!"

"Don't move her, you idiot. Somebody call 9-1-1!"

"Is she breathing?"

"No. Wait. I'm not sure. I can't find her pulse."

The pain eased away as she drifted toward a distant light. Somebody called her name. She tried to answer but could make no sound.

"Lady, please. Hang on."

"She can't hear you."

"Well, do something!"

"In the Name of the Father, and of the Son, and of the Holy Spirit…"

"You're not a priest, you ass. You can't do that."

"Anybody can say it."

"Shut up. I hear the ambulance!"

Sassy heard it too.

CHAPTER 39 – WELCOME HOME

Carrie's watch showed the time was five minutes past ten when the train pulled into the station. She walked past the clock on the wall without noticing it was after eleven.

Someone was following her. Carrie hid among the strangers. Everyone looked guilty. She quickened her pace but couldn't stay ahead of those watchful eyes. She hurried toward the exit, hoping Sassy was outside waiting.

The bench by the newsstand was empty, like it had been when Carrie looked out the window of her departing train, nearly twenty years ago. They had sat here together, before Carrie left, promising to visit each other often. Sassy had waved good bye, with the lonely bench in the background. Carrie sat here now, in the spot they were supposed to meet.

Carrie watched the faces passing by. She wondered if she would recognize Sassy. The pictures looked so different from the girl she grew up with. She tried not to enjoy the granny glasses. She hoped Sassy, in turn, would forgive the dark circles under her eyes. Hiding small vanities was easier when she could click and edit before anyone saw her.

The crowd thinned. She looked at her watch again. 10:30am. She reached into her pocket for her phone but didn't feel it. Could she have left it on the train? Was she even in the right place? The panic crept in. The eyes were on her, an open target. Time passed as strangers hovered. *This was a mistake. I shouldn't have come.*

Hiding behind an open newspaper, she watched a pair of men's loafers coming toward her. They moved slowly, then stopped. She gripped the newspaper like a shield. The loafers were looking for her.

"Carrie?" he asked.

"Daddy!" Dropping the paper, she jumped up and hugged her father with the relief of a pardoned felon. He squeezed her hard, kissed her on the cheek, then delivered the message.

"Sweetie, David called. Sassy's been in a car accident."

"W-what? Where is she? What did he say?"

"He didn't know much yet. The doctors were still with her."

"Take me there. Please take me!"

Thirty minutes later, they burst into the hospital's emergency room. The woman behind the desk was sipping coffee and gazing at a magazine. Obviously annoyed at the disturbance, she looked over the edge of her bifocals. Her voice twanged the same stale question she repeated fifty times a day.

"May I help you?"

"Sassy. Sassy Lingle," Carrie pleaded.

"It's Mrs. Martin. Brought by ambulance from a car wreck," her father helped.

"Are you family?"

"Yes...no...yes..." Carrie bit her thumb.

"I'm sorry, Miss. Only family is allowed back right now."

"They're family," David interrupted.

Carrie turned to see him. "She'll be okay," he said. The man from Sassy's pictures suddenly came to life, replacing the younger man she had known. He fell into her arms. She envisioned him alone; no family, no children, no wife.

"She'll be okay," he repeated. Carrie sniffed. She straightened his tie. He took her arm and led them through a maze of intimidating machines, past the nurses' station, and down the long corridor of rooms.

Smells of illness and pain mingled with the good intentions of disinfectant. The aroma of coffee broke through for a moment, then drifted away like a busy nurse. Beeps and moans begged for attention throughout the "sterile" halls.

A mother rocked her crying baby. An elderly gentleman yelled for a bedpan. Each room held its own drama. Theirs was behind the door at the end of the hall.

"She'll be okay," he said again.

Carrie hid her shock when David opened the door. Sassy's face was swollen and bruised. Her neck was in a brace. David wiped some drool from her chin as he announced her visitors. Her mouth tried to smile.

"She, uh, had a little trouble with a squirrel," David spoke for her. I guess it ran in front of her. She swerved to miss it and hit a tree."

Sassy scratched, "WELCOME HOME!" onto a notepad.

Carrie moved some hair, ever so gently, away from Sassy's face. Her friend looked out through the injuries. Carrie smoothed her blanket, making sure her feet didn't stick out. They had shared so many words over the years. The stored laughter, frustration, excitement and tears, all nestled together into one glorious hour of silence. They were together again.

CHAPTER 40 – TRUTH BE TOLD

In the dark, it felt like the same old room. Carrie couldn't see the simple beige walls or the rich burgundy accents. In the middle of the night, her bedroom was still pink. The furniture was white and girlie, not sturdy oak. The long, freestanding mirror she used to dress in front of was still in the corner. She was the girl with the ponytail. Darkness entertained the past, but it couldn't hide the man.

His unspoken presence filled her. The silence was more frightening than his roars. "Don't be crazy," she told herself out loud. "Don't be crazy. He's gone. It was in your head. You're safe." She pinched the bridge of her nose. The pain wouldn't budge. Truth was the only cure.

She thought of the headless dolls. She had no right to hurt them like that. They were there for her. They never laughed at her or called her a kook.

A kook, Carrie thought. *Oliver had used that word.* She could picture him here, in her room. "Carrie, you're too old to play with dolls," he had said. The memory felt foreign as scattered bits trickled through her mind. "Adam's grandfather says your mom's a kook."

Oliver had never known her mother. Carrie had never known her

mother either. *Adam wouldn't let his grandfather say bad things. Adam*

didn't know. She wasn't supposed to know. She knew. Oliver had told her.

"Carrie, you can't do this," Oliver had said. "Don't be like her."

He had said a lot of things. She hated him for telling her that her

mother killed herself, and she loved him for it. Nobody else did that.

Giving in to the nightmare of being awake, she slipped on her

clothes and picked up her shoes. Tiptoeing out into the hall, she stopped to

listen for the snoring that had allowed her to escape so many times before.

Her father's door was shut. She crept down the stairs, carefully skipping

the step near the bottom. That one always creaked. When she opened the

door, she was almost disappointed not to see her friends there waiting for

her. She sat on the stoop and wiggled into her sneakers. There would be no

hiding on the hill to spy a drive-in movie tonight. No cars could be

"borrowed" for a midnight joyride. She wondered if the tree house still

existed.

She followed herself across the street, past the house, toward

Sassy's backyard. Her mind didn't let herself think about the fact Mr.

Lingle had sold the place two years earlier. Whacking her head on a

hanging flower pot, she took a second to readjust her bearings. That used

to be a basketball net, and it was much higher. A garden took over the spot where they used to park their bikes. A gazebo replaced the picnic table. Mrs. Lingle would have been pleased to know her yard was still beautiful.

The wide-open grass made her long for the days of running through sprinklers and tossing water balloons. The tree had aged gracefully. The weathered boards and rusted nails left by the tree house were covered by its growth. She tugged on the tattered old rope ladder. It broke off in her hand, requesting her guilt. As she placed it on the ground, an image of wilting yellow roses flashed in her mind.

A twig snapped under her foot, rekindling forgotten paranoia. *The dolls' heads are under this very ground*, her mind told her. She had buried them herself. Fear tried to protect her as memories of youth invited her to safety, then slapped her away.

Go back, she thought. He was out there. Again, he was watching. She felt naked and dirty. Every inch was exposed, begging for cover. The wooded area behind the yard dared her to enter.

Nature offered no sympathy as she twisted her way through the maze of rocks and fallen branches. She had a shovel. The dirt felt cold. "No!" she told her empty hands. She ran.

Don't look back, she thought. *Okay, stop. Rest. No, he's too close. Keep going. The heads. Keep going.* She kept moving deeper into the woods. *I shouldn't have ripped off their heads. Keep going.* Their little

plastic faces had never stopped smiling. *Kook.*

Carrie pleaded with her feet to move faster, cursing her middle-

aged stamina. Her muscles mockingly responded to the strain with tight

sarcasm. Gasping for breath, it felt like every doughnut she had ever eaten

was clinging to her heart. She couldn't stop. She was too old to play with

dolls! She ran harder, gradually overriding the protests. Defying her body,

she picked up speed. As she sought refuge, echoes of the past rang through

her mind.

"You following me?" a voice demanded.

"I was worried," she heard herself say.

"Don't need your worry," he said.

Another voice spoke to her now. A woman. "I'm sorry…I'm

sorry," Carrie heard. "I'm sorry, too," she said.

"Don't need your sorry neither," Stranger said.

"Kook," a new voice sounded like Adam.

Her body began to retaliate. Carrie couldn't outrun the memory.

Collapsing behind a tree, she pressed her back against the mossy trunk,

trying to be as invisible as possible. It was no use. Stranger was with her.

He was always with her. Her pounding chest grew tighter. Everything

ached. She covered her ears, desperate to silence the voices.

"Let me take you home," she heard her own voice in her head. "You're in no condition to drive."

"I said don't worry! Go home and play with your stupid dolls, little girl. Don't pretend to care 'bout me now," Stranger said.

But she did care. Feelings of deep love, and bitter hate encompassed her. The voice that had been with her for so long sounded newly familiar. Carrie cringed. The man was a boy. He was not her enemy. He was family, someone that she loved. Twenty years of verbal abuse exploded into the words that finally broke her, words she had heard before.

"I love you, Carrie," he said, and he wasn't a stranger anymore.

Her broken heart guided her broken mind as she relived a twisted memory. Hallucination resurrected the beast. Carrie could hear him as if he was alive. She could see him with her eyes closed. And she could feel him dwelling in her soul.

She stiffened like plastic. Alone against a tree, she felt his control. Her little rubber head wanted to pop off. Her painted eyes wouldn't close.

His shadow lifted and dropped her. "You're too old to play with dolls!" he said.

She was twenty again. "Your mother killed herself because of you," she heard. She slapped at the air, her hand searching for a face.

"You're lying!" she screamed. "Adam wouldn't let his grandfather say that." She punched and kicked. "It's not true," Carrie cried.

Memories had her pinned. Invisible hands ripped at her clothing. Darkness kissed her lips and a taste of alcohol swam across her tongue. She turned her head away from the monster as her body thrashed on the ground, fighting the hallucinations. Her mind could no longer bury him. His strength was too much for all of her.

Carrie's outer body stilled, and she lay motionless under the tree. The man came to life as her sanity imploded. His mouth wrapped hers, eating her screams. Then, he struck hard between her legs. The man said nothing as he plunged his weapon into her and stole her innocence. She could feel him inside of her, moving... and moving. The pain was real.

There was no need for speech now, as the voice took back its face. A shy grin spread across his lips. His cheeks flushed around one perfect dimple. The familiar boyish charm was unmistakable. Carrie searched for the steely grey eyes she had known, those eyes that could once behold beauty in a rainy day.

"I'm not crazy," she heard herself say. "I'm not my mother."

Madness crushed memory. This face had no eyes. She stared into the black void. Allowing herself a role in the hallucination, she reached out. At the touch of her fingertips, the face shattered and crashed upon her.

As she scrambled to salvage the broken pieces, shards of his flesh cut into her. She raised her bloody hands toward Heaven with cold, red streams draining down her arms.

"Not yet," a voice boomed down.

The faceless man claimed her hand from the air and kissed it. He pulled off his sweaty shirt. Very gently, he put it over her head and covered her naked chest. He handed her a small black velvet bag, then picked wildflowers and placed them in a circle around her. Swigging some more poison, he stumbled to his car.

Her fingers slid up and down the soft velvet, then settled on the tie that bound it shut. She pulled it as if in slow motion, allowing an eerie light to escape. Two steely grey eyes glowed from inside.

"Kook," she heard, in the voice of her husband.

"He knows," Stranger said. "Adam knows."

Sanity fought back, allowing the present to intervene, and reclaim its rightful place. She awakened; a forty-year old mother, alone in the woods, longing for her husband. A warm summer breeze hugged her trembling body as Carrie repeated aloud the last words she had ever said to Oliver.

"But, I did love you. You were like my brother."

CHAPTER 41 – GUILT TRIP

Adam had been on the road for seven hours, maybe eight…or nine. His eyes were getting heavy. When did the sun come up? His thermos was long since empty. The sandwiches had disappeared at least a hundred miles ago.

He pulled his car to the side of the highway. Not a single car passed him as he got out and did ten jumping jacks. He stopped and hit redial on his phone. Carrie still didn't answer. Maybe she had forgotten to charge it again. He tried Sassy's number. No answer there, either.

He returned to his travels, driving a little faster now. The road was flat, straight, and impossibly endless. He wished he had flown, but that would have taken planning. He'd get there. Everything would be fine. He passed a sign and calculated the distances. *Great!* he thought. *Already halfway there.* He picked up the empty thermos and shook it. *Oh my God. Only halfway.*

Fighting sleep, he carried on. Soon, his head dipped. The steering wheel jarred him awake. He opened all the windows and blasted the Bon Jovi CD Carrie had left in the player.

Muddling through the words, he joined the band. As he tried to keep up, he wondered, "What does she see in this guy?" Then he turned the same question on himself. His tired mind couldn't answer. Instead, he asked the boys in the band a sarcastic, "What do you drive?" The platinum rock stars responded with another song that always stirred his wife's heart. Adam gave up his singing career and made a mental note to buy her their next CD as soon as it came out. In the meantime, he settled for listening to some of her favorite songs.

Each one took him a little bit closer to Carrie. His eyes cooperated until the end of the last track. The second time around wasn't as helpful. He drifted and bobbed his way to the nearest rest stop. He parked in the shade and reclined his seat. Just thirty minutes, he promised himself.

An hour later, he woke up sweating. The heat had him glued to the soft leather. He opened the door and pealed himself from the car, stretching away the stiffness. With a yawn, he grabbed a dry shirt from the trunk before proceeding to the facilities for a quick clean up. Twelve minutes later he left the building eating a hot dog and admiring the pink beaded bracelet he had bought for Carrie. Refreshed and somewhat rested, he felt a little better about everything. Maybe they could work it all out.

In an instant, his world fell apart again. He dropped his dog and ran toward the pitiful white clunker that was now parked in his spot in the shade. There was no sign of the sleek black Mustang that had brought him this far. He stood in front of the sad little car, dumbfounded. Instinctively, he felt his pockets for his keys. All that jingled was loose change.

The clunker's frightened teenagers ducked with their cell phones as the lunatic with the pink bracelet, and mustard on his shirt, ranted. The target of the tirade shifted back and forth from the unknown thieves to the idiot who had left his keys sticking out of the trunk. Exhausted, he slumped on the curb and buried his face in his hands.

"Gone," he said.

He looked up when he saw them coming. Two stern officers walked toward him. Dark glasses covered their eyes. The sight of the approaching policemen gave life to the images hidden in his nightmares. He could feel the contempt radiating from the weapons clinging to their hips. His strength turned on him.

Fear banished logic. Carrie must already know. Revenge was here for him. It seemed the "someday" he had been avoiding had finally found him.

"I'm sorry… I am so sorry," Adam said holding out his wrists to be cuffed.

"You been drinkin' sir?" The officer asked.

"No, I-I…No."

"Hear you been causin' a ruckus. These kids say you lost your car."

Adam climbed to his feet. The six-foot-four inch, two-hundred-thirty-pound jock slipped the lovely pink bracelet into his pocket. He dried his face in his shirt as his stomach rudely reminded him of the half-eaten hot dog he had attempted earlier. Reality returned. Guilt had been playing tricks on him. He wasn't a murderer today. He was a normal lunatic whose car had been stolen.

Four hours later, he was driving a midgrade rental car up the interstate. With the confidence of a virgin, the car followed his lead. He eased it through gears it didn't know it had. The engine roared. It wanted to perform for him.

The usual racing fantasies tried to lure him. His mind wouldn't go. It was stuck in the distant past. The memories that slept with him on so many nights were awake now. This time, the alarm clock couldn't save him.

#

Sometimes, the twenty-year-old memory of their last night with Oliver allowed itself to-sneak in. The long ride home, however, pulled

Adam's thoughts back through that night as if he was living it all over again. There had been an awful argument with Carrie, a raunchy party for Oliver, and a coward (himself) sneaking out the back door when the love of his life came looking for him. Adam's shame in such things could have faded over the years, had the night ended there.

When he found Carrie on the ground wearing nothing but a bloodstained shirt that wasn't even hers, he had seen the pure heartache in her young eyes. Her own clothes were scattered. Her body was so cold. She was mumbling incoherently. He'd held her in his arms. His doll was broken.

He had gathered her clothes and carried her away. The pain both led, and followed. Every step had been too late. If he hadn't fought with her, she would have been home in bed.

She cried when he tried to remove the bloody shirt. "No! Oliver, please. No more."

Her cry struck him like lightning. The name she spoke rocked him to his core. He hadn't let himself believe this storm would come.

He should've been surprised when she said his best friend's name, because deep down he'd already known—Oliver had a dark side.

"Baby, I'm so sorry," he said. "Don't worry. I'll take care of you. The hospital is only a few minutes away."

"No, no! Please, take me home."

"But Carrie, he…"

"He couldn't help it," she said. "It was my fault."

"How can you say that?"

"I shouldn't have led him on. He's leaving in the morning. He's scared."

"He's drunk off his ass and you gave him a ride. That doesn't give him the right…"

"Adam, please. Please! Take me home."

Carrie hugged her knees and rocked. "I'm not crazy. I am not my mother," she said.

"What are you talking about?" he asked.

Carrie mumbled the very words Adam had shouted at her earlier, "Too old to play with dolls," she said. "Too old."

Adam hadn't meant to hurt her like that. When he had come to tell her that he was going to go to the party with Oliver, she had been lying on her frilly pink bed, clutching some doll. He had been embarrassed for her.

As she rocked, half-naked in the back of his car, Adam tried to apologize. But she shut down. She wasn't mumbling anymore. Only rocking.

"Damn it, Oliver," he said to no one.

If he hadn't gone to the party, she never would have been there. He vowed to never let her down again.

Carrie didn't want to go to the hospital. He imagined her trauma being dragged out for months. Doctors and lawyers would poke her and her whole life apart. He could at least protect her from that. His rage boiled with Carrie's every whimper. He would handle this himself.

He was going to drive Carrie home, but as soon as he got her settled into the car, she fell asleep in the backseat. Adam crammed the pile of telltale clothing under the seat and assumed his position at the wheel. Instead of taking Carrie home, he drove around, looking for Oliver. Adam was looking for a criminal, not his best friend. The search felt misguided. He stopped the car and watching Carrie sleep, tried to settle his thoughts. He wanted to think that the Oliver he knew would at least be feeling guilty.

Guilty. He had a hunch where Oliver might go if he was feeling guilty. Sassy talked about a place on the mountain. Their profound hangout. Jerry Rock, she called it. He got back in the car and headed toward the overlook at Chippi's Park.

He drove a little faster. When he pulled into the parking lot at Chippi's Park, he was only partially surprised to see Oliver's car was actually there. It was still running. Adam kissed Carrie's hand and locked the car doors. Then he approached Jerry Rock like it was an enemy encampment.

The sight of Oliver, there on his knees, sickened him. Adam stepped closer. He needed to hear a confession. Oliver was silent.

"Praying for forgiveness?" Adam asked.

Oliver didn't look up. He stayed on his knees with his hands folded. Adam slapped him in the back of the head to get his attention. Oliver's head dropped further. The next whack was angrier.

"Talk to me you bastard! How could you do this?"

Still, he got no response. Adam pulled Oliver up by his ear.

"What's the matter? You only fight girls now, friend?"

Nothing. Adam wrapped his arm around Oliver's neck, putting him in a choke hold. Not even a squirm. Adam spun him around. Oliver's head hung. Adam lifted his chin, forcing him to look him in the face.

"I ought to toss you over this edge," he had said, and meant it.

An older Adam forced his thoughts back to the rental he was driving. Stupid car. It was like driving a mule compared to the horsepower he was used to.

CHAPTER 42 – FORGOTTEN, BUT NOT GONE

The brass plaque by the door almost looked like an award. If Adam didn't know better, he would have been impressed. A black, oak leaf border framed the words. A rich, dark background held the engraved letters as if they made sense together. The display was distinguished, classy and completely naïve. The loving memory of Oliver Lingle was flawed.

"Oli's House." The stains Oliver had left on his sister's life appeared to be well-treated. Adam rubbed his finger across the line, "My brother, my protector, my friend." He banged on the door. The girl that opened it looked about seventeen. Long strands of purple hair hung over her eyes, barely covering the bruises. She stood with her hand gripped on the doorknob.

"Hi," Adam said. "Sorry it's so late."

"You the night watch?"

"I'm looking for Carrie Jenkins." Adam tried not to stare at the bruises as he spoke.

"Never heard of her. You a cop?"

"No. I just need to see my wife."

"No wives here."

"Of course she's here. She came to see…"

"You callin' me a liar?" The girl moved her hair back over the marks on her face.

"Okay, then… Sassy… Mrs. Martin. Please tell her I'm here."

"She ain't."

"Sassy's not here either?" He looked at his watch. "It's almost midnight."

"Dude. It's like one o'clock."

"Where's David? Who's in charge here?"

"Me. The lady they sent to stay with us split."

"Nobody's here?"

"That's me. Nobody." She tilted her head up just enough to add extra attitude to her words.

"Damn. Did they say when they'd be back? Leave a number? Anything?"

"Let it go already. They got enough trouble."

"Trouble?"

#

The bruises Oliver had left on Carrie weren't on her face. Adam had seen them when he stood her in the shower. She had been so numb by then, she hadn't resisted when he washed her. Her body accepted his soapy hands as he scrubbed Oliver from her flesh. He held her in the water as the suds went down the drain. She flopped like a rag doll when he dressed her in his clothes.

When she woke up in his bed, she was a little disoriented. Considering the trauma, and the sleeping pills he had given her, he figured some confusion was normal. She asked how she had gotten to his house. He simply said he thought she'd feel safer. When she noticed she was wearing his sweatshirt and pants, all he could say was she had been cold.

#

Adam's rental car moved faster. The lake was behind him. The girl with purple hair had finally told him Sassy was at the Wayne Valley Hospital. As he drove there, he could see the mountain. In the distance, it didn't look so high. He stuffed his conflicted feelings for Oliver. He hadn't wanted to care back then, and he certainly didn't want to care now.

#

When David had come over to break the news of Oliver's accident, Adam had acted surprised. But as he listened to the story David told, genuine shock finally weakened him. His tears had mourned the loss, for Carrie, for Sassy, and for himself. He hadn't cried for the stranger at the bottom of the ravine. He cried for the friend the stranger had stolen. He was stunned by his own reaction.

At first, he supposed Carrie's grief was similar. She wept in his arms as they consoled each other. David said Sassy was finally asleep and asked them to wait to come over. After he left, Carrie made tea and rubbed Adam's back. She spoke lovingly of the younger Oliver that climbed trees and dropped water balloons. Adam couldn't listen any longer.

"Carrie, it's okay. You're allowed to be angry."

"I don't want to be angry. Sassy's going to need us."

"Don't you want to talk about last night?"

"I'm sorry, Adam. I had a headache and I couldn't sleep. I took one of my father's sleeping pills. You must hate me for asking you not to go to that party with Oliver."

"What are you talking about? Are you feeling okay?"

"Don't worry. I'm going to take care of you, now. You and Sassy."

Carrie's voice had sounded more lost and insecure than usual.

#

The hospital was bigger than he remembered. Adam clutched the cheap chocolate rose he had bought for Sassy in the mini-mart up the road. Red foil covered the flower. A hard wire poked through the plastic stem, scratching his hand. The gesture he gripped felt as hollow as the chocolate.

She might know, he thought. It didn't matter right now. He imagined his wife's face, soaked with fresh tears. He stepped into the elevator and pushed the button for the third floor.

When the doors opened, he could see David in the lobby down the hall. He was sitting with a younger man. It looked like they were arguing. The man looked familiar, but he couldn't place him.

Carrie wasn't there, so he slipped past them. He counted with the numbered rooms until he got to 128. The name on the door felt wrong: Martin, Elizabeth. The girl he was looking for was Sassy Lingle.

He tiptoed to the bed. The sleeping woman stirred. He stood there motionless, afraid to wake her. He waited. When she was still again, Adam turned for the door. As he moved, she grabbed his wrist.

"Pig," she barely said.

"Hey, you. Are you okay?"

She squeezed his hand. The effort was comforting. He set the rose on top of her bedpan. A slight air of laughter lifted the room. Sassy reached for her note pad.

"Her Dad's," she wrote. "Go to her."

Adam kissed the tip of her pen. "I'll be back," he promised.

#

Memories plagued Adam as he continued making his way back to Carrie.

"What are we going to tell Sassy?" he had spoken to Carrie's back as she opened the teapot and hung teabags over the side.

Oliver had been gone for less than twenty-four hours. Mixed thoughts had plagued his mind. The dominant idea hovered around the guilty hope that Carrie would also want to keep the ugly secret. The kettle whistled. She poured steaming water into the delicate china pot.

"Flowers," she had told him.

He'd been so surprised. She wanted to send flowers. Their world was falling apart, and she wanted to call the florist.

His angry attempt to storm out of the room failed as he tripped over his shoelaces, into the table. The hot teapot fell to the floor and smashed, scalding Carrie's bare feet. She covered her mouth to hide her scream.

An image of her screaming at the mercy of his best friend flashed through his mind. He eased her feet into a bowl of ice water, silently vowing to never make her talk about that night. But for days, every time he looked at her he had wondered if she even knew.

#

After leaving Sassy, Adam chose to go down the back stairs to avoid David. He skipped every other step, hurrying to the parking lot. He clicked the rental car's radio on as he pulled out of the lot. Fumbling for song, he wondered who was listening to Carrie's Bon Jovi CD. The hip hop music the local station was playing did little to ease his nerves.

By the time he walked up to the door of Carrie's old house, he felt like he had a rock in his stomach. He reached for the glowing doorbell, then stopped when he noticed that the door was open a crack. He pushed it open further and went inside. He froze as the first step creaked, then eased his way up to Carrie's room. He kicked off his shoes and crawled into her bed. With one hug, he discovered his soft, snuggly wife was a bunch of lumpy pillows.

The open door now panicked him. She used to do that when she snuck out so she wouldn't wake her father. Where could she have gone? He crossed the street and searched Sassy's backyard. Guilt had taken her there before.

The last time Carrie had wandered out in the middle of the night, it was shortly after Oliver's death. Her father was still out of town, so Adam had been staying with her. When he went into her room to check on her, she wasn't there.

He found her asleep on the grass beside the memorial of flowers that were left underneath the tree house in Oliver's honor. Her hands were muddy. When he lifted her to carry her home, he saw that the ground underneath her had been freshly dug.

"Wow, Carrie. Planting flowers in the middle of the night? You can't be doing this," he had said. She didn't wake, but he noticed some stiff blonde hair sticking up through the dirt. He set her in clean grass. "What have you done here?"

"She shouldn't have reproduced," Carrie said through sleep.

He pulled the hair. The head that came out of the earth had been filled with maraschino cherries and walnuts. He shoved it into his pocket, took Carrie home and put her back in bed. He locked the doors, grabbed a trash bag and crept back into the Lingles' yard. The thirty some heads he dug up all had the same filling. He knotted the bag of heads and did his best to cover the little patch of broken ground. He locked the bag in the trunk of his car.

Carrie didn't wake up until the next morning. He had waited for her to comment on the dirty clothes she had slept in, or the dirty sheets. But like the morning after the rape, she had acted like nothing happened. Like the morning after the rape, neither of them spoke of it.

He finally realized she didn't remember any of it. It was like she couldn't handle knowing. The idea of helping her recall what had happened seemed cruel. He wished he could forget himself.

#

All these years later, he wished a lot more. This time she wasn't asleep under the tree house. Adam stared into the empty darkness, cursing it for keeping his wife.

"Carrie!" he called. "Are you out there?"

He stood very still and listened. Through the silence, he could hear her crying in the distance. As he ran through the woods, following the sound of her voice, guilt had yet to release its first prisoner.

Unprotected by sleep, fragments of twenty years' worth of bad dreams played through Adam's mind. Carrie was in the back of a small Air Force plane. The pilot had a crewcut and was wearing a football uniform. Storm clouds filled the cockpit. Despite Carrie's pleas, the pilot refused to land. The plane headed straight toward a mountain. Adam's grandfather strapped Carrie into a parachute. The door opened and sucked her out. As she fell, the parachute wouldn't open. Oliver was on the ground laughing, holding baby Daniel.

CHAPTER 43 – A MAN OF HIS WORD

Earlier, David had pampered Sassy with a lavender sponge bath. He wrapped her in her favorite afghan from home and painted her fingernails with deep red polish. Soft rock music played through a small portable stereo. Her eyes sparkled through swollen pockets of bruised flesh as she sucked her dinner through a straw. When he told her she was the most beautiful woman he had ever laid eyes on, he absolutely meant it. For years, he had tried to protect her from pain. He wasn't about to let a squirrel win.

At least he'd gotten rid of Jack for now. David stretched out on the hard sofa in the waiting room down the hall from her hospital room. He lay awake listening to two nurses gossiping about Dr. Wendell and Karen from X-ray, whoever they were. He heard a mop swishing about the lobby, but his feet were already up, so he didn't bother to open his eyes. A fly landed on his nose. He swatted it away, again and again.

Yesterday's newspaper was on the table, the headline shamelessly mocking him. He didn't have to read it again. He knew the whole story, and he'd never be able to change the fact that Joseph knew it too.

When David had called him from jail that night, he knew his friend, Joseph, was good for more than a ride home. His visit had certainly softened the blow when David told Sassy he had been arrested. Joseph backed his lame story when he said he'd fought with a guy who cut him off in traffic. He told her not to worry, and coming from him, she couldn't debate.

Joseph had bought him time. That was all David had wanted.

Despite his efforts to ignore the article, David couldn't sleep. He reached for the newspaper.

"Body of Sixty-Seven-Year Old Man Found Locked in Closet," he read. David sat up and confirmed the important details in the article: *Anonymous Tip, Jack Martin, Dead, No Leads.*

David pealed the front page away from the rest of the paper. He folded it twice, then rolled it. He sat very still, listening for the insect's faint buzz. With one swift whack, the pest was eliminated. He brushed the fly into the trash and dropped the newspaper on top of it.

Again, he tried to sleep. This time his conscience buzzed. He wanted to hate himself for losing control with Jack, but he didn't.

#

As he tossed and turned on the hospital sofa, David's closed eyes weren't watching dreams. He saw memories of Joseph, the boy who had been abused by an asshole. And Jack, the scumbag he never should have let into Joseph's life. David opened his eyes, trying to avoid the image of Jack's hands around Joseph's throat. But it was still there, and it made him want to kill the bastard all over again.

Joseph shouldn't have been there, David thought. *I told him to stay away.* That didn't matter. Joseph was there because of him. Again. This time he had seen David kill.

#

For love is strong as death; Jealousy is cruel as the grave.

David felt like he understood now. Oliver had written part of a Bible verse on the back of a picture of himself with Sassy, Carrie, and Adam. In his own twisted way, the guy had loved all three of them.

The picture had been locked in the drawer of Oliver's nightstand. David didn't regret burning Oliver's creepy little treasure chest. He never wanted to see any of it again. He didn't want to know anymore. Oliver's reasons for keeping some weird mermaid doll, Sassy's green scarf, and a bunch of hair ribbons wouldn't get to matter to Sassy. She'd never have to see anything that was in that box, not even the letter that had been scribbled on pink stationery.

David had spent countless hours trying to read that letter, but could only make out the words, "Dear Mom."

It was all a pile of ashes now, along with the file Joseph had given him.

David thought about Joseph's file. It didn't prove Adam killed Oliver, but it supported the suspicions he'd carried for the past twenty years.

Officers Kane and O'Brian hadn't agreed with each other that Oliver's death was an accident. According to Joseph, O'Brian had talked to five different people who claimed to have seen Oliver leave the party with Carrie. But, in the report Kane had filed, there was no mention of Adam and Carrie being at the party at all.

O'Brian had also told Joseph, that Kane questioned Adam, who explained he and Carrie had been to dinner with Oliver and the Lingle family earlier in the evening, but he had taken Carrie home from there. Oliver's own mother had confirmed the story, and Kane insisted it was a dead end. Carrie had never been questioned.

Joseph's file further noted that young Charles Kane had played football for Adam's grandfather at Wayne Valley High School. He'd even attached a newspaper article highlighting a full scholarship upstate.

In the article, Kane was quoted as saying, "Coach Jenkins was like a father to me."

David found some comfort in knowing he wasn't the only one covering for Adam. Still, there was a math problem that continued to bother him. He took out a pen and scribbled the numbers running through his mind, the date that Sassy had been quietly celebrating for the past nineteen years. Again, he did the calculations, confirming the timing. *Roughly nine months after Oliver died.* Next to the date, he wrote, "Happy Birthday, Daniel Jenkins."

#

David knew what rage felt like, wild rage that could take a person outside of himself and make him watch as his self-control exploded into mayhem. It was a feeling he'd craved as a small boy, when behaving meant absorbing Jack's anger. When he got older, control had developed into the strength he needed to avoid becoming the monster he'd wanted to destroy. He feared losing it.

Then he'd walked in on Jack as he was attacking Joseph, and the rage came. It wasn't power, or weakness. It was David, saving Joseph. The rage was excessive and ugly and final. It was done.

Jack was a dead monster. Maybe Oliver was, too.

CHAPTER 44 – CLEARING THE CLOUDS AWAY

David rolled over, unconsciously aiming to wrap his arm around his wife. Instead, he fell off the couch, banging his head on the table. Shifts were changing. Despite the never-changing fluorescent lighting, he deduced it must be morning. Sassy was probably already awake, waiting to drink her breakfast. He didn't want to miss it. He slipped into his shoes and tucked in his shirt. She'd never get her strength back if she didn't eat. Maybe today the nurse would let her have chocolate.

He was still deciding which nurse to ask, the one with the blue eye shadow or the short one with bad breath, when he stepped into the hall. Suddenly protein shakes didn't matter. There was a flurry in front of Sassy's room. Nurses were scrambling. He could only make out a few frantic words. "NO PULSE," and "STAT," hung in the air. David ran to her room. Someone tried to keep him out, but he wouldn't have it. He pushed past to be by her side. Her hand was like ice. She wouldn't open her eyes. Why wouldn't she open her eyes?!

A man in a white coat entered with some kind of machine. Her doctor followed. Or did he lead? The scene was a jumble of panic. David resisted when two security guards attempted to remove him from the room. A nurse took his hand and eased him into the hall. Her calming touch suggested a better way. The door closed behind them. She stayed with him as a small army of strangers performed unspeakable acts on his wife. The nurse held a stiff hand up to the guards. They stepped back but remained in view as he paced through eternal minutes.

"What's happening?!" he demanded. "What are they doing to her?!"

"It's called a defibrillator. They're trying to restart her heart."

"Her heart? She was in a car accident. The doctor said she would be fine! There's nothing wrong with her heart. You're wrong. There's nothing wrong with her heart! She's going to be fine!"

"Mr. Martin, they know what they're doing. These people have done this treatment many, many times. They're going to do everything they can to…"

A second nurse came out of the room. She avoided David's eyes. He didn't wait for permission. He ripped the door open. Nobody tried to stop him. They didn't have to. The panic was over. Sassy's doctor sent everyone else from the room.

"I'm very sorry, Mr. Martin," the Dr. began. "We did all we could. Her heart…"

David didn't hear the rest. He pulled a chair beside her bed and took her hand between both of his and rubbed, trying to bring back the warmth.

"Mr. Martin, I'm sorry. Your wife has passed."

David didn't look up. There was nobody else in the world to him at this moment. He reached into her bag and pulled out her favorite lip gloss. He dabbed a hint of the sweet vanilla to her still lips and kissed her soft mouth good bye. Then, without a word, he left.

Joseph was outside the door in tears. The two men embraced, then parted with nothing to say. Joseph walked with David to the parking lot. He wouldn't accept a ride or company. They were about to go their separate ways when they saw Adam and Carrie walking toward them. Joseph put a hand on David's shoulder.

"Good morning, David. How's she feeling today?" Carrie asked.

David stopped to ponder the question. There was no answer. "It doesn't make sense," he said. "They said she was going to be okay." He picked up a rock and threw it at the trees. "Hey, squirrel!" he shouted, and the energy of his anger grew. "You in there? Show yourself, you little bastard! I want my wife back, dammit! How is this fair? You get to live, and she doesn't? What the hell? There's nothing wrong with her heart! She can't be dead. It doesn't make sense."

#

Carrie didn't know where to put herself. She looked around for Sassy. David was yelling about something. She couldn't make out what he was saying. His voice was so angry. A hazy vision of Oliver floated through the air. A piercing noise rang through her ears.

The image persisted. The rest of the nightmare introduced itself with memories of Oliver. He was on his knees. She saw Adam pulling him up by his ear. She saw herself moving closer. The guys struggled.

Adam was falling.

He caught a branch.

She remembered wanting Oliver to help. Instead, Oliver's foot moved toward Adam's desperate fingers.

She reached out… and pushed with all of her might.

There had been screams, terrible screams. It was so far down. Oliver kept falling. Her hands could still feel his bare shoulder.

After twenty years of torture, the villain was revealed. She digested the vile truth like poison. It had been her all along. She killed Oliver. Fresh delusion exploited her guilt.

The Stranger. The voice. She could feel his spirit leave her. She let him out. She shouldn't have let him out. The man was finally gone, but now Sassy was gone too. Carrie crumbled. She couldn't control him anymore. How could she let this happen? Her freedom wasn't worth losing Sassy. Hysteria finally had its way with her.

"It was me!" she yelled. "I killed Oliver. He's gone now. But he took Sassy."

Sobbing uncontrollably, she shrunk to the ground with her confession. David and Joseph stood back in horror as their speculations twisted into unthinkable truth. Adam picked Carrie up and rocked her. She rested her head on his chest. He was humming the theme song to Sesame Street as he carried her into the hospital.

CHAPTER 45 – CELEBRATE THE LIFE

Sassy's funeral was quite appropriately untraditional. David knew how much she had hated saying good bye to her mother in that stuffy room, with eerie organ music and red velvet chairs. "Why not celebrate the life?" she had asked. He knew she would have liked the arrangements he made. A picnic with hot dogs and cheeseburgers was one of her favorite ways to celebrate.

Friends and family reminisced about the roles she had in their lives in the open beauty of Chippi's Park. It was a sunny day full of music, laughter and many tears. Their pastor read a letter she had filed with her will.

My Dear Friends,

Please rejoice with me for I have made it! I have been blessed with a fabulous life. Though it seems like it could never be long enough, I am thankful for the time I've had and for the people I've shared it with.

My mother was a strong and courageous woman. She taught me a lot, and she told me to follow my dreams. She lived a life I didn't always agree with, but she was proud, honest, and very real.

With the help of my incredible husband, David, I was able to see my dreams come true. He taught me the beauty of acceptance as we shared our mission. Even though some times were hard, he loved and supported me through it all. I can't imagine having a better life.

Through my brother, I learned the treasure of time. Our childhood together held many laughs and many lessons. The laughs made the lessons worth learning. In losing Oliver, part of me was lost. I realize though, the loss was yet another lesson. Too much of his short time on this earth was wasted with anger.

When he was killed, his death made me face the toughest challenge I've ever known. I had to forgive something I didn't understand. I had to let go of the anger, to get through the pain, for both of us. That precious tool, forgiveness, has been the root of my strength for years.

We've tried to honor Oliver's memory through Oli's House. With the money he left, and David's financial wizardry, we've been able to spread his care. I have found that giving care, and receiving care, both nourish the ground faith stands on. It is my greatest wish the care of Oli's House will continue, at David's discretion, for many years to come.

As I say good bye, I thank you, my friends. And I ask you to share these lessons: Embrace the world you are in. Laugh whenever you can laugh. Cry when you need to cry. Don't waste too much time on anger or regret. Love, learn, grow and care. Always, always be real.

God bless you all!
Sassy

The letter was rolled into a neat little scroll and handed back to

David. He adjusted the tie clip Sassy had given him for their tenth anniversary. It was simple and elegant with a small diamond, the stone

from the earring he had worn at their wedding. Inscribed on the back were

the words, "You are my stud, my love. Forever."

The pastor said a short prayer. David stood up and thanked

everyone for coming. Then he lifted the urn and kissed it. He raised his

head and moved onto Jerry Rock. Stretching his arm out, he sprinkled

Sassy's ashes over the ravine. As much as David wanted to follow, he

wouldn't dishonor her memory.

The crowd eventually thinned. Beth and Daniel went off to play

volleyball with Joseph and his family, leaving Adam alone. David walked

over and sat beside him. He set Sassy's letter in front of him on the table.

The tiny golden cross Oliver had given her was wrapped around it.

"Sassy would want Carrie to have this," David said.

"I'll make sure she gets it." Adam sipped his soda. "Your wife was

a special lady."

"She seemed so strong, so healthy," David said. "Her heart. It's

hardest to believe her heart failed her."

David adjusted his tie clip again. Maybe her heart hadn't failed

her. Maybe it saved her. She never had to learn the truth about Oliver. She

never had to see the effects his actions had on her best friend.

"How's Carrie doing?" he asked.

"Last night she was hunched over in a chair in the corner. She kept rambling about Oliver. I tried to put my arms around her and she freaked. They had to sedate her."

"All these years, she didn't know…she couldn't remember?"

"She buried everything. Her mind even created a fantasy that we were together so she could justify her pregnancy with Daniel. She needed it to be true. I let her believe it. I thought I was protecting her. I should have seen what it was doing to her."

"What did you tell the kids?"

"The truth. I finally told them the truth."

Daniel ran over to retrieve a stray ball. His shirttails were flapping, and his knees were dirty. Adam tossed the ball to him. Daniel head-butted it back. The ball went back and forth from father to son until Beth hollered for her brother to get back in the game. Adam handed it to him. Daniel started to go, then turned back.

"Thanks, Coach… Thanks, Dad."

"Good game, Son."

CHAPTER 46 – REALLY

Carrie sat, strapped in a chair, being spoon fed by an overworked nurse. Her beaten mind didn't need Oliver to torture her anymore.

My best friend died because of me. I should have stopped Oliver, she thought. The silent ramblings continued. *I did stop him. It was an accident. He would have killed Adam, right? I had to do something. Oliver was Adam's best friend.* She twisted in the chair.

He wouldn't have hurt him. But he hurt me. Maybe I deserved it. He only loved me. But how could he do that? It didn't feel like love at all.

Carrie crossed her legs. *It was humiliating and painful. He was right. I am a kook.* Applesauce glided down her throat. *The fight was because of me. Adam never fought with Oliver. They were best friends… Best friends… Sassy is dead… Dead like my mother.*

She locked her lips shut. *No more food. Sassy can't eat anything. I shouldn't either.* The nurse became agitated. She tried to push another spoonful of applesauce into her mouth. After several attempts, she gave up.

"She'll have to be fed through a needle," the nurse called out. "You're making this harder on everybody," she said to Carrie. "You need to cooperate. You want to go home, don't you?"

"Home," she said. The word felt foreign.

"That's right, honey. This place is only temporary. You'll go home. First, you have some work to do. But that's why we're here. We want to help you."

Carrie gazed past her through the lunchroom window. In the distance, she could see the top of Chippi's Mountain. The murder scene still looked lush and beautiful. A kite lifted above the trees. Her mouth opened. The applesauce was lukewarm and sour, with a hint of cinnamon.

As she ate, her mind wandered to Sassy's old room. There were dozens of shoes, a lavender boa, a poster of a giant cheeseburger. She could imagine every detail but couldn't hear the music. Sassy always had music.

The nurse released the straps on her wrists and put the spoon in her hand. She sat up a little straighter and finished her breakfast. She pulled at the belt holding her to the chair.

"No, no. We can't have you getting lost on us again," the nurse said.

She vaguely remembered crouching in a closet in another patient's room. *I should have been at Sassy's memorial service.*

Talk of electric shock therapy had terrified her. Adam wasn't with her. She had to hide. They found her. The doctor said she didn't have to have the treatment. Then they gave her something to make her sleep.

She woke up the next morning and Adam was by her side. He had something in his hand. He tried to give it to her. She could see it. She knew what it was, but she couldn't take it. It didn't belong to her. He placed it on the night stand.

After she ate, the nurse put her back in the room with the bed. "Dr. Charles wants to talk to you this afternoon. Remember, he can't help if you won't talk to him," she said as she left.

"No doctor could change what happened," Carrie said to the door as it closed. And with that thought, her mind entertained a chorus of words that had been neglected for years. A new voice begged to be heard. One word touched her heart like never before.

"Forgive."

"Who?" she asked herself. "Sassy is gone. I can't even tell her I'm sorry."

She sat in her corner of the seventh-floor psychiatric unit of the Wayne Valley Medical Center. Adam was out there, somewhere on the outside of her cage. Daniel and Beth were out there too.

How they must hate me, she thought.

She imagined David, alone at the lake house. Time disappeared.

The nurse came back to take her to lunch. Carrie needed to walk on her own. With a promise of good behavior, she was allowed the small but giant dignity of being released from the straps. The lunchroom felt different this time.

Two young girls pretended to eat, pushing food around their plates. Their hair was broken and brittle, their cheeks sunken, their eyes vacant. Carrie could see their veins through the skin on their arms.

Another patient spoke to his meatloaf. He was sitting by himself. She walked toward his table, but he barked at her. Literally barked.

She sat with a gentleman who was wearing a baseball cap and hooded sweatshirt. He reminded her of Adam. Home. She wanted to go home.

Another man joined them. He didn't speak at all. He ate quietly. She noticed his utensils were plastic. Even so, he didn't have a knife. He reached for a spoonful of butter and his shirt sleeves inched toward his elbows. She had to excuse herself from the table when she noticed the bandages on his wrists.

She returned to her room alone. The colorless walls that held her away from her family gave her new peace. The pictures Adam had hung didn't look so scary. The smiling faces of their children again gave her purpose. "Daniel and Beth, my sweet babies," she said aloud. She reached out to touch their images and the scroll Adam had left on her nightstand fell to the floor. She picked it up with unsteady fingers. The golden cross took her back to another time.

"Help me find something for Sassy," Oliver had said.

"Are you sure you have to go?" Carrie asked.

"Are you going to miss me?"

"Of course I am. We all are."

Back in the present, she slid the necklace off of the scroll. Sassy's letter rested curled on her lap. She unraveled it and read, repeating the last paragraph out loud.

"Embrace the world you are in. Laugh whenever you can laugh. Cry when you need to cry. Don't waste too much time on anger or regret. Love, learn, grow and care. Always, always be real."

"And forgive," Carrie added.

When she saw Dr. Charles that afternoon, she didn't feel like he was her enemy anymore. They talked for an hour. He asked if she'd talk to him again. She promised she would.

Beth and Daniel came later that week. They stayed for about ten minutes. Beth clung to her brother like she'd drift away without him. The barking man stared at her. Carrie told them she had a headache and asked them to leave. Then she hid in her closet for an hour. This time Adam found her.

"Honey, what happened?"

"They can't be here," she cried. "Please don't make them come again."

"Carrie, I didn't make them come. They wanted to see you. They want their mother back."

"They do?"

"Of course they do."

"Adam, I'm so sorry."

"We love you. No more hiding, okay?"

"Thank you," she said. She didn't know what else to say.

He held her in his arms and told her about his conversations with their children and with David. They talked about spending summers at her dad's and taking the kids out on the lake. She said she'd like to take some classes. He thought it was a good idea and said Daniel and Beth had a little surprise for her at home. Then he had to leave. She walked with him to the nurse's station.

He squeezed her hand as he waited for the guard to unlock the big double door. She cringed when it banged shut behind him. Through a six-inch square window, she watched him walk away. She wanted him to look back one more time. She knocked on the window. He didn't hear.

"Adam!" she yelled. "I love you!"

He didn't look back. He got on the elevator.

"It's hard for him to leave here alone," the guard said. "Hold on to that feeling. The love. This place is meant to be temporary. Soon you'll leave here together."

That night she gathered her belongings and put them in her pillow case. She made the bed and slept on the floor, where it felt less permanent. Then she woke up in the morning and got ready for the day. She continued the pattern for the rest of her stay until finally she was strong enough to be released.

Before returning home, they celebrated with her father and Jane at their wedding. It had been postponed long enough.

Their last stop in Wayne Valley was the cemetery. She had yet to pay respects to Mrs. Lingle. Adam and the kids agreed to wait in the car while Carrie placed fresh flowers on her grave.

As she pulled a tattered handkerchief from her purse, a picture of her mother drifted out with a breeze. She watched it float, as if in slow motion, before catching it in the air. Then she flipped it over and reached for a pen as an old friend reclaimed its place in her heart.

Accept What Is

We cannot forget what we cannot forgive,
We cannot love if we are afraid to live.
Illusions will find the truths we ignore,
Hearts cannot rest if they always need more.

CHAPTER 47 – TEN YEARS LATER

Beth stood in front of the mirror biting the nail on her little finger. She closed her eyes and imagined she was on the stage. Everyone knew their lines. All costumes fit. The scenery couldn't be more perfect. The orchestra was in the pit. When the curtain came up, she would be ready.

The chewed nail broke loose and fell to the floor. She gasped like she had lost the whole finger. Not today. The music had already started. She had to get out there. This would be the role of her life.

"Mom!" she shrieked.

"What's wrong?" Carrie asked as she hurried to her daughter's side.

"It's ruined. The whole day is ruined," Beth said, holding up a stubby pinky finger.

"Don't be silly. He's not marrying you for your manicure."

"Mother, you don't understand."

"You're right. I'll send everyone home."

"Real funny. I just want everything to be perfect."

Carrie turned her away from the mirror. "Take a minute to look past today. Imagine yourself coming home from your honeymoon and starting a real life together. You and Jason share hopes and dreams. Can you work together to find those dreams?"

"Mom, he is my dream."

"When you both come home from a stressful day, will you be able to comfort each other? When your plans don't go as expected, can you make new plans together?"

"Remember the time my voice cracked on opening night? I heard Jason in the audience cheering. It kept me from running off the stage."

"Is he the same man you want next to you beaming with pride the first time you hold your newborn baby? Is he also the man who will put up with you and take care of you through nine months of pregnancy?"

Beth glowed.

"Do you want to nurse him when he's sick? Can you work with him, laugh and cry with him? Beth, do you love him?"

"Everything is a little bit better when we're together."

"Honey, that is what perfect is. Now relax and enjoy your special day."

Carrie handed Beth her bouquet and adjusted her veil. Then she stood back and snapped yet another picture. Adam came in and put an arm around Beth. Together they waited for one more click. Carrie winked at them and left to find her escort.

#

Daniel stood at the back of the church in his tuxedo. Carrie's two young grandsons fidgeted, preschool versions of their father. Daniel straightened their little bow ties and stood his boys in line with Abby. He reminded them to keep their fingers out of their noses and not to pull on Mommy's gown. Carrie stuck her arm out. "Don't fuss. They'll be fine," she said.

Daniel warned them with one last stern look, then took his mother's arm and walked her to her seat in the front row. He gave her an extra hug, and then moved to his position among the groomsmen. Her dad handed her a pack of tissues as her two little gentlemen started their march up the aisle, beginning the procession.

So long ago she had feared this moment. Years of therapy helped her reach a point where she could enjoy the natural therapy life brings. Her last baby was moving on. Now that the time was here, she rejoiced. Like Daniel was when he left, Beth was ready. Her children weren't leaving her. She would always have them. As her best friend once told her, she didn't have to let go. She had to adjust her grip.

Later, as she arranged the wedding photos into her ever-growing collection of albums, she imagined the new camera she had given Beth as a shower gift would help continue the tradition. She sat with her new memories, pleased she had given the same gift to Abby.

A picture of her two grandsons hanging upside down on the monkey bars stood among her favorites on the mantle.

With their children settling comfortably into lives of their own, Carrie and Adam were set on a path of rediscovery. He joined her for therapy once a month. Her days of hiding were over. Together they faced their lives in open honesty.

With David's help, the surprise she had been dreaming of could finally happen. When Adam came home to their recently emptied nest, she was waiting for him.

"A package came for you today," she said.

"What is it?" Adam asked.

"They left it in the garage."

Testosterone bubbled within him. The good stuff was always in the garage. He had a slight spring in his step as he went out to investigate. Carrie followed at a safe distance, almost giddy. She held her breath as he opened the door. She waited for his reaction but heard nothing. Maybe she had made a mistake. She stepped cautiously into the garage.

Before she could speak, he grabbed her in his arms. They hugged excitedly, gratefully wiping each other's sentimental tears. This was their moment. No secrets hung between them. The night was theirs. Carrie handed Adam the key to Grandpa's shiny black Mustang. A new road lay ahead.

CHAPTER 48 – GOLDEN

Fifty candles flickered in the dimmed room. Lace tablecloths adorned every table. The man at the piano was taking requests. Carrie sat in silence, drinking in the elegance of the evening, as she listened to the party around her.

Beth's daughters were whispering something about a handsome waiter. Their older brother was already nagging Jason to let him drive home later. Carrie grinned when her grandson promised to use his mirrors this time. Abby saved her brother-in-law from the debate, asking her nephew for a dance.

Basking in the peace of settled years, Carrie watched her family weave about the room. Daniel's eldest son and his wife clinked glasses, enjoying a quiet minute of each other's company, as Grandpa Daniel showed off his brand new granddaughter. His younger brother soon interrupted the couple's moment alone with an introduction of a new girlfriend.

The piano music stopped. A roomful of cameras clicked into duty as Beth walked onto the stage. Carrie applauded in advance, expecting her daughter to sing something wonderful.

"Thanks, Mom," she said. "But tonight, it's someone else's turn to dedicate a song to you. In honor of your fiftieth anniversary, we have a little surprise."

Carrie searched the room for Adam. He should be here for this. Every other family member was accounted for. The children and grandchildren looked to her as if she could make him appear. The piano didn't wait. Through its melody she heard it, the sound of Adam's cane tapping across the floor. He had a wiggle in his step as he walked out onto the stage.

"What's this? What's Dad doing up there?" she asked Daniel as he approached her table.

"Do you have time to dance with your tired old son?" he asked extending his hand.

"Of course," she said.

As Daniel took her hand and helped her to the dance floor, Adam stalled with a short speech.

"Thank you all for coming. My wife loves this kind of fancy stuff. Isn't she beautiful? This song is for you, honey. For fifty years of sharing, babies and beyond. Love and life, you're the only one I could do this with. I love everything about you, Carrie. From snuggling on the couch to sharing your last few bites of lasagna, you are my girl. I love the way you let out a sweet little sigh when your bank card is approved at the grocery store and your saintly tolerance when I lose my glasses. Most of all, like the man says, 'Thank you for loving me'."

Adam's senior citizen rendition of her favorite song sealed the romance that wrapped their entire relationship. She couldn't have dreamt a more perfect fantasy.

#

That night Carrie closed her eyes for the last time. She thanked God for the incredible love in her life. She thanked Him for every minute, good and bad. She was so grateful she got to be there for all of it.

Her story meant something. When she left this world, it was on His terms, and it was right.

She never even felt a bump.

The End

44125738R00225

Made in the USA
Middletown, DE
05 May 2019